BY WAY OF WATER

CHARLOTTE GULLICK

www.sfwp.com

"In the Valley" by Marty Robbins, © Copyright 1959. Renewed 1987. Mariposa Music, Inc./BMI (admin. by ICG). All Rights reserved. Used by permission.

"Big Iron" by Marty Robbins, © Copyright 1958. Renewed 1986. Mariposa Music, Inc./BMI (admin. by ICG). All rights reserved. Used by permission.

Library of Congress Cataloging-in-Publication Data
Gullick, Charlotte.
  By way of water / Charlotte Gullick.
    pages ; cm.
  ISBN 978-0-9882252-8-2 (alk. paper)
  1. California, Northern—Fiction. 2. Jehovah's Witnesses—Fiction. 3. Dysfunctional families—Fiction.
  4. Rural families—Fiction. 5. Loggers—Fiction. 6. Girls—Fiction. 7. Domestic fiction. I. Title.
  PS3607.U53B9 2013
  813'.6—dc23

                              2013001186

Published by SFWP
369 Montezuma Ave. #350
Santa Fe, NM 87501

www.sfwp.com

For my family
For the community
For the land

For all our different strengths

In memory of too many

***

This is when *it* happened. When Justy was left speechless, her quiet ways easing her task, when she gave over her voice, swam to the bottom of the Eel River, slipped her tongue in among the rocks and fell into the currents of their minds.

J ake drove the truck from the house, tuned for a flicker of animal movement. The Willys whined in the cold and it seemed as if he'd entered a kaleidoscope, the snow flying at him. He stopped the truck at the Cedar Creek opening, pushed his glasses up the bridge of his nose with his pinkie and stepped into the night. With Kyle's .30-30 in one hand, a flashlight in the other, he walked from the truck, trying to think like winter deer. The rifle felt good in his hand, like it might bring him luck.

Snow whispered the land white and he felt large in all that stillness. Only the tree trunks loomed dark at him. It confused him, this blanket, making his world a place he didn't know. Jake walked the hill, snow packing under his weight with small crunching sounds. He wanted to whistle to make the night less lonely, but he kept quiet. The flashlight beam cut the flakes, revealing a trail, and Jake followed the muted hoof prints to a young black oak tree. The lower branches were nibbled down in spots, and Jake took off his glove and dug his thumbnail into the tender skin of the tree. He imagined a deer's soft muzzle stretched up to scrape its teeth along the branch, hunger extending its reach.

He let go of the tree and sighed, holding his palm upward. Snowflakes landed on his bare skin and melted. It had been a lone deer and had paused here hours before. Jake put the glove back on and walked down the hill.

The engine sliced the quiet and he blinked, trying to see beyond his fogged glasses. He pulled off his gloves again and looked at his hands. They seemed so useless in the winter. The black hairs on the backs of his fingers looked like limbless trees bending over the knolls of his knuckles. Under those trees, the land was pale, like the falling snow. The red soil under the blanket of white contained nickel, and the mining company wanted it, wanted to sink their big machines into the mountain and take out its insides. He'd seen pictures of strip mines, the way the earth seemed naked and weak.

He flexed his fingers and put the truck into gear, considering where to look next. He decided to head toward the old hunting cabin another mile uphill. The tires rolled over the unbroken snow, and he tried not to pay attention to how the tree branches beckoned him. He had to shift into low four-wheel to make it up the last incline, and still the back tires slid when he came to a stop.

The cabin looked tired, barely able to hold its shape under the burden of snow. He walked to the structure and flashed the light inside. All was how he had left it last; on the far side of the wood table, the small stove remained tucked in the corner. The stovepipe hung away from the hole in the ceiling, and snow drifted in. He walked the interior, steps softened by the heavy layer of dust on the floor. Mice droppings lined the corners of the room. Something glimmered under the window. He assumed it was a bullet casing left by the hunters who used to own the land, but stepping closer, he saw it was a penny. He kicked it, sending it flying.

Instead of reckoning Sullivan, Jake leaned against a wall and thought about the hunters who used to come here. Wealthy folks from the cities, coming to the land once or maybe twice a year, shooting deer they never ate. Jake wondered if those men had somehow created this night, when he and his family had gone days without food, when the freak storm blew in snow, when all he wanted in this world was to find one deer. Maybe those lawyers and doctors had committed an offense for which Jake now had to pay. He wasn't sure if he believed that, but he was willing to consider it. Anything seemed possible tonight, with the land he loved covered in white and his wife breaking promises to God.

The waiting, that's what made him think such crazy thoughts, made him want to scratch the inside of his skin. All the time waiting, for the winter to be over and the falling jobs to start up again, always counting the days of rain, and now this snow. Waiting for that one break, waiting for the mining company to hand over the orders to move, the mine finally approved. Each day without his chain saw in his hands seemed like standing at the edge of his life and watching it stream by. He pushed off from the wall and rubbed his hands together, feeling jumpy, thinking about the hunters who'd sold the land to the mining company without a thought for what the company would do. If Jake could buy this chunk of earth, he'd treat it like one of his children.

He walked in the quiet to the Willys, grabbed his fiddle case and brought it back to the cabin. It didn't make any sort of sense, but he figured he'd try. Playing music made him feel like he had wings, and there was nothing he wanted so much in the world as to get away. He opened the case and brought the instrument to his chest, hoping to settle the spirits.

***

Dale sat in the rocking chair by the woodstove, swaying with silent prayer, blond hair framing her face. Justy still stood by the window, alternately looking out into the night after Jake and watching Dale's eyelids and her fingers tracing the looped letters, *New World Translation of the Holy Scriptures*. Justy knew that finger dance; she often passed time at the Kingdom Hall following the same route.

Time creaked by, filled by the sound of the rocking chair and wood burning. Micah lay curled in a ball, watching the flame of a candle, head resting on his arm. Lacee sat next to him, thumbing the edges of *The Red Pony*. Micah twisted to look at Lacee and then stood. His movement made the candle between them dance, and his shadow hung huge on the ceiling.

"Mama," he said.

"Just a minute, child." She didn't open her eyes. Asking for forgiveness, asking for a miracle, one undermining the other, that took attention. But Micah couldn't know this, so he called her again. Dale moved her head the slightest bit, telling him to wait a few more minutes. She slid away from the weak spot that'd shown itself outside Sullivan's store; she wished herself safe passage from that memory. Even as Justy watched Dale, she felt Jake's music flow through his own dark hollows.

Micah's stomach growled and Lacee stood, too, her older, slender self stretching up above him. She tapped her foot and watched Dale for an instant. Then she shook her head and placed an arm around Micah's shoulder.

"Let's make tea," she said and walked to the front door, guiding Micah along. They went out onto the porch, and Justy could hear them talking. Behind her, Dale called for Jehovah's guidance, and Justy could feel the Scriptures storming through her. Justy moved to the kitchen table and pulled a shiny coin from the coffee can. Walking back to the stove, she flipped the penny over and over, feeling the grooves of Lincoln's face and the word "Liberty" and the year "1970," the year of her birth, seven years before.

A knock came at the door and Justy opened it. Lacee and Micah came back in with their cupped hands full of snow.

"Get us a pot," Lacee said, and Justy went into the dark kitchen and found one by habit. She brought it to Lacee, who nodded toward the stove. Justy placed the pot on the warm surface, aware of Dale's distance and her silent stream of prayers. Lacee dumped the snow in and it immediately began to melt. Micah emptied his hands, and Lacee brought the candle from the floor and the three of them watched the white crystals turn liquid.

"Here," Lacee said, handing the candle to Micah. She went to the kitchen and fumbled in a drawer. Then she was back, a package of food coloring in her hand. A grin rode her face and she tossed back her straight black hair. "Green?"

Micah nodded, crowding close, while Lacee opened the fat tube of dark color and squeezed out a few drops. Dale shifted in the rocking chair but remained gone. Justy focused her attention on how the deep green swirled in the heated snow, on how the water danced around the strands of color until it became the color.

Lacee brought out three mugs, filled them with the green liquid and handed them out.

"It's a spell," she said, raising her cup toward the ceiling. The candle flickered and Micah scowled.

"Once there was family," Lacee said, while bringing the mug back down and looking sideways into Micah's face. "This family, they were hungry. And then it began to snow white, fat flakes from the sky, and they were still hungry, and the lights had been off for days and they thought about eating the candles, especially the oldest girl child." Lacee smiled and reached her hand toward the candle and passed her finger through the flame.

"Stop it," Micah said, whispering.

Lacee winked at Justy. "The children, they were smart, and they knew how to make things happen that the adults didn't. When the parents looked outside, what they saw was snow, little bits of ice on the ground, but the children, they knew it was more than that. You just had to add the right ingredient to turn the snow into the most delicious food in the whole universe."

"What is it?" Micah asked. His body leaned forward, and his eyes flitted between Lacee's face and the mug. Lacee shrugged her shoulders and took a sip.

"Lacee," Micah whined, and looked at Dale to see if she'd heard, "what's the secret ingredient?"

"All right, then, but I can't say it very loud or an adult might hear and the spell will be broken." Lacee's face was serious and she leaned to whisper into his ear: "Green."

Justy smiled. Micah shook his head, looked into his mug and smiled, too.

"See?" Lacee said. "It's a spell. A spell to make the snow stop, to make a deer show up, to have Mama make us blackberry pie." She shrugged. "Anything different, it'd be good."

Micah half reached for the Bible on Dale's lap. His brown hair fell over his eyes when he looked down at his mug, considering.

Lacee twisted her lips into a smile and reached a hand to his shoulder. "Listen, kiddo." She took a sip. "It's just some snow and some food coloring, and it's all we got. But we can pretend it's anything we want it to be."

Justy thought about the falling snow and wondered why it couldn't turn into manna. She looked to the window and saw their reflections. They stood in a line according to their age, Lacee on the outside, Micah next to her, still staring into his mug, and Justy, holding on to her cup with both hands, the penny pressed in her right palm.

Lacee walked away and brought back the can of pennies. She set it at their feet and reached in, letting the coins slide through her fingers. She sat down, and the others followed and took sips from their mugs, the warm water filling them up like magic. Even if something so simple could be the work of the Devil, it felt heavenly in this moment.

Lacee brought her mug over the red coffee can, tipping it so the water almost spilled out. Candlelight wavered over the letters that spelled Folgers. A drop fell onto the coins.

Justy set her mug down and felt the music and the prayers swirl inside her. She went back to turning her penny over and over in the fingers of her right hand. Lacee let another drop slide from her mug into the can. The tiny blob of green liquid clung to one coin before it slid onto the next.

The pennies were glossy and looked new. Dale had soaked them in vinegar the day before, and the grime had floated to the top of the pan. Then she had dumped them on a towel and the children had helped dry them, making them even shinier. Each penny polished was one step closer to filling the widening hole of hunger.

Micah looked to the windows and said, "I want him to come back." They all nodded.

"With a deer," Lacee said. Justy closed her eyes and sensed Jake finish a song, pause, then start another. Dale continued to loop her thoughts and fingers. Justy felt a tap on her shoulder. She opened her eyes to see Lacee looking at her.

"What do you think?"

Justy looked to Micah, who stared at her, his mug poised at his lips.

"Do you think he'll get a deer, Justy?" Lacee's other hand now stirred the coins, creating a small song.

Justy shrugged and wished she could see into the future—but not the way Dale looked forward to another world, one of Jehovah's perfect making. What Justy wanted to know was whether Jake would come home tonight and if he'd come with an illegal deer.

"I wish he'd done it." Lacee stared into the coffee can, moving the water over the pennies.

"No," said Micah. "It would've been bad. Dad would be in jail if he'd done it."

"I don't think so," Lacee said.

Micah shook his head. "Did you see his face?" he asked, his mouth hanging open.

"Yup. It was terrifying."

At Lacee's words, Justy felt Dale's prayers stop. Dale had opened her eyes and was watching the three of them.

"Time for bed," she said, standing and pulling the can of pennies from Lacee's hands and placing it back on the table. The children stood, and Justy hid the coin in her mouth, her tongue filling with the metallic taste. When they were in their beds, Justy heard Dale pacing in the living room and imagined how the shadows jumped at Dale's movements. Lacee began to snore lightly and Micah rolled over, saying amen in his sleep. Justy tripped her tongue over the edge of the penny, thinking about Jake playing in the night while the snow fell.

Dale came and tapped Justy on the foot. "Come sit with me," she said. Justy slid from under the covers, making sure they didn't leave Lacee's shoulders, and followed Dale to the couch where Dale would read Scriptures, whispering the words. Justy clenched the coin between her teeth while she slid into a spongy sleep.

***

Part of her dreamt the river, how it curled around and over rocks, gathered into the tiniest of spaces, traveling to the Pacific all the while. Part of her rode the ebb and flow of Jake's music, swaying nearer and farther from the moment at Sullivan's. A rivulet of Dale's scriptural words trickled over the countryside of Justy's sleep, making the quietest of noises. When Jake stopped playing, his silence swelled in her dreams, and she knew he was remembering, wishing the children hadn't gone along, hadn't seen.

***

Hunger had ridden with them as Jake drove the Willys through the white landscape, the children squeezed between him and Dale. She sat on the outside, Justy on her lap, the can of pennies in between their legs. Micah had fallen asleep against Lacee's shoulder, and she sat up as tall as her fourteen years would let her next to Jake. She held *The Red Pony*, but she didn't read. Every few miles Dale dipped her fingers into the can, checking to make sure each penny had come clean. Justy tasted the metallic smell of the coins whenever Dale stirred them.

They drove past the two service stations at the south end of town. Jake pulled into the slushy parking lot of Sullivan's and killed the engine. No other vehicles waited and he decided to count this in their favor. He reached across Lacee and Micah and took the can from Dale without looking at her. He glanced at himself in the rearview mirror and ran a hand through his short black hair. The few wrinkles around his eyes eased into crow's-feet then, and his glasses magnified the lines, making his face a dry riverbed. Snow eddied into the truck when he opened the door and floated in the cab as he walked toward Sullivan's.

"Good luck," Lacee said, and Dale frowned—Jehovah's Witnesses believe that luck is the work of Satan. Dale looked next door at the second story of the building beyond Sullivan's. Above the beauty shop, the tiny room known as the Kingdom Hall had a view of the parking lot, but the windows were dark. Tomorrow Dale would be looking down at the memory of herself sitting here, her hungry children piled around her.

Jake finally pushed open the door to Sullivan's, and Dale began praying while Lacee twirled the ends of her hair. Micah rubbed his eyes, looked around and asked, "Why'd we come to Madrone?"

"Less people know us here," Dale said, watching the store. Justy imagined Jake asking Mr. Sullivan if he could buy some food with the pennies. She hoped he'd get some ice cream—not what she was supposed to want, she knew, but what her body craved. Vanilla ice cream that she could swirl into the deep purple of a pie made from blackberries she'd picked herself by the creek behind the house. Berries so black they were purple, and when she put them in her mouth, she would taste the summer sun.

Five minutes passed, and then the door opened and Jake walked back, his steps fast. Dale inhaled sharply, and Justy pretended he carried a half-gallon of ice cream instead of the stupid can. He set it in the new snow on the hood and pulled out a penny. Dale pushed Justy off her lap and got out to stand next to him. She didn't step too close, unsure yet where the anger was settling in his body.

"Sullivan said he'd rather throw pennies in the street for kids than take money from an Indian."

Jake cocked his arm and flung the penny at the storefront. It hit a window with a zing. Flakes landed on Jake's red-and-black-checkered wool shirt, on Dale's thin blue windbreaker and on their hair, making them seem like angels or ghosts. Justy looked to see if Sullivan was watching, but there was too much stuff piled up in front of the windows for her to see.

Jake picked up another coin and cocked his arm again. He turned to Dale and said, "He asked if my wife was that Jehovah blonde."

He released the coin. It hit the window with another zing. Dale looked at her feet, fingering the end of her braid. A truck drove by and honked. Maybe a logger buddy of Jake's, heading south to the next town.

A boxy blue car pulled up next to them. A woman with a flowered scarf tied around her long brown hair talked to a boy in the passenger seat. Rocks, leaves and feathers decorated the car's dash, and beads hung from the rearview mirror. The woman climbed out. She wore sandals with no socks, but she didn't seem to notice the slush as she walked into the store after looking at Jake and Dale and the can. The boy turned to look at Justy and nodded like adult men nod to each other. She looked away, pretending she didn't see him or his blue eyes or his long brown hair in a braid down his back.

Jake pulled out a third penny, weighed it, cocked his arm and let it fly. When Dale took a step closer, Jake spun at her and grabbed her arms.

"He said he'd rather take food stamps than pennies from me," Jake yelled. Justy sat back against the seat, fear pulling her shoulders in like a fallen bird. Dale took quick, short breaths and looked up to the Kingdom Hall. Snow continued to fall on their heads, and Jake's spiky hair seemed to spear the flakes.

Jake released her and said, "I'm going to beat the hell out of him." Dale didn't turn as he started walking, but as he reached the door, she took a deep breath and said, "Maybe you could hunt."

Jake stopped and looked at the back of her head. "What?" He cocked his head as if his ears needed cleaning.

"Whoa," Lacee said. Micah looked at her and then nodded.

Dale turned to Jake, standing a little taller. "Maybe you could hunt." She seemed surprised by her mouth, how easy those words ran from it. Jake placed a hand on the door, removed it, looked at the boy in the car and took two steps closer to Dale.

"You told me you'd leave."

She cast a glance at the Kingdom Hall and said, "I've changed my mind."

Jake looked at his hands, fists that knew how to find the solid soft parts of the stomach, the crook of the nose that would break. He clenched and then released his fingers. "And you won't call the company like you said?"

She shook her head. Her lips formed the word no.

"You serious?"

Dale nodded. Silence filled the afternoon and Jake stood looking at his curled hands. The woman from the leafy blue car came out from the store. She stopped and took a long look at Dale; then her green eyes ran over the children in the truck and over Jake, and finally back to Dale. She opened her mouth but shook her head. She tried to meet Dale's eyes, but Dale looked only at Jake, who gave the woman a curt nod before she climbed into her car. Her bracelets jingled and her deep blue dress flowed around her pale limbs as she moved. She and the boy watched Dale pick up the can and walk to the passenger door of the truck.

"Make room," Dale said to Justy, who stood and pressed herself to the dash. Dale then pulled Justy onto her lap, placing the can back between their legs. Jake stood looking at his hands, and Dale's heart surged in her chest. Justy looked at the blue car and saw the kerchiefed woman's mouth shaped in a tiny oval.

"Don't look at them," Dale said. Justy sat up straighter, noticing that Micah was now in Lacee's lap and that the two of them were almost on top of her and Dale. Jake climbed in and started the engine without a word. As they pulled away from the parking lot, Justy turned to meet the boy's eyes once more.

∗∗∗

"I don't know what you want from me," Jake said to the dark of the hunters cabin. His stomach lurched, and he decided to go to the orchard pasture by the old homestead. Maybe a deer or two would be out looking for a fallen apple. He walked to the cabin door and then stopped, the fiddle's weight solid in his right hand. He moved back to the table and set the instrument and the bow down in the darkness. His fingers slid the smooth surface of the fiddle's body as he remembered the night Kyle had given it to him, Jake's eighth birthday. He and Kyle had lived in the house out at the Reese Ranch. There was a bottle of rotgut on the table that night. Kyle handed him a shot of whiskey, told him he was growing up now and produced the fiddle case from under his bed in the living room. Jake took a sip, shook his head against the hot sting and smiled. The family fiddle, one of the three things that had made it on the trip west. He reached for it, and Kyle held it from him for a minute before handing it over, a sloppy grin on his face.

"It's time," Kyle said and took a straight shot from the jug. "Daddy would've wanted you to have it." Kyle wiped his mouth with the back of his hand and said, "And you're old enough."

He took another drink and seemed to slip away. Jake wanted him to come back, to show him how to play, but he knew not to bother Kyle when he was remembering. So Jake plucked at the strings until his father returned to show him how to tune the instrument, how to bend the bow when he tightened or loosened the strings. It had been a good night, Kyle playing and teaching and not too far gone.

Jake picked the A string, heard the cold air bending the note and walked to the door. He thought maybe now that he'd left the fiddle, he'd find a deer. Hoping, he moved through the night back to the truck.

***

The orchard was empty, the trees looking like skeletons in the overgrown rows. Each tree trunk was pockmarked by woodpeckers. The snow was too deep to see what he knew was there, the decaying apples and pears—fruit that Dale had wanted to can but hadn't had the equipment. He'd promised her that next summer, he'd find a way. He wouldn't have her borrowing the stuff from that scrawny JW woman, Joella. He walked from tree to tree, looking for deer signs. Two sets of faint tracks paralleled the fallen wooden fence, but it looked like they were passing through, not nosing the snow for fruit like he'd hoped.

As always when he came here, he thought about the family who had tried to homestead seventy years before. Maurer, that's all he knew, their last name—that they'd moved away after fifteen years, after planting these trees and building a house that was only an ash pile and a few rusted cans now. Jake shined the flashlight up; snowflakes glowed as they passed through the beam. He wanted to know what had happened to their dream, where they went from here.

So stupid, he thought, to leave the fiddle—as though the world worked that way. He walked back to the truck and drove recklessly home, his earlier cautions about scaring deer, about spinning off a cliff, gone.

The truck whined up and down the hills, and Jake turned his situation again and again in his mind. There seemed no way out until the spring and the work came. The other rifle from Kyle was in the pawnshop. Jake needed to get it back in the next two weeks before the owner sold it. He thought about pawning his chain saw but knew that didn't make sense, especially if a firewood job came up. He could put the fiddle in with the gun, but the thought caused a sharp pain in his belly. He remembered the animals he used to trap with Kyle, the raccoons, the coyotes, sometimes even skunks. The traps Kyle used were metal and snapped shut on a leg when the animal reached for the bait. As he drove, Jake wished for the sudden snap.

Less than a mile to the house, something pulled him from his thoughts. He slowed and the headlights revealed her, twenty yards ahead, standing in the middle of the road. The doe watched him, one foreleg poised for action, tail flashing its warning white. Jake left the engine running and climbed out, rifle in hand. Her eyes glowed brown and the petals of her ears stood erect. He leaned across the hood, bracing his elbows on the cold metal. He brought the rifle to his shoulder, right index finger on the trigger, left hand on the barrel rest.

Waiting, she watched him. He lined up the sights, switched the safety off and breathed, like Kyle had taught him. She lowered the leg and her ears flicked once. He pushed his glasses back and sighted again, looking away from her face. When he pulled the trigger, the silent night exploded with the sound and the deep orange flash of the shot. She crumpled where she stood, her front legs folding underneath her as if she were kneeling.

Jake walked to her, sliding the second bullet into the chamber in case she wasn't dead. But he knew he'd shot her between the eyes. Blood ran from the wound, staining the snow around her ears. His head rang from the bullet, but he could still hear the snow adjusting to her weight. He knelt and placed a hand on her neck. The hide was scratchy and warm under his palm. He followed the arc of her neck to the body, and his fingers felt a little less on fire.

***

Justy woke suddenly and watched Dale worry her wedding ring. Dale stood when she heard the sound of the truck, and Justy remembered dreaming the river. The headlights curved out of sight as the truck neared the house. Dale paced the room, hoping against herself and her promises that he'd gotten a deer. Her shadow leaped in the candlelight. Justy wanted to tell her not to worry, but she caught herself and placed a hand over her mouth. Her tongue licked the edge of the penny she still held in her teeth. Dale sat back down on the couch and picked up her Bible.

Jake walked into the house, blood on his hands, his knife and his jeans. Dale calmly set the book aside and stood. Jake walked to the kitchen and washed his hands, dried blood flaking off in the water. Dale worked her palms together, fingertip to fingertip, her mouth hovering above the steeple of her hands. Justy watched her face, wanting to know how to compose her own.

He walked back into the living room, his candle shadow roaming the walls.

"What's she doing up?" He pointed the knife at Justy.

"She couldn't sleep."

"Then she can help."

Dale shook her head. "No. She shouldn't see."

Jake walked to the door. With his free hand on the knob, he said, "Bundle up. It's cold." He went out.

Dale worked her slight body into the windbreaker and brought in wood for the fire. Then she wrapped herself in a denim jacket and went into their bedroom. She came back with a quilt she laid on top of Justy, kissing her on the forehead before heading out into the night with a deer bag—two old sheets she'd sewn together last fall that they'd wrap around the body after it was skinned.

Wood shifted in the stove and Justy stood. She picked up the nearest candle and walked to the bedroom. Neither Micah nor Lacee stirred as she searched for Lacee's cowboy boots. Someday the boots would be all Justy's, but for now she usually wore them only when Lacee gave her permission. Justy returned to the living room, placed the candle on the floor and slid the too-big boots on her socked feet. She walked to the door, grabbed Jake's logging jacket and stepped into the night, the boots clicking on the wooden porch. As she moved slowly in the dark, she smelled the old sawdust, gasoline and earth worn into the pores of Jake's jacket, what she thought of as his summer smell. At the edge of the porch, she stopped.

Before her, caught in the headlights of the truck, Jake and Dale worked on the body of the doe hanging upside down between them. The deer's hind legs were suspended by short lengths of rope from the lowest branch of the ancient Douglas fir just outside the fenced yard. Justy stepped down into the snow, placing the boots in Dale's footprints. Neither Jake nor Dale heard her approach, and she stood back, watching them work.

Jake cut the skin away with quick, deft movements. He wielded the knife with precision, pulling on the hide after a series of horizontal cuts. Dale pointed the flashlight at the point of contact between knife and hide. They moved their way downward, each yank of skin separating from the body with soft tearing sounds. They worked without speaking.

Snowflakes landed on Justy's hair, melting their way to her scalp. She remembered the look of amazement on Dale's face in the parking lot and felt the waves of relief and regret washing through Dale now. The deer's eyes were clouding over into a smoky green, like the river in springtime. Behind the smokiness, the doe's eyes watched them from a farther and farther distance. She's swimming away, Justy thought. It made her think about the photos Jake kept tacked on the barn wall. He had ten of them, stories that marked the years of his life. In one, he and the grandfather Justy didn't know squatted, both holding rifles in their left hands. With their right hands, they each supported the head of a buck, holding on to the many-pointed antlers. In the photos, the men smiled similar smiles, but Jake was the darker of the two, his mother's blood tinting his skin the slightest bit.

"Over here," Jake said and pointed with the knife. Dale stepped closer and brushed into the deer's ears. Justy shifted her weight quietly and did a quick tally of the pictures both Jake and Dale guarded. Dale kept her five photographs in a white envelope in the towel drawer, under empty paper bags with the towels on top. Dale looked at them only in the morning, after Jake had left for the woods in the dark of early day. Justy had seen her from the hall, sliding her fingers over the past. Justy knew both sets of pictures, knew Jake refused to look at the one wedding picture because Dale's adoptive mother had hidden it when a neighbor remarked that Jake looked like an Indian.

These people confused Justy—this man and woman before her in the night. She wanted to know why they each kept a photograph from the year before her birth, when Kyle had still lived in town, when Jake and Kyle still played music and Dale sang—"like a bird," Lacee said.

Lacee also said that it was during the pregnancy with Justy that Dale had stopped singing, when she promised two things to Jehovah. And here Jake and Dale were, standing in the middle of one of the broken promises, hovering on the edges of legal life once again. A poached deer didn't seem that bad to Justy, not when she was this hungry. For her own sake, Justy wanted Dale to break the other promise, too, just once, so she could hear Dale and Jake in harmony. She shivered inside Jake's jacket.

The deer's hide was almost off and its head kept disappearing behind its own skin. Justy wanted to see its eyes once more, but she stayed put, wiggling her toes to keep warm.

Jake grunted and Dale moved again to shine the light where he wanted. Blood dripped from the cut jugular vein onto the snow at their feet. Crisp air and the odor of warm flesh swirled around them; they were almost done. Justy watched Jake's hands, saw the strength in them when he yanked on the hide, watched his face to see how this day and night were settling on him.

Each time he pulled at the skin, he thought of Sullivan and his smug smile. Dale was worried about the double offense—how it was not just a poached deer but also female. She tried to keep her thoughts from the mining company, how they'd written a formal letter about any poaching on the land, making eviction entirely clear. Dale returned to her favorite passages from the Psalms, sliding away from the reality of her own bloodied hands.

When the deer was relieved of its skin, they both stepped back. So did Justy.

"You'll want the liver," Dale said without looking at him.

"Yes." He wiped the blade on his right thigh. "It's in the bed of the truck."

She turned and started to walk away.

"Dale," he said. She stopped, and Justy backed up some more.

"We ain't got shit in this world."

Dale paused, then said, "We are being tested, Jacob. And I failed today."

Her words hit him and he stared. "What are you talking about?"

Justy retreated farther, feeling the rage build in him, run into his fingers.

"God offered us a test and I failed," Dale said.

Jake threw the knife on the ground. "Dammit, Dale. There ain't nothing wrong with a man feeding his family. I thought you finally saw the light on this."

"I didn't see that it was a test then, and I've been praying while you've been gone, and I see now. There are other options."

"Bullshit there are other options. Don't you think I've thought about this?" His words came from a lower and lower place in his throat. Justy moved back again, biting the coin, hating herself for not being able to step forward.

"There's government help," Dale said, taking a small step away.

"You know how I feel."

And Dale did know, knew he'd never accept any help, not when his body still worked and there was the land to tell him who he was.

"In the old days," he said, "it didn't matter."

"Tested," she said, "like Job."

"We used to take what we needed. We didn't need anybody telling us how to live, how to fill out paperwork."

Dale closed her eyes.

"I am not in the Bible." His hand shot out and punched the deer. It swung in a wild arc, the branch creaking under the weight. "Dale, I've done this all my life, and I stopped for you after Kyle left, but now we don't have time to think about God."

"Jacob. It's wrong, even if I was the one to suggest it." She started to walk away, but he caught up with her, grabbing her shoulder and spinning her around.

"It ain't wrong."

Justy turned her back on them and waited for the silent wrestling of bodies. The deer finally stopped swinging, and all Justy heard was Jake's breathing. She walked to the porch, listening for the fight to turn physical. Her stomach hurt beyond her hunger as she wished for the violence to come, just so it would be over.

J usty swam the emerald Eel, sliding through the bends to the ocean. The water filled her senses and she tasted the faint tang of salt as the river flattened out, getting ready to join the Pacific. Like a salmon, she left the clear water and dreamed herself free. Standing at the mouth of the river was the doe, leaning to take a drink. As the deer looked at her, Justy broke the surface, suddenly out of breath.

"Justy. Wake up."

Jake's voice pulled her from the water and she slid out from under the covers. She still wore the clothes from the night before, and the penny was clenched in her right palm. The space next to her where Lacee slept was empty; so was Micah's bed across the room. She heard no sound in the small house.

"I want to go to town." Jake leaned against the doorframe, looking at the ceiling. "Meet me at the truck. Food for you on the stove."

She nodded and he left. She found tennis shoes under the bed and went into the living room. The can of pennies still sat on the kitchen table. The snow had stopped, but the world outside glared.

She squinted while she laced the shoes and then slipped the coin inside her right one. It was Sunday, and Dale had gone to meeting with the others. Joella Mills must have driven the extra twenty miles to pick them up again. Justy's stomach somersaulted and she looked to the woodstove. Two plates, one inverted over the other. When she lifted the top plate, she saw venison steak. Her thoughts flickered back to the deer dream and then to the real deer hanging upside down in the night. She heard the truck start and reached for the steak, sinking her teeth into it while sensing that Dale had not eaten, that she sat at the meeting with a week-empty belly, trying to pay attention to the public talk.

Justy chewed and wondered whether Jehovah begrudged her this food. She closed her eyes, knowing most Witnesses felt Him deep in their hearts. All Justy could feel was hunger and Jake waiting in the truck and Dale waiting at meeting. Maybe there wasn't any room inside her for Him to grow. She opened her eyes to the glare and blinked. Twenty feet from the house, the dormant garden drooped. Black-and-white chickadees hopped in the snow, picking at the dead plants Dale had sown last spring. The biggest bird flew to a beanpole stake, its little body sentinel to the morning. The stakes leaned into one another, forming a row of triangles—a perfect tunnel to get away from the summer sun. Beyond the garden, the valley lay covered in melting snow, a wandering ribbon of black creek water breaking up all the white, moving to join the Rattlesnake. Oaks, firs, madrones and pines stood heavy in the snow, their branches bowing to the ground like devoted followers of the weather.

Jake honked and Justy went to the door, venison in one hand and his logging jacket in the other. She liked wearing his jacket; it made her feel closer to the trees he felled. She moved to the truck, feeling the penny in her shoe. After getting in, she saw the body of the deer, looking barely like an animal anymore. It was wrapped in the deer bag, and the only parts she could recognize were the hind legs attached to the ropes. The head was gone, and Justy wondered what the eyes looked like now. She chewed carefully as Jake backed the truck up. A foil package on the dash caught her eye, and she knew meat from the deer was inside.

As they drove down the road, Justy looked at the land to push out the image of the deer. Jake tapped his fingers on the wheel, a song surging through his thoughts. They crossed a ditch and the land changed, the soil now red and dark. It bled into the puddles of snow creating water the color of pumpkin innards. They left the dirt road, and Jake took the old highway into town, still angry over the freeway, even though it had been finished more than ten years before. The old road curved along the Eel, following her lines from hundreds of feet above. Thick fog hung over the river canyon, and Justy pretended it was cotton candy, pillows of spun sugar she could reach out and eat. The steep hills were covered with white-layered trees. It looks like Christmas, Justy thought, and smiled, even though she wasn't supposed to want Christmas or any other holiday.

Not wanting Christmas made her think of Dale, who was at the moment trying to pay attention to the brother's words while part of her stretched out to Jake and Justy in the truck. Dale had hoped her decision to leave her youngest with Jake would anchor him home. She looked at Micah and Lacee, seeing her son lean forward in his seat, a small smile pressed to his lips; Lacee slouched in the wrinkled skirt that she hated, her eyes roaming the corners of the Kingdom Hall. Dale frowned at Lacee's thumbs playing leapfrog. The other people in the room seemed to have no problem focusing on the talk, and Dale sat up straighter.

***

Jake pulled up in front of the Hilltop Tavern. Off to the right of the building, a snowy shoulder waited. Sometimes he parked there, and when he did, Justy both loved and feared it. She loved that she could see the river far below, the canyon walls reaching skyward. As the afternoons passed, the canyon darkened and she began to feel like she might fall into the shadows. Even though she cherished the river, she also knew it could be dangerous. She knew it had taken some of Jake's classmates, had heard that water was the reason Dale didn't graduate from high school.

Jake eased off the white straw cowboy hat and checked his hair in the rearview mirror. Justy thought again how strange it was for him to wear that hat when he'd sold his horse two years ago. She thought maybe he was just staying ready for when the four riders showed up. He replaced the hat and turned to her. "Let's go."

As they walked to the door, snow stained the canvas of Justy's tennis shoes dark, and the penny slid forward under her sock. The parking lot was empty, and they weren't surprised to see only Helen Martinez in the bar, smoking while she swept near the pool table.

She looked up when they entered. "Jake Colby." She spoke around the cigarette. "And Justy. Hello there." Helen placed a hand on Justy's head for an instant, then she blew smoke toward the ceiling. Her curly brown hair framed her wrinkled brown face. Justy liked the gentle weight of Helen's hand, knowing it was this same one that sometimes telephoned Dale to warn her about Jake's moods.

"Ay, Jake, it's been a while."

"Well," he said.

"Could have used some of your music here last night."

He remained silent, mindful of where the fiddle lay in the hunter's cabin, the cold air warping the instrument. Justy looked at the picture on the left wall and smiled a hello to Helen's son, Francisco. Helen went behind the bar and snapped on the radio. A man sang about Daddy Frank, the blind guitar player, and his family—the music their only means of survival. Sometimes Justy pretended this song was about Jake and Dale.

Justy sat on a stool in the dark room, watching the Hamm's beer sign above the cash register with its eternal waterfall. Her face looked tired in the huge mirror next to the sign, black circles under her eyes. She kicked her legs against the counter and felt the heat coming from the woodstove in the corner. On the door that led downstairs to Helen and Juan's house, a Tucker's Logging Supply calendar read 1977. The New Year had come and gone since she'd been here last with Jake. He stood next to her, fingertips worrying the seams of his back pockets. "How you been?" Helen asked and lit another cigarette from the remains of the first.

"Surviving."

"I hear that."

"How's Juan?" Jake placed a boot on the bottom rung of the stool.

Helen shrugged. "This year, this weather."

Jake nodded. Justy ran her hands over the lacquered surface of the redwood bar, feeling the grooved names and initials. She wanted Helen to talk more; she liked listening for the hint of the woman's accent.

"You got something against sitting down today?" Helen gestured with her cigarette. The song ended and the announcer spoke from the mill town of Eureka, sixty miles up the coast. His smooth voice commented on the snow, and then he said something about it being God's dandruff. When he stopped talking, a woman began singing about a crumbling relationship, spelling out her troubles in the form of a crossword puzzle.

Jake took his foot from the stool. "You in a trading mood?"

"It's been years since you asked me that, Colby. Your dad back in town?"

Jake shook his head and smiled in the corner of his mouth.

"Well," she said. "It depends on the trade."

"Let's just say I came across some venison and now I've got a thirst."

Helen studied the cigarette. Justy felt the letters D.J.—Dwayne James. She knew him from when he came into Hilltop, friendly at first, happy for company since he lived in the backwoods. As the hours passed, he'd start talking about 'Nam, and the villages he'd bulldozed with a Cat tractor. When the stories and the whiskey ran thick, something would snap and he'd start a fight with whoever sat next to him, and if the person moved, he'd continue to fight with the air. Justy had watched Jake step into that space and fight D.J. back more than once.

Reflected in the bar mirror, Jake's body looked tense, his shoulders drawn into his chest, both hands gripping the cowboy hat. Helen smiled at Justy, who returned it, knowing her child's face sometimes helped. Helen slowly shook her head and said, "I sure do like the taste of fresh venison."

Jake smiled and his shoulders eased. "Justy," he said. "Run on out and get that package."

She slid off the stool. As the day neared noon, the canyon looked less menacing, and she imagined the river full and muddy now. She grabbed the package and walked back to the bar. The sun cast a warm glow on the trees and mountains. She tried to make out Jake and Helen through the bar's front window, but the contrast from the bright day to the dark bar didn't allow her to see them. Then, like the moments in dreams when the river became real, she saw herself peering, a small face shaded and searching through the glass.

Justy reentered the bar, her eyes stinging from the smoke. As she walked across the faded linoleum, she watched Francisco watching her. The picture was signed, she knew, "To Mom, with love, Paco." A rosary hung from the right corner. Justy knew he was missing, in a place that D.J. said was greener than even Mendocino County. Jake now sat, a shot of whiskey and a bottle of Coors in front of him, and Helen held a Coors instead of a cigarette. Justy placed the cold package on the bar and climbed back on the stool. Jake slid the meat over to Helen.

"To trades," she said, and raised her bottle. Jake raised his and they both drank. Justy returned to exploring the bar's letters, and a man on the radio sang about how by the time he reaches Phoenix, she'll be rising.

"I'll take this to Juan," Helen said. The calendar on the door swung when she shut it. Jake downed the shot and took a swig of beer. Justy watched his reflection and the way his Adams apple galloped in his throat. He stared into his own brown eyes as he swallowed. She tried to scratch a line in the bar with her fingernail, to mark his first shot. The bottle hit the bar with a clink and he ran his fingers through his hair, adjusted the cowboy hat on the bar to his right, then pushed his glasses up the bridge of his nose with his pinkie. Without taking his eyes from his own face, he reached out his hand and clamped it around the back of Justy's neck. She braced herself against the bar.

"Look," he said. The pressure of his hand increased while the Phoenix song ended and the familiar strands of "The Streets of Laredo" began. Jake stared at his reflection, his eyes tunnels to a faraway place. Justy slid forward on the stool.

"Look." He drank. And her eyes traveled the room, seeing the Budweiser light above the pool table, Paco's young face, the wood rosary, the cobwebs tucked into the corners of the room. The radio sang to them, telling them to play the fife lowly and beat the drum slowly, and promising to sing them a sad song about a cowboy who'd done wrong. Justy looked, away from her own sharp face, brown stringy hair, green eyes open wide. Her gaze was caught by the waterfall in the Hamm's sign, by the way the water seemed to forever move though nothing really changed.

"This is all you get," Jake said, and released her. She almost fell off the stool. He moved to the radio, switched it off and walked to the stove. She watched his reflection open the stove door, saw how the flames cast him in a glow she imagined the Devil might wear. Keeping her eyes on him, she reached over and brought the bottle to her lips.

She swallowed the beer, letting the harsh taste fill her mouth. Her eyes watered, but she kept drinking. Three long pulls, wanting to taste what made him see the world the way he did. She set the bottle down and wiped her mouth like she'd watched him do before. Her head felt light and the room suddenly seemed much hotter.

He added more wood and closed the stove door just as Helen came back with a plate in her hands. On top was a towel folded over what Justy knew from the smell was a pile of fresh flour tortillas. Helen set the plate down and pulled back the towel. Steam rose from the white circles. Justy's stomach lurched at the smell of the butter and cinnamon.

"Thought some food should remain in the deal, and Juan, he likes to cook." Helen nodded and her brown hands rolled the top tortilla in a tight curl. She held it out to Justy, who took it, smelling cigarette smoke on Helen's fingers. Justy flicked a look at Jake in the mirror, but he was smiling at Helen. She bit into the splurge of tastes and sensed Dale rising to sing with the others in the Kingdom Hall. Justy chewed and chewed her first bite, willing Dale to feel the glory in the warm tortilla.

Helen rolled another and offered it to Jake. He took it with a whispered thanks while Helen rolled a third for herself. "Juan doesn't do half bad," she said, holding the tortilla as if it were a cigarette. Jake and Justy nodded. The fire swelled, and Jake took off his jacket.

"Dale at her meeting?" Helen asked.

Jake nodded. "I never should have let them JWs come around in the first place." He finished the tortilla and drank the rest of his beer. "That Luke Mills coming to the house every month is what took Dale in."

"A woman of faith is a good thing," Helen said, lighting another cigarette. Helen looked at Paco, and her face rearranged itself around her sadness, lines near her mouth puckering. She crossed herself took a deep breath and looked back at Jake and Justy. The quiet swelled, and she walked to the radio and switched it on. Another singer told them about the something in the Sunday-morning air that makes a body feel alone.

"You heard about the petition, Jake?"

"No."

"Some people are protesting the mine."

Jake placed both hands tight around the beer bottle. "Who's protesting?"

"Started out with some of those new teachers at the school, you know, wanting to save the trees and all that." Helen rolled her eyes.

"Any locals?" Jake took a swig, watching himself in the mirror, fingers tapping a fast rhythm on the bottle.

"Only Lefty Fry, but you know him. He'd join anything that'd have him."

Jake let this new information settle. Justy thought about Lefty and his river-green eyes. She felt his first name carved into the bar, big and blocky on her far right. She'd heard he lived on crazy money, doing one officially insane thing each year to keep his government check. Last summer he'd driven his truck into the post office, telling people the voices told him to do it. Justy liked Lefty because sometimes he bought her a soda and a bag of chips when he saw her in Hilltop. She couldn't see anything crazy in his warm smile or his missing teeth.

When the song ended, Helen cleared her throat. "Gaines was in here last night."

"You say?" Jake sat up straight. It was unlike Gaines to come to Hilltop unless he had work for somebody.

"Yeah, he was in here, talking about that mare of his like he does." Jake snorted.

"When he finally shut up about her, he said he's looking for two men."

Jake nodded. Justy finished her tortilla, then returned to the carved letters. Leaning over the bar's ancient surface to see the whirled reflections of Jake's face and beer bottle and the tip of Helen's cigarette, she wished she'd seen the tree when it had been standing.

"He mean falling jobs?"

Helen shook her head and leaned to fetch Jake another beer.

"Graves," she said.

"The bastard's finally buckling." Jake drank from the new beer.

"The water's getting close to his family."

Helen drank also, and Justy realized Helen drank with her customers only on the first sip.

"Justy."

She looked up to see Helen offering her another tortilla. At Justy's nod, Helen handed it over. "Gaines said he'd guarantee crew jobs to whoever did the graves," she said.

"The coast job? Falling?"

Helen nodded. Justy chewed, watching her face in the mirror, sensing the quickening of Jake's pulse. "Juan got any interest?"

"Ay, we may be hard up, but Juan, he don't dig up bodies, no matter what." Jake took a drink. Helen ran a rough palm through her hair and said, "But it's paying work."

Jake cleared his throat and asked, "Gaines need two men?"

"Yep."

"Do his work now, falling jobs come spring?"

Helen laughed and said, "As long as you don't get near his precious horse."

Jake smiled. Wood shifted in the stove and the fire burned louder. Justy watched the waterfall, wave after wave, as her fingers slid the surface of the bar.

***

A half hour passed with Helen, Jake and Justy quiet, listening to the singing storytellers. And then the boxy blue car from the day before pulled in next to the Willys, and the sandaled woman climbed out, a red scarf over her hair today. A tall, thin man unfolded himself from the passenger seat. His blond hair was pulled back into a ponytail and his heavily bearded face smiled. Different colors of paint smeared the dirty white of his overalls.

"Hippies," Jake said.

Helen said, "There's more coming all the time. Harris keeps bringing them in. He sells more real estate than anyone in this county, and that includes Ukiah." Helen shrugged. "These two don't seem bad, though."

A wave of cool air swept into the room; Justy could feel it swirl around her ankles and up her pant legs.

"Helen!" the woman said. The man wore a beaming smile.

"How are you two?" Helen set the glass down she'd been cleaning and lit a cigarette.

"Good, good," the woman said. She walked behind Justy, who kept her eyes on the woman's reflection. "Except for we're going a little crazy, with the snow and all, and the tipi..." She shrugged.

"It gets small some days."

Jake cocked his head at her, eyebrows raised. "Did you say tipi?"

"Yeah. It gets small, like I said, but it's pretty mellow."

Jake smiled at his beer.

"Didn't I see you yesterday, down in Madrone?"

Jake's smile slid away and he shook his head. The woman tried to meet Justy's eyes.

"Yeah, in the parking lot of Sullivan's."

Jake watched the woman's reflection, his brown eyes glittering.

"My name is Sunshine Raven."

The woman held out her hand, but Jake did not turn.

"Used to be Laura, but I realized it wasn't warm enough."

"What can I get you?" Helen tapped her cigarette into an ashtray.

"Couple shots of tequila would be great," Sunshine said. She dropped her hand and swayed to the song, her eyes roaming. She bowed slightly to Paco's picture, her hands pressed together in front of her. Helen watched this while she filled two shot glasses. Sunshine turned from the picture and pulled a wad of cash from a woven rainbow-colored purse. Jake watched the woman in the mirror, his face struggling to remain calm.

"Thanks," Sunshine said.

She and the man took the shots, and then pool balls thundered through the tunnels of the table. She cleared the table in a matter of minutes, her hair falling over her shoulders. The man sat in a chair against the wall, smiling and watching her.

Jake took a breath and said low, "Where'd they come from?"

Helen didn't look at him but said, "Berkeley. They bought part of the Hermitage, the piece closest to the Eel."

Justy looked at the people who'd chosen to live next to her river.

"They working?" Jake asked.

Helen shook her head. "Don't seem to need to. He's an artist of some kind, and her, she's supposed to be good with herbs."

"Herbs?"

"Natural medicine, she called it. I don't know. Maybe a *bruja*."

They fell back into silence and the pool table spilled forth another crash. This time the man broke, his manner slow. Justy imagined him a turtle that liked to sleep in the mud or the sun.

"Helen," Jake said. She looked up from cleaning spotless glasses.

"You figure there's room in this trade for a few coins? I got to call north."

She raised an eyebrow and then walked to the cash register, pulled out some change and set it in front of him.

"Thanks," he said.

"*No problema.*" Helen watched Jake roll the empty glass in his hand. He caught her eye, and she poured another shot of whiskey, which he drank down in one swallow. Justy tried to make a third mark in the bar. Jake lined up the coins, glancing at Sunshine's reflection every time she laughed. He tapped on each one, six quarters, four dimes, two nickels— presidential faces marching bodiless toward the wall. Every coin said "Liberty." Justy tilted her foot back and forth, making the penny slide.

***

Two more shots of whiskey, two more beers and Jake continued moving the coins. Sunshine and the man played game after game, shuffling their sandals on the linoleum. When Helen caught Justy's eye and winked, Justy relaxed some.

Helen left through the back door again and Jake stared at the money, looking up only to meet his own gaze in the mirror when he took a drink. He slid Washington after Washington in an arc, placing the advancing coin in the lead. Helen returned with three plates of enchiladas, setting the smallest serving in front of Justy.

"No thanks," Jake said, and tried to wave away his plate. But Helen set it near him.

Justy waited for Helen to begin a story, but she lit a cigarette and smiled at Jake. He didn't look at her. She cleared her throat and started telling them about when she and Juan used to live in Mexico, about how her mother used to test Juan to see if he was worthy enough for her beautiful daughter. "Yes, if you can imagine it," Helen said. She went on and Jake began smiling at her tale, nodding at her Spanish phrases. Helen told them about Juan trying to make an impression by bringing flowers, but what he didn't know was that Helen's father was deathly allergic to bees and thought all flowers brought bees with them. By the time she got to the end of the story, Jake had cleaned his plate and was smiling fully.

Helen knew how to keep people safe, and Justy wanted to walk behind the bar and hug her. After they had finished eating, Justy felt a stab of hunger from Dale. She turned the stool and watched Sunshine's red skirt flow like water around her bare ankles. Then a truck's lights glared through the window and stopped. Jeff Harris climbed out of his new red Toyota and walked in, his boots clunking; he dragged his left foot from a logging accident years ago. He flashed a smile at the bar, hugged Sunshine and shook the man's hand. The three of them huddled together, then Sunshine laughed, long and loud.

"A shot for our main man," Sunshine called to Helen, who already had it on the counter. Harris walked over and grabbed Jake's shoulder in greeting. Jake turned to meet his gaze. He seemed to smile at Jake from a faraway place, his mouth almost lost in his bushy red beard.

"Hey, Colby. What's shaking up on Red Mountain?" Harris reached in front of Justy for his shot and didn't seem to notice she was there.

"Not much," Jake said. He turned his back to Harris. Justy thought about his wife, Mamie, the only other Jehovah's Witness in Sequoia Valley. That's what Jake and Harris shared, wives who'd fallen into a religion no one else at this end of the valley seemed to understand. Harris and his wife had twins, a boy and a girl, in Micah's class. Justy liked Mamie, but something about Harris smelled wrong, and he never noticed Justy, like she was just another tree in the way of his view.

"What's with this change?" Harris said. Jake swept them into his palm and said, "I got to track somebody down."

"Well, you let me know if you ever get enough coins together to buy that land. I'll take care of you." Harris clunked away to Sunshine and the man.

Jake shook the coins in his palm and said softly, "How can she do that?" He stood.

Justy looked at him and knew Dale was now in Joella's car, waiting to come home and see if Justy had kept Jake tethered.

His dark eyes looked to the hippie woman, talking and laughing. Helen moved away to stoke the fire.

Jake placed a firm hand on Justy's head. "You don't believe that stuff, do you? Luke coming by every month in that suit of his, trying to make me one of them." He paused, and then said, "Micah, he seems to have taken to it."

Then he took his hand away and said, "Phone call." Justy nodded and he walked to the door without looking at the pool table. Justy watched Harris's reflection. Dale and Mamie had found Jehovah, but Harris and Jake had not. She closed her eyes and checked again, but He wasn't there.

***

The cold plastic of the receiver felt good in Jake's fiery hands. He didn't know the number, but the operator found a K. Colby in Bellingham, Washington. She connected him and the phone rang. He tried to imagine what the room looked like, if Kyle still carried those three masks from

Mexico, if he still hung them on the walls of whatever room in whatever town he found work. Jake leaned his forehead against the cool glass.

On the sixth ring, a muffled hello.

"Kyle?" Jake pressed his left palm to the glass.

"Who is this?"

"It's Jake."

"Jacob. That you?"

A brief silence, and then, "Yes."

"What's happened?"

"Nothing. That's the trouble."

"Dale?"

"She's fine," and Jake flitted away from the memory of why Kyle had left.

"The mine?"

"Not yet."

Kyle waited and Jake shifted his weight, rolled his forehead on the glass.

"There's work here."

"You say?"

Jake watched a moth dance outside the booth, eager for the light.

"How many years, boy?"

Jake cleared his throat. The operator came on and said, "Time's up."

"Dad?"

"Two weeks." Kyle's words hung in the air, then the connection was cut.

***

Helen played a game of solitaire, smoking and casting glances at the pool players. Harris and the man were teamed up against Sunshine. Jake stood in the phone booth, head still pressed to the glass, the receiver hanging at his side. Sliding her sandals over the floor without picking up her feet, Sunshine moved to Justy and placed a hand on the bar next to her. Helen flicked her a look, then one at the door. Sunshine was warm, and Justy could smell oranges and something deeper, like the clean aroma of fresh dirt. Sunshine spun the bar stool around, her hand light on Justy's arm.

"What you doing, baby?"

Her voice was smooth, like rain over stones. Justy looked into the woman's blue eyes and Sunshine stared back, not smiling, not frowning, just there. Her face was brown from the sun, and wrinkles lined the corners of her eyes.

"I got a little boy," she said. Justy nodded, remembering his face from the day before.

Jake walked into the bar, saw Sunshine bending over Justy. He stopped at the pool table and pointed at the man. "Jesus sandals don't make no sense in the snow."

"The name's Nolan," the man said, and smiled.

"Your mom's pretty," Sunshine said to Justy, but loud enough for Jake to hear. He walked close.

"Let's hit it," he said. Justy moved off the bar stool, away from Sunshine and into the jacket Jake held. He placed the cowboy hat on his head.

"Helen, I appreciate your understanding."

She waved her cigarette at him. "You got it, Colby." Justy looked at Helen and snaked her a smile, grateful for the food and the story. She wanted to look at Sunshine but didn't as she walked in front of Jake to the door.

***

Justy leaned her head against the cool window, watching the white lines of the highway to make sure Jake stayed inside them.

As the day edged toward late winter afternoon, she looked away from the lines every few minutes to check the progress of the mountains. The way they looked in the twilight felt like they'd come from her dreams—only silhouettes, suggestions. Soon they would be tall mounds of nothingness, the opposites of their daytime selves, places she could walk into and disappear.

On this drive, Jake went outside the lines only in the tight curves, something he did even when he hadn't had anything to drink. Still, Justy knew that one corner a little farther north had grabbed the wheel of a different truck before she was born. Coming home from a high school reunion, Jake hadn't made a turn, and he and Dale and the truck had rolled down an incline covered with boulders, stopping halfway between the road and the river. Dale had been wearing a seat belt, but not Jake, and he landed on a boulder, a gash in his forehead that took sewing up. The Willys didn't even have seat belts, and Justy tried to make it stay in the lines by not blinking.

When they reached the dirt road and the fork that led to the back-country of the ranch, Jake stopped and considered going after the fiddle. He looked at the gas gauge, decided against it for the moment, and then headed to the house.

Dale, Lacee and Micah sat at the kitchen table, a plate filled with red strips of meat in the middle, next to the Folgers can. Two candles burned low, and the shadows they cast jumped as Dale cut through a hunk of flesh. Lacee salted and peppered the strips, and Micah unbent paper clips, then slid one end of each through the tips of the meat. In the hallway, one coat hanger was already full. Drops of blood fell to the newspaper below.

"Hey," Jake said. "Jerky, huh?"

Dale gave a curt nod. "You smell like smoke."

"Hey," Micah said, and smiled at Justy, who went to the couch and unlaced her shoes, careful to keep the penny inside. From where she sat, she couldn't see the others but watched their shadows on the wall behind them. Jake stood there for a minute and then went to the kitchen sink.

"What's this?" His voice cut through the house, stopping Dale's slicing.

"Peanut butter."

Justy knew Dale didn't look at him. "Mamie gave it to me today at meeting," Dale said. Micah and Lacee exchanged looks, and Lacee stood and hung another full coat hanger.

Dale cleared her throat and said, "It's for the kids' lunches, so they can go back to school tomorrow."

Jake rolled the can between his palms, the commodity letters disappearing and reappearing in his hands, the alcohol focusing in him. Lacee sat back down at the table.

"Peanut butter." His words were tight and clear. Blood dripped on the newspaper, and Justy imagined the black-and-white print, the gray pictures of people she didn't know covered in a slow pool of red.

"Where does Mamie get off giving us handouts? Her husband is the biggest dope grower in this valley, and they've got the nerve to apply for government aid and then give it to us?"

"Yes, peanut butter," Dale said. She ran her tongue over her teeth, thinking he might look and see that she'd finally eaten something. The taste still lingered and it made her warm—to eat legally—but she still didn't look at Jake. Justy wiggled her toes and thought about Harris, his big beard and his funny smell, like summer tarweed. She took turns closing one eye, then the other, wondering how Dale and Jake each saw the world. Her left eye revealed the shadows of her family, the right eye the strips of meat hanging in the doorway. Back and forth between the shadows, the tension gaining power in her belly and making her want to run from it. The stain spread on the newspaper, the drip seeming to fill the house.

The silver can of peanut butter sailed over the counter that separated the kitchen from the living room and hit the far wall with a solid thud. The can rolled toward Justy and stopped a few inches from her toes. Dale nodded at the bedroom. Micah and Lacee left, but Justy felt frozen to the couch.

Jake leaned over the counter.

"This goddamned government. It'll hand me some peanut butter, but I can't go out and feed my family."

Dale's knife went back to work, shaking the table with her efforts.

Jake spun toward her. Justy's eyes moved to the reflection of a candle, stretching over the silver surface of the peanut butter can.

"Don't you have anything to say?"

"Not really, Jacob."

She began using the salt and pepper on the strips. The couch beneath Justy was solid, a place she could locate herself while their words swelled into her. Jake walked back and forth in the small space between the sink and the kitchen counter.

"Dale. I called Kyle."

She stood.

"He'll be coming shortly."

"Jacob."

He faced her, the cowboy hat in his hands. "Gaines has work for two men."

She pulled at the end of her blond braid. Bits of deer flesh from her hands caught in her hair. She stepped toward him. "I don't know what to say," she said.

He shrugged and wished for another drink. He looked at her a long minute and said, "Hell must have froze over." He walked past her and out into the night. The truck started, and Dale wondered if he was returning to Hilltop. Don't worry, Justy thought, he's just going to get the fiddle.

***

Jake drove the back roads for the second time in less than twenty-four hours, thinking about Kyle and their last fight. If only Kyle hadn't gotten in the way and confused Jake, then Jake wouldn't have hit Dale.

Justy joined Dale at the table, working paper clips into the strips of venison. Time was marked by the sizzle of wood from the fire, dripping blood and the thick give of the meat when the paper clip edged through. In the candlelight, Dale's eyes were dark and shadowy, nothing like the pictures of when she and Jake used to sing together, when her face seemed full of light. She didn't look at Justy.

At the cabin, Jake stumbled over the snow. His hands found the fiddle and bow where he'd left them, but the room felt crowded by things he couldn't see. He walked back to the truck, turned off the lights and played a warped song of his own, free for a few minutes.

***

The children readied themselves for bed and still Jake had not come home. When they were under the covers and Lacee had blown out the candle, Dale came to stand in the doorway, her silhouette sagging into the frame. The strips of meat hung behind her, curing in the heat. She walked over to the bed Justy and Lacee shared and sat near their feet.

"Thank you," she said, her voice wispy and faraway. "For giving us this day and for feeding us." Dale paused, cleared her throat and took a deep breath. "We hope that Jake will open himself up to the Truth. May we learn from your Word and apply it to our daily lives." Again she hesitated, and the room shrank with her silence—then the joy she felt about Jehovah's knowledge filled her and she struggled to share it.

"Please watch over my children and help them follow the Truth. We ask these things in Christ Jesus' name. Amen."

Micah echoed her and then fell into his own eight-year-old prayer, his words a string of whispers. Lacee curled tighter, her copy of *The Red Pony* tucked into her arm. When morning light began to fill the room, she'd be reading, taking herself away with a story. Justy couldn't see more than the lighter shade of Dale's blond hair. Micah drifted off to sleep, and Justy tried to make her breathing like his and Lacee's. Dale finally relaxed into the wall, her strong back curved into a soft question mark.

Justy heard a match being struck. She sensed the presence of light as Dale cupped her free hand around the match, studying the arch of her children's eyebrows, the planes of their features. Twice in the last year she'd done this—trying to find evidence of herself in the children's faces. Now Dale's hands were walking her own face, wanting to soothe the ache inside. Dale wished she'd been studied as a child, made known to the mother who had given her up for adoption.

Justy prepared herself not to startle when Dale's hands leaped from one child mirror to another. Justy pretended she was a stone in the Eel and that Dale's hands were the water, gliding over her surfaces and passing on.

A piece of wood rolled in the stove with a thump. Dale's cool fingers found Justy's hair, then gently brushed her eyebrows, her cheekbones, her nose, her lips. Justy took deep, even breaths and became aware again of the jerky dripping. Dale leaned back into the wall. She sat still for a moment and then went to the kitchen drawer. The white envelope was where she had left it, and she brought it to the bedroom. In the dark, she removed the pictures. She could tell two of them just by their feel: the Polaroid from Carl Walters and the wedding picture, not just because it was bigger, but because the corners were worn smooth. She held herself and Jake and thought about that day, how she'd been so nervous, how she had to borrow the dress from the school teacher she was staying with at the time. Her bare arms had seemed so naked in the fall air, but she loved how she looked. Like a young woman should, she thought.

She shrugged her arms inside the flannel shirt she wore now, suddenly aware of the entirety of her skin under her clothes. Her adoptive mother hadn't come, but Kyle had. He and Jake had been good that day, laughing and full of music and jokes. It seemed so long ago. And he was coming back, after seven years of anger between him and Jake—because of her. Her thoughts ran away from her and she flashed to that night, when Jake had slapped her across the face. She'd been pregnant with Justy, and Kyle, he'd had enough. He stepped in and beat Jake. Dale shivered now, confused by Kyle's consistent warmth to her and his unpredictable coldness toward Jake. There'd been talk after Kyle left, but no one knew the truth of it except the three of them. And how could she explain to the phantom rumors that it was only violence that sent Kyle away, nothing more?

Justy's left foot began to itch, but she didn't dare move, not when Dale had done this, brought out the secret pictures, not when Justy sensed her own story lurking in Dale's thoughts. Dale forced herself away from the wedding picture, still angry with her mother for her harsh response to Jake's Indian blood. Dale flipped through the pictures and imagined the scenes—the last picture from Carl Walters's visit, checking on them for the mining company, Dale and the children standing on the front porch in summer clothes. Another photo taken in Los Angeles when they'd gone to Jake's birthplace for his mother's funeral, five years back. The picture of Jake and Kyle playing while she sang, some community barbecue eight years ago. And the picture of her baptism, right after Kyle left. She looked happiest in this one, she knew, because she was filled with confidence about her decision to lead a legal life and to use her voice only in praise of Jehovah. The legal life had been a requirement, but the choice to give up singing with Jake, that had been her own, one most people didn't understand.

Justy finally rubbed her feet together, pretending to roll over in her sleep. Dale sat up straight, wishing she could see herself better in her children. She sighed and put the pictures back in the envelope.

"Jacob," she said. Justy sensed Jake coming back, coasting downhill to save gas.

"Jehovah," Dale said then, and Justy was confused. She opened her eyes and saw that Dale was more ghost than mother in the dark. Her calling of His name meant Satan or his demons were close.

"I'm asking you…to help me do the right thing."

Justy closed her eyes again. Dale was saying some kind of prayer, a kind Justy hadn't heard before but a prayer all the same.

The children waited at the bus stop, returning to school after being gone a week. The sun lingered behind them, threatening to break free of the mountains. Lacee stood where she'd stopped, reading in the cold morning air. Justy also loved when books carried her away, riveted her from the chaotic world of Jake and Dale.

The bag lunches of celery and peanut butter and jerky waited at Lacee's feet. Every time the children heard the sound of a car, they turned to the south, waiting for the yellow of the bus to rise out of the horizon. Their breath pooled in white clouds, and Justy pretended she was making her own fog, just like the Eel. She looked down the old road and saw the coastal fog curling over the tip of the forested mountain on the other side of the river canyon. She sniffed deep, searching for the salt smell of ocean water as she jiggled the shoe that carried the penny.

Micah threw rocks at the back of the highway sign that said "Drive-Thru Tree Road." The rocks hit the metal with a zing, sounding like pennies on glass. Not many tourists took the old road anymore; the freeway sped them along faster to the Tree. But every once in a while, a car stopped and the driver asked the way. The looks on the people's faces usually matched their license plates. People from Missouri and Kansas couldn't imagine a tree big enough to drive through. Seven miles from here, they'd have their perspective changed as soon as they drove down toward Sequoia Valley. At first nothing seemed that different, but once the road curved past Hilltop and the huge expanse of the river canyon, the trees stood so tall that tourists sometimes had accidents from looking for the tops while they were driving. Justy loved the ride to school because she got to follow the Eel and then the trees. Deep in the Drive-Thru Tree Park, the ancient chandelier redwood stood, its heart cut out so people could drive their cars through it. The limbs of these trees hung in the air like fancy lights Justy had only heard about. She knew this was where Jake had taken Dale on their first date, after dinner.

Micah hopped in place, tired of waiting. They heard Emmet shift down and then the bus appeared. When it stopped at the sign, they each took different seats. Lacee and Justy sat near the back, Lacee returning to her book before the bus began moving. Justy took a seat on the west side, wanting to watch the Eel. Micah sat in the middle with Caleb Harris, Mamie and Jeff's son. Caleb's twin sister, Sky, perched right behind him, watching his every word and move, playing with the hem of her dress. Justy thought the twins looked like watered-down versions of their father, with their pale red hair and tapioca skin. The bus lurched and rolled forward, under the freeway overpass and down the old road.

Justy alternated between watching the river and thinking of Jake and Dale. Dale waited on the couch, darning a hole in a sock stretched over a useless light bulb. She was grateful it was quiet; it gave her the time to figure out how to move in this world when it was filled with so much confusion. Jake was in the barn, a hundred yards from the house. He leaned against a sawhorse and stared at the pictures he kept tacked to the wall, putting off a visit to Gaines.

The bus stopped at the road leading to what people called the Hermitage. The boxy blue car waited there, the woman and the boy inside. Sunshine wore a flame-orange scarf around her head, and when she leaned over to kiss the boy, Justy squinted and imagined that the woman's head was on fire. The braided boy wore green corduroy bell-bottoms, hiking boots, a black turtleneck and a denim jacket that had different symbols and animals embroidered on it. He carried a green woven sack, and Justy felt herself liking him already because he didn't have one of those fancy, expensive lunch boxes with pictures of Barbie or Spiderman that she'd seen on the shelves at Safeway. The boy smiled at Emmet and walked toward Justy's seat. She didn't look at him but watched his mother smile up at the bus. He sat opposite Justy and she could tell he was trying to catch her gaze. But she sent her mind back to Jake and Dale.

She peeked only once. He looked up from his book when she turned toward him. She closed her eyes but listened when he turned the pages, when he said "Sure" to Jennifer Sloan's request to sit next to him. The bus was only half full when they reached the school, and Justy waited until the boy walked off before she moved. The few high school kids headed to the building on the right, and Justy followed the boy into Ms. Long's first- and second-grade classroom. He had a seat two rows away from hers. His desk nametag said Ochre Raven—he must have joined the class sometime last week. After Justy sat down, Ms. Long came to her desk and kneeled. Justy blinked at her teacher, who was braiding flowers into her frizzy blond hair. She probably had a greenhouse where she grew all kinds of things.

"It's nice to see you, Justine." Ms. Long smelled like the vanilla that Dale sometimes put in French-toast batter. She wore flowing black pants, a black turtleneck and brown sandals with black socks. Her pale skin glowed pink from the cold, and she sniffled. Justy lifted the lid to her desk and placed her lunch inside, seeing her pencils and an eraser exactly where she'd left them. She couldn't tell she'd been gone a week.

"Were you sick?" Ms. Long's fingers played with the edge of Justy's laminated nametag, glued to the top of the desk. The letters were simple and big and they annoyed Justy. She watched Ms. Long's hand.

"Is everything okay at home?" Ms. Long tucked a strand of Justy's hair behind her left ear. She had a silver ring on each finger and a tattoo of a rose on the back of her right hand. Justy looked at her shiny white face. Even if Justy had the words to tell anyone why her quietness had become silence, Ms. Long wouldn't be the one she told. Maybe Jehovah would be the one, and maybe He already understood. But Justy still didn't find any sign of Him.

The bell rang, and Ms. Long stood and went to the front of the classroom, where she sat on a white rug. She closed her eyes, and her hands rested on her folded knees, the thumb and forefinger creating a circle. Her black sweater and her chest underneath swelled with her deep breaths, and the students sat waiting. She did this each morning, and she told the students she hoped her meditations helped them focus their minds for learning. Once she'd tried to lead the class in a guided meditation, but Justy knew better. While Ms. Long used a soft voice, telling them to create a sacred space inside, Justy let her mind slip to the river and she swam it again, playing out the curves in a fast-forward version of the water until it reached the Pacific. When Ms. Long had talked about white light touching their auras, Justy had left the water for a moment to look at the teacher. Ms. Long wore a serene smile as she talked quietly to the students, and Justy had closed her eyes and her mind against her. Ms. Long didn't even know she was doing the Devil's work, inviting him in whenever she opened her thoughts in meditation.

The new boy was watching Ms. Long with a smile. The teacher took a final deep breath and greeted the students with a warm hello and asked them to stand for the pledge of allegiance. Justy remained seated and was surprised to see the boy sitting also, playing with the end of his braid. Ms. Long asked Jordan Fry, Lefty's nephew, to lead the pledge, and the class joined together to say what Justy knew was a mistake. She'd never said the pledge of allegiance nor sung the national anthem. Dale and the Witnesses had told her that to do so was to put man's government before God's. Justy knew Dale didn't vote, either, but sometimes Justy got confused, since it was Dale who insisted that Jake shooting a deer when they were hungry was wrong because it was illegal.

After the pledge, Ms. Long handed out math worksheets. Justy completed hers within a few minutes and then set her pencil down. She usually had to sit for the longest time before anyone else finished, and like always, she watched the clock to see how long it would take for the next pencil to stop. She smiled when the boy finished one minute and thirty-three seconds after she did. Both of them watched Ms. Long water the many plants in the room, humming. Justy felt Jake leave the barn and drive into town, heading toward Gaines's place. Her eyes roamed the room and she saw hearts cut from red and pink construction paper taped to the wall next to the blackboard, which was green and didn't make any sense. Sixteen valentines decorated the wall, shapes the children had colored or pasted other shapes onto. Justy's and Ochre's names were not up on the wall. Hers was missing because she didn't participate in any of the holiday activities, and she figured he must not have been here for the Valentines Day preparations. Cards illustrating the sounds of the alphabet hung on a wire that encircled the room. Today Justy was drawn to the one with the pale-skinned woman placing a finger to her lips, demonstrating the "sh" sound.

***

At lunchtime, Justy walked to the cafeteria by herself, looking for Micah or Lacee. When she entered the noisy room, she saw Micah sitting with the Harris twins, the three of them praying before they ate. Lacee sat with a group of kids around her, but she didn't seem to notice, her nose in another book. Justy sat by herself and felt good about it. As she chewed her jerky, trying not to think about the deer and its eyes clouding away, Justy looked at the different-aged students in the room. Most of the kids ate hot lunches—meatloaf and mashed potatoes served on metal trays by skinny Sally Ferris. Justy knew if Jake would let them, they could have hot lunches, too. He refused to fill out the paperwork that Dale brought to him at the beginning of each school year, hoping he'd changed his mind. He didn't take charity, he said, and threw the papers in the stove. Justy watched the children eating and she didn't know how Jake thought the Colbys were any different. Every hot-lunch kid who had a dad living at home depended on the timber jobs just like Jake, and every winter, those families ran out of money, too. Jake thought the Colbys were different somehow and Justy wondered how they were, aside from being one of two families in which the mothers had decided that the children wouldn't celebrate holidays or salute the flag.

Ochre entered the lunchroom minutes after the other students, and came to sit opposite her. Justy became interested in the creases of her paper lunch bag and didn't look at him. She wiggled her feet and remembered the penny in her shoe, and it made her smile, to have a secret so close. It helped her attend the comings and goings of Jake and Dale.

Ochre pulled a sandwich from his woven bag and began to eat without looking away. She could feel his stare and finally glanced back. He had the same face as Sunshine, though his skin was fairer from less time in the sun. His stare was the same as hers, too—not smiling, not frowning. Justy pulled another piece of jerky from her bag and left the table, still chewing, happy he hadn't said anything. She escaped the noise of the cafeteria, and instead of going to the playground like she was supposed to, she went to the library. The big dictionary on the stand waited, and she looked up Ochre's name. She smiled when she read the definition—his name meant "yellow."

On the page before "Ochre" was a color illustration of the earth's oceans, without the water. The naked planet fascinated her. Maybe people had a world of landscape inside them and maybe they carried a version of the earth. She studied the mountains, valleys and canyons of the deep oceans, sensing she had the same inside her. She walked away from the book and went to the playground, her tongue working at a piece of meat stuck in her teeth. The dictionary had said that even though the waters of the planet were divided, they were all connected. Seventy percent of the earth was covered in water—the same amount she carried in her body. Justy now felt better about the new thing that had happened inside her, how she was able to swim in and out of Jake's and Dale's worlds.

***

After lunch, when the children had plowed back into the classroom with muddy feet and chilled hands, it was story time. When they took off their shoes, Justy pulled the penny out and kept it hidden in her right palm. The children gathered in a circle, and Ms. Long sat under the green blackboard. Justy sat opposite Ms. Long, and Ochre sat three students away on Justy's left. She loved story time. Even though the tales were simple, she was still able to flow away on the words.

While Ms. Long read a story by Dr. Seuss about a thing called a Lorax and cutting down too many trees, Justy kept looking at Ochre's jacket. She liked the bright colors of the signs and symbols, but she worried that some of them might be Satan's work. She wondered if it had been Sunshine's pale hands that stitched the shapes.

Ms. Long read on, and Justy could see that the vivid colors in the world of the book had faded into dark purples and yellows. The thing called the Lorax sat in a lonely house in a treeless landscape. Ms. Long finished the story and smiled brightly at the students. Then she said, "Now, wasn't that lovely? And aren't we lucky to live in among all these beautiful trees." She sighed. "Lucky indeed."

The students all seemed to have the same look on their faces, except Ochre. Their daddies cut down trees, and Ms. Long had just read them a book that said that was bad. Justy looked back at Ochre and his jacket, almost too full of information to sit still. Ms. Long said, "Okay, now, my little light beings, I want us to go around the circle and each say something about nature that we like."

Jordan Fry was on her immediate left and he looked uncertain.

"Go ahead," she said. "Tell us something you like about Mother Nature." Ms. Long folded her hands in front of her chest, waiting.

Jordan's blond hair fell into his eyes and he blew it. His mouth seemed to start working before any words came out. "I like hunting with my dad."

Ms. Long frowned. "What do you like about hunting? The deep smell of the forest floor? The sun rising over the mountains?"

Jordan blew his hair again. Justy didn't think he looked much like his uncle Lefty. "I like the guns," he said. "Daddy's got a twenty-two he lets me carry, and when I turn eight, it'll be mine."

Ms. Long frowned more and asked Jennifer Sloan, who twirled her hair around a finger and said, "I like the flowers."

"Exactly. Me, too," Ms. Long said, and beamed. The circle continued, with Ms. Long being frustrated by most of her students. Justy wondered where Ms. Long had come from. When it was Justy's turn, she just looked at her socks, saw where Dale had darned a hole on the left heel. Ms. Long prompted Justy three times before she glanced at the clock. Justy looked at her and noticed that the flowers in her frizzy hair had wilted.

"Justy." Ms. Long used her firm voice. "Please answer the question."

Justy shook her head no, once.

"Well then, we'll just have to put your good little head to work. Write me a poem about it, due tomorrow." Ms. Long nodded, affirming her decision. The other students stared, then looked to Justy's left for Buddy Stewart's response. The children were used to her being different, mostly because she couldn't participate in the holiday activities and because she got to do different assignments, ones that let her go to the library by herself and leave for other classrooms every once in a while. When Ochre refused to speak as well, Justy sat straighter and sneaked a look at him. He was smiling at her. Ms. Long stood up with exasperation and told him he had to write a poem also.

"Back to your seats," she said, and handed out handwriting worksheets. Justy flew through them as Jake approached Shelby Gaines's house, rang the doorbell and waited, his cowboy hat in his hand. Dale looked through recipe books Mamie had given her, letting the pictures take her from the four things she had to cook with: peanut butter, celery, food coloring and deer meat. Justy laid her pencil down and waited for the school day to end so she could ride along the Eel and return to Dale.

***

Eight days later, Jake picked up the kids after school and then stopped at the post office, leaving them in the truck while he went into the one-room building for the mail. The five-foot-wide bulletin board that stood between the store and the post office held a few handwritten signs, two of them offering cordwood for sale. One advertised herbs, and Sunshine's name and post-office box were listed. Justy guessed they didn't have a phone in the tipi. Jake tried not to smile when he saw the envelope from Kyle marked "Jacob Colby, General Delivery." Inside was a check for two hundred dollars written in Kyle's blocky handwriting, and Jake took a deep breath, feeling suddenly lighter.

He returned to the truck and smiled through the window. Justy gently shoved Lacee, who looked up from her book and smiled back at Jake's rare show of teeth. He opened the door with a flourish. On the way home, he sang cowboy songs the children all knew by heart. Lacee mouthed the words and Micah sat next to Jake, smiling. When they reached their dirt road, Jake traded places with Micah. "Let's see you drive, boy."

Micah's legs barely stretched to the pedals, but Jake told him how to work them. Lacee pretended not to notice, but Justy could see her watching from the corners of her eyes. Jake felt a surge of pride at his son, at all his children with their good grades and all. When they pulled up to the house, he told Micah he'd make a good Tonto any day of the week. Lacee and Justy went inside, and Jake showed Micah the carburetor, the battery and the spark plugs. Justy wanted to learn these things, too, but Jake didn't think girls needed to know such stuff. Lacee went into the bedroom and began reading again, taking herself away from Jake. Justy walked to Dale, who sat at the kitchen table with a needle and thread, fitting a dress for her. A candle fought back the approaching afternoon dark while Dale sewed. The dress and other clothes had come in a black plastic bag from people in the congregation last Sunday, and Dale had spent her days changing the clothes to fit her family. She was almost finished, and Justy watched her strong hands making quick work of the thread and fabric, sewing a hemline.

"Hello," Dale said through the pins in her mouth. Justy wondered if it mattered to Dale that she'd grown speechless. Dale hadn't once said anything about it. Justy was surprised at how easy it was to leave the world of speech. If only Ms. Long would leave her alone and stop asking her to participate in the circle talks. Ochre hadn't remained true to his circle silence, staying quiet only on the first day. Jake and Micah entered the house, and Dale set aside the sewing, pulling the pins from her mouth as Jake walked close.

"Look what he sent." Jake held out the check and Dale's eyes widened. "I know. It's a chunk. I can get the rifle from the pawnshop." Jake walked away from her, taking big goose steps. He poked Micah in the ribs, and Micah laughed. Dale watched them play. Justy wondered if Jake would like her and Lacee more if they were boys.

"Jacob?" Dale said.

He looked at her and went back to tickling Micah for a few more seconds before walking back. "Yeah?"

"Can we go to town and get some things?" Dale leaped inside at the thought of being able to make a real meal.

"Yup. You can have fifty. Why don't we go to Safeway?" He smiled and tousled Justy's hair. She looked to the can of pennies still sitting on the kitchen counter and wondered what she could do with them.

***

They rode though the darkening day. The fifty miles passed quickly, with Jake singing to himself and Dale holding tight to Justy, considering the different food she'd buy. Micah and Lacee were quiet, each reading a book. The dirty snow melted along the road, no longer looking like something good to eat. When they had to stop at a sign, they entered the north end of the town of Willits.

The lights of Safeway stung Justy's eyes as she followed Dale and Lacee inside. Jake drove away with Micah to the pawnshop, on a back street in the front room of a man's house. Dale took a cart and pulled out a pencil and a piece of paper from her purse. Lacee began reading a fashion magazine, scowling at the pictures of women wearing too much makeup and not enough clothes or flesh. Justy drove the cart and Dale considered each item. If she put it in the basket, she added it to her tally, making sure she didn't go over her allotted fifty dollars.

When she had placed milk, eggs, flour, sugar, bacon, potatoes, rice, bread and a few nonfood items in the basket, they entered the cereal aisle. Dale picked out oatmeal and Cheerios, but Justy's eyes were drawn to the colors of what Dale called the sugar cereals—Froot Loops, Cocoa

Puffs, Sugar Smacks. Justy knew these weren't good for her, just like the holidays, but she still liked to look at the packaging. Ochre never ate meat or candy, but he seemed to like the lunches Sunshine prepared for him. He kept sitting next to Justy at lunch but never said anything.

Dale paused in the baking aisle and studied the numbers on her paper. Then she grabbed a package of baking yeast; she'd seen a recipe for sourdough bread, and if she could figure it out, she could keep the starter in the fridge and make bread instead of having to buy it. Justy closed her eyes and felt the ways Dale spread herself thin; she didn't know when money would come in next, so she tried to figure out how to buy the right things to last. Justy thought it was almost like a spell, Dale's ache and ability to feed five mouths. Dale put the package in the cart, smiled and said, "It's not even a dollar."

Justy nodded. Dale's love for her children felt like the ocean to Justy, wide and without end. Lacee approached them with a magazine. "Look, Mama." She held out a picture of a woman dressed as a girl.

"We can't afford that," Dale said, and looked away.

"I just wanted to show you this article." Lacee gritted her teeth and started to walk away. Justy tapped Lacee on the elbow. She looked at Justy as if she weren't there. Justy felt Dale waver; she didn't mean to come across so harsh, but she wanted to stop hope before it had time to fill the sails.

***

Jake walked into the pawnshop while Micah waited, playing with the steering wheel and singing, just like Jake. The man who answered the door nodded at Jake without smiling and said. "I've had to fight off some good offers."

Jake panicked, and his eyes ran the room full of guns, giant televisions, radios, guitars. Behind the counter, his Krag .30-10 waited, and he relaxed a little.

"I reckon you have." He pulled out the cash, tried not to think about Kyle's need to send the check and laid out a hundred dollars in tens.

"One more day and I'd have sold you short, friend." The man rubbed his large belly.

"Good thing I got here, then," Jake said. The man counted the money again and handed the rifle to Jake. The gun's weight was pure in Jake's hands, and he grinned. Despite his dislike for someone who thrived at the expense of other people's failures, Jake dipped his head and left the pawnshop, feeling better than he had in months.

J usty sat in the barn, looking at the pictures tacked on the wall. She stood in Jake's territory like he stood in hers every day, he and Dale filling her up and making her confused all the time. In the growing afternoon dark, the people in front of her were hard to see, but she liked the clean, white edges of the pictures—the way the borders made the photos seem complete, whole stories she could tell herself. Today she was trying to gather from them something of Kyle.

Justy leaned on a saddle, a stirrup hitting her behind the knees. Around her, cobwebs lined the things in the barn—the wooden kitchen table Jake had cracked one night when he was mad, a grandfather clock that had never worked, boxes full of what, Justy didn't know. The air remained chilly and she chewed on the inside of her turtleneck. Most of the photographs tried to curl into themselves. Off to the right, four blue and two red rodeo ribbons hung. In one rodeo picture, Jake's arm blurred as he quick-wrapped a calf's hind legs; a horse pulled another rope taut, keeping the calf's neck strained.

In an old tomato box, Jake kept his high school yearbooks. Justy had pored over them and learned it had been Jake's ambition to be either a rodeo star or a professional fiddler. And she found out he'd played all the sports in high school, even football when the town had been big enough to have a team. His nickname had been Fiddle, and in the yearbook pictures, he didn't wear glasses.

A raven cawed from one of the drooping live oaks that surrounded the barn, and Justy looked away from the yearbooks and concentrated on the photo of Jake's mother when she was young. Lila—the grandmother Justy hadn't known—and her three sisters stood outside a shack, their hair in black braids that disappeared down their backs. Each had her arms folded in front of her chest, the gingham of the dresses faded. They didn't look like the Indians Justy had seen on television or in comic books. Their faces were lined with stories she would never know—lines that were echoed in Jake. Justy scrunched up her cheeks to see if she, too, carried stories in the canyons of her face, but her skin felt smooth. Her fingers left her face and she thought about the Indian who sat on every billboard advertising the big trees. He was a silhouette on his horse, spear at his side. The way he sat made him look completely defeated, and it took her the longest time to realize the spear wasn't lodged through his body. She didn't understand why a sad Indian was the symbol of the giant trees. Maybe it had something to do with the red of the bark and the supposed red of an Indian's skin. But that didn't make much sense to her, either.

She touched the picture of Lila and her sisters. Jake didn't know what had happened to his aunts, and Justy wondered if they'd grown up, married men with blond hair and blue eyes, whether they had had children. She didn't like it—that there might be family somewhere in this world who didn't know about hers. Justy imagined the girls' parents standing with the photographer, too shy to be in the picture but still proud. She thought maybe they had been people who knew how to sing and play stringed instruments, and that Jake had inherited an appetite for music from both sides.

The sound of a truck broke her gaze. She knew it wasn't Jake. With a sigh of relief she stepped back. If he caught her here, she'd get it. She remembered back to the night, years before, when Helen had called and they'd had to leave, Dale shaking them awake and all of them running down the road. It had been strange, to run away from the power in Jake's drunken hands. Now someone drove the quarter mile to the house, but when she checked the filaments of her shadowy senses, she knew Jake was still at Gaines's place, digging ditch until the grave job began. Dale punched down a loaf of sourdough for the second time, pleased she'd taught herself this new skill. The sound of the truck grew, and Justy looked at the picture of Kyle, a dashing young man in military dress, a world of white behind him. She considered hiding in the trough—like she did when Jake drove home and she was here—and decided against it. She took the picture down, knowing how vivid Jake's anger would be if he knew. Something lurked beneath Kyle's absence, and Justy had been given only a hint of it that night Dale had visited the pictures in the dark.

Justy held Kyle in her hands and was not surprised when she heard the truck turn toward the barn. She walked to the barn door. Kyle's eyebrows arched, wonder riding his features, but he smiled. She glanced down at the photo and saw that most of his good looks had run into the wrinkles by his eyes. He looked at the row of barn supports that caught the edge of the roof, creating a protected overhang for cattle or horses to feed. Three of the five supports simply hung in the air, like rootless trees, the cement blocks that used to meet them gone.

Kyle shook his head and walked toward her. "Hello," he said, then squatted on his cowboy boots before her. She nodded and felt lost in his hazel eyes. Their color reminded her of the Eel in late summer. He pushed back his white straw cowboy hat, and she could see sunspots dotting his pale forehead. His long legs were clothed in faded jeans, and over his lanky torso he wore a white western-cut shirt. They studied each other and then his eyes darted to her hands. He smiled and walked to the back of his old Chevy pickup. He pulled out a saddle and brought it into the barn, the straps and stirrups dangling around him. A few feet into the building, he stopped, letting his eyes adjust. He slung the saddle over the edge of the family baby crib and slapped his hands together.

"Crazy, ain't it? This saddle with no horse." Kyle sighed. "I see Jake's are all gone."

Justy tried to see through Kyle's eyes, someone who'd been here before, now returned to the skeletons. Jake had sold his three saddles over the last three winters.

"Where are we gonna go, anyway?" Kyle asked. She just looked at him, wondering if she should be afraid of this man. He walked the length of the barn, past the cobwebbed tack hanging from the large nails in the wall. His footsteps rang hollow until he reached the other end and the dusty remnants of hay, now more silhouette than person. Small slivers of vertical light seeped through the spaces in the boards. This was her grandfather, a man she knew only from pictures, pieces of stories and whatever feelings Jake and Dale allowed concerning him.

He pivoted a slow circle on his boots and held out his hands. "What a man don't own…"

Justy wasn't sure his muffled words were intended for her. He stood quiet another while and then walked back to her. "You must be Justine."

She nodded, wishing she could open her mouth and tell him she preferred Justy.

"Nice to meet you." He stuck out his hand and smiled. "I remember when you was just a growing thing inside your mama's tummy."

She studied his palm, saw the callused softness of it and stuck out her own. They shook hands, his warmth easing her shoulders. Her hand seemed so tiny in his large grip, and she grimaced, feeling like she could tumble into him.

"A pleasure," he said. "What you got there?"

She looked down to his young black-and-white face and then held it out to him.

"Time sure does get you." Kyle took the photo. He studied it and then grinned. "United States Army," he said. He cocked his head, and his words seemed to fall out of the lowest portion of his mouth. "Wanted to be a horseman." He gestured to the saddle.

"Figures that the year I join so I can be in the cavalry is the year the army decides to phase it out." He handed her the picture and looked to the rest of the photos. She moved closer. She wanted to keep her stories of her family intact. At the same time, she wanted to know the people Jake and Dale were before she was born and whether their stories could help her bridge the gap between them now.

Kyle squatted and rested his palms on his jeans while his eyes traveled the pictures. He considered each one, blinking only when he moved to the next. The nine pictures on the wall were almost all the Colbys had to show themselves they had a history. Kyle looked at himself as a young man sitting in an army jeep, snow covering the landscape, military sheds in the background and behind the sheds, radio towers. He took the picture down. Justy took a deep breath. This was Jake's place first, and then hers, and here was this stranger boldly touching the photos. Kyle turned the jeep picture over and held it out to her. In pencil, it said, "Daddy wishes he could take his Jake boy for a ride. Daddy burns up the road with this buggy."

Justy blinked, realizing that was Kyle's handwriting from years ago, the same as on the check he'd sent two weeks before. She didn't know words lingered on the backs of any of the photos.

"So, they sent me to the Aleutian Islands instead of giving me a horse. Had to keep a watch against the Japanese, the Russians, anybody that might try an attack through the Bering Strait." He shook his head, and Justy tried to remember where these places might be. "Ridiculous, when all I wanted was to be a cowboy, not an army hero."

Justy didn't understand his words and looked at the picture of Jake playing the fiddle. He must have been a year or so older than Justy was now. She tried to imagine Jake receiving the picture of Kyle in the jeep, thinking about his daddy off in some islands.

Kyle sighed and tacked the jeep picture back in place. He pointed to the fiddle picture. "Jake still playing?"

Justy nodded.

"Good. Keeps a man sane." He reached to the picture of himself, Lila and Jake. She was so much darker than he was. Her hair now kinked and almost fuzzy, Lila barely looked like the girl standing outside the shack with her sisters.

Kyle stood. "Gets to be too much. All those memories."

He took the picture from Justy and tacked it back. She worried that Jake would be able to tell the pictures had been touched, but Kyle brought up some old hay from the floor. He blew on the straw, motes whirling in the air. He sneezed and laughed.

"That ought to cover our tracks."

They stepped back, and Justy felt something inside leap toward this man. He might be able to help her bring Jake and Dale back together. They closed the barn door and then he stood looking around. Justy tried again to imagine how he might see the corrals, which were nothing but rotting poles held together by baling wire. She knew Jake and Kyle had once worked cattle together. They'd logged in the woods during the week and tended cattle on the weekends. Their branding iron still hung inside the barn. Kyle sighed, and Justy felt a sadness creep into her chest. Most things felt so empty, as if the Colbys had already moved somewhere else but had forgotten where.

"Hear that?" He tilted his head and Justy stretched her hearing.

She heard a faint rustle in the breeze.

"That's what they call rattlesnake grass. That's because the dry seed pods look and sound like a rattlesnake tail." He pointed to the grass on the far side of the wrecked corral. The grass talked to itself in the wind, a calm voice soothing the air. Kyle placed a hand on her shoulder.

"We got work to do."

***

Kyle drove to the house and Justy walked, shaking her head at his offer for a ride. She'd noticed the guitar sitting on the passenger side of the truck and wondered if Dale might sing now that he'd returned. The motorcycle strapped in the back of the truck jolted in place as he rolled away.

She closed the barn door, thinking about Jake and Dale and their old music, stuff she knew only from inside the womb. As she walked through the blossoming twilight, she kicked a rock that skittered in front of her until it veered off the road into a winter-dead blackberry bush. The cold stung her eyes. The bare branches of the oaks made the trees look cold, too, especially the huge oak leaning out over the pond. She stopped at the tree and shimmied up its length so she hung with it out over the water. The pond was full but murky, like the Eel. Catfish and turtles snuggled deep into the mud bottom. The turtles remained curled into their shells to keep in the known. Come warm weather, they'd be out of the mud, crawling from the water to sun their bodies. It made her think about Ochre's dad, the blond man she'd seen at the bar.

Justy pressed her face to the tree, feeling its scratchy bark, its spring moss. She heard muted sounds from the house, knew Dale and Kyle were greeting each other with careful hellos, delicate questions, furtive looks to see what new pains had been endured. A twig dropped from the tree, hitting the pond's surface with a splash.

Justy watched the rings of waves moving out and away from the original circle. She watched until the waves hit the shore and the water was calm again.

***

Her grandfather, Lacee and Micah sat at the kitchen table, peeling oranges, Kyle's cowboy hat now off. On the table sat a box full of fruit and vegetables. The colors hit Justy and she smiled. She loved how very orange the oranges were, how the banana curved yellow and the broccoli was two different colors of green. It felt as if Kyle had brought a piece of early spring to them. Lacee and Micah chatted with Kyle while he peeled oranges. Citrus and baking bread filled the small house.

"You'd like some, Dale." Kyle held out a peeled orange. She looked at her children from the kitchen, lips thinking about a smile, and shook her head. Her hair was pulled back into a ponytail, making her look younger, showing the delicacy of her ears. Kyle watched her play with the edge of her black T-shirt and then held out the orange to Justy. She tried to compose her face like Dale's and shook her head.

Kyle grinned and split the orange in half. "Get over here and eat this, girl."

She took it from him. Lacee reached for a second orange and told Micah she'd split it with him. He said yes through a full mouth. Justy considered the orange half in her hand, then split it again, walked to Dale and placed the orange sections on the counter. Dale looked at Kyle and smiled. He shrugged. Dale took the fruit and sat at the table. Justy studied Kyle, filling in the empty space she had for her grandfather.

"So, how old are you, Lacee?" Kyle asked.

"Fourteen." She ran a hand through her straight black hair, leaving a bit of orange in her part.

"Thirteen? That's a good age. Do you remember me?" Kyle grinned at her and winked at Dale.

Lacee nodded. "I'm fourteen, and you took me on my first horse ride."

"And you showed me the catfish in the pond," Micah said.

"That's right," Kyle said, and Justy wondered what he had heard.

"I'm eight," Micah said.

"Well, little man, that's a good age to be."

Micah smiled, his fair face riding a wave of pink.

"Aren't they good-looking?" Dale said, pride raising her face.

"You said it, woman. Spitting image of their grandfather, if I do say so myself." Kyle winked at Lacee.

"And I remember you and Jake used to play music together," Lacee said.

"Music? Yes, Jake and Dale and me, we used to raise some ruckus."

Kyle sang a line from a spiritual, about the Lord taking a body up. His sweet, deep voice filled the room, and then he smiled. He looked at Dale with a tilt of his head, waiting. Her fingers found their way to the bottom of her T-shirt again. The fabric soothed her, and she tried to smile.

"Mama don't sing those songs anymore," Micah said.

"What do you mean?" Kyle asked, looking at Dale like she'd hit him in the stomach. She opened her mouth, closed it, then left the table to check the bread in the oven. Kyle reached into the box, pulled out an apple and began cutting it with his pocketknife.

"She just sings at meetings now," Lacee said.

"Well, I'll be," Kyle said. "If that ain't a crime in this world, I don't know what is."

Dale still wouldn't look at him. The house grew quiet, and Kyle seemed faraway. He finally said, "And how old does that make you these days, Dale?"

She turned to meet his gaze and shrugged.

"Mama's thirty-one," Lacee said.

"Hard to believe that." Kyle offered Justy a piece of apple and she took it. She thought maybe part of how she had learned to be quiet came from watching and hearing people answer for Dale.

"I think little Justine must be six or seven," Kyle said.

"She'll be seven in a couple of months. April twenty," Dale said.

"She likes to be called Justy," Lacee said, and Justy flashed her a smile. "She'd tell you herself but something made her grow so quiet a while ago that we can't hear her anymore. At least not right now." Lacee looked at Justy as if they'd just met, considering this silent sister and her strange but forgivable ways.

"Justy, then," Kyle said. "Or maybe we should just call you string bean." He winked and said, "We'll have us a birthday party with some good old chocolate cake and homemade vanilla ice cream." He grinned, and Justy could see that he and Jake had the same teeth, maybe even the same cheekbones. But Jake's eyes and nose came from Lila, what Justy considered his Indian features. She thought she had the same nose as Jake.

Micah and Dale shook their heads. "We don't celebrate birthdays," Micah said. Lacee bit into another orange section and rolled her eyes.

"Oh." Kyle looked at Dale. "You really took that Jehovah stuff seriously, didn't you?"

Again she opened her mouth to explain all the changes she'd made since he'd left. She wanted to tell him that Jake had been good because of those changes, not once laying a hand on her in the seven years Kyle had been gone, not if she didn't count the other day at Sullivan's and those times she'd run away to escape. But he hadn't hit her, and she knew it was because of her decision to dedicate herself and her voice to Jehovah. And the joy she felt from knowing the Truth filled up every empty space she'd ever had. She swallowed, and Kyle turned from her.

"Kyle," Dale finally said. He tapped his fingers on the table in a lively rhythm. "There's no way we can thank you for the food."

He shrugged and opened his arms wide.

"And the check. We were able to get the lights back on, and that was nice, having hot water again."

"I don't want you to worry about it," he said after a while, something sad blowing into his voice.

"But I do." She did not look up.

"I know, Dale. I know you worry."

Beneath his words, Justy felt an acknowledgment of all the other worries Dale carried: whether Jake and Kyle would get along, where they'd go if the mining company got their permits, if the jobs Gaines had promised would be enough. All of it passed between them quickly.

"I'll show you the cabin."

"I know where it is, Dale." Kyle stood.

"It just seems like the proper thing to do." Dale walked to the back door.

"All right, then."

Justy followed them both, feeling more like a shadow than a person. They walked the fifteen feet to the slick ramp spanning the creek and leading to the cabin. The creek ran high and fast, full with the snow-melt. Justy dropped a bit of orange into the water, wishing it well on its journey. The room had no electricity, so it was dark and damp and had the rich, musty smell of redwoods and moss. A small stove hunkered in one corner, and two tiny windows faced each other from opposite walls. Cobwebs tangled in the ceiling corners, gray strands almost black in the dim light. Justy looked and saw a tiny brown spider balancing on its web, waiting. The cabin was cold, tucked into the shade of the trees.

"It isn't much," Dale said, playing with her shirt once more. Two days after Jake had told her Kyle was returning, she'd swept the floor and stacked kindling and wood by the stove.

"Seems grand to me," Kyle said, and rocked on his toes. She sighed and walked to the tired mattress sitting on rusted box springs. They creaked when she sat, and she rubbed her arms against the chill.

"Dale, them logging camps up in Washington and Oregon, they seem like hell compared to this." Kyle watched her face. She held her chin in her hands.

"How's it been, Dale?" His voice was low and calm, and he glanced at Justy, She studied him, trying to decide whose side he was on or whether he knew that the way out was not to be on anyone's side.

Dale looked away and shook her head. "Fine. You know..." She took a deep breath.

"I'm sorry, Dale."

She sat up and said, "Don't feel sorry for me, Kyle. I've made my choices and I'm sticking by them."

Kyle turned and tried to open the west window. It stuck and he rested his elbows on the sill, looking out at the valley and the mountains on the far side of the river canyon. "I didn't mean it that way, Dale. It's just that, well, I'm the one that taught him to fight."

Dale continued to look at the floor.

Justy felt a downpour of confusion. She knew Kyle's words were part of the puzzle, but she didn't know where or how to fit them in. His sadness filled her and she tried to keep it out. He stared through the window and finally said, "It's a sin to age, Dale. And I'm not even talking about how your physical body starts breaking down on you. It's a sin that my memory can't even hold on to the good days."

It seemed that he was struggling to find words.

"I remember when Jake first came to stay with me, when Lila sent him north. I remember building him a rope swing so he'd have something to do when we were in the woods all day long." Kyle's eyes were closed. Dale slumped on the bed, and Kyle floated in his memories.

"Next thing I can remember, he's seventeen and got more attitude than I know what to do with, and we got into it, over something that escapes me now, and I hit him, like a man, and he was still just a boy. He fell to the ground, crumpled like rag doll, and then he was on his feet, fists up, ready. It was raining, dead of winter, and that house out at Reese Ranch grew smaller every day and we just fought... I blame myself."

He opened his eyes. "That wasn't the only time, I have to admit."

Justy wanted to run, but the story held her. Dale reached a hand toward Kyle and then stopped. Justy felt too small to contain everything that swirled in the room. The sound of the creek swelled.

"Anyway, did I mention in that last camp, there were black widow spiders in all the bunks, every night a fellow went to bed?" Kyle winked at Justy, suddenly seeming to see her. His voice had changed, smoothing the space left by his earlier words. He turned to Dale, a grin riding his wrinkles. "One guy, he took to sleeping in his truck, he got so sick of them spiders."

Dale shook her head and walked to the door. I'll get to fixing dinner."

They both stood quiet, and the sound of the water again filled the cabin.

"It's good to see you, Dale," he said.

She nodded and turned to him. "I hope it all goes well." She walked down the plank and to the house. Justy felt herself cleave a little, the different water in her trying to run in opposite directions.

Kyle sat on the bed, his lean, tall frame folding in on itself. Justy turned to follow Dale, and Kyle cleared his throat.

"Where are your words, girl?" He smiled, resting his palms on his knees.

She studied the wrinkles on his face.

"Can't be no harm in not talking if you don't have nothing to say."

Justy blinked. The softness in Kyle bent toward her, and she tried anew to keep him out.

"But I reckon with the way you listen, there'll be a time when you will have something to say."

She nodded.

***

Lacee, Micah and Justy helped Kyle bring his few things to the cabin. Justy carried his guitar and tried to absorb all the music he'd played. She wished Jake would let her touch his fiddle, even if just once, so she could feel the songs. Lacee and Micah asked Kyle about the motorcycle and when he'd take them for a ride. "As soon as your mama will let me," he said.

Jake made his way home, confusion bleeding into a slow anger as he drove. A stop at the bar helped him ease the torque building in his guts about seeing Kyle. The alcohol allowed him to slide away from his anger for a window of time, just like the music did.

When all of Kyle's possessions found a place in the cabin, he began arranging his clothes in the built-in closet while Lacee made a fire. He pulled three masks from one of the boxes and found nails to hang them on. The faces were carved from wood, and the lips were large and all curved upward. The last one Kyle hung had a piercing set of eyes, so that Justy had to look away. Kyle lit two candles, rigged up a tottering bench with pieces of firewood and a board, then took the guitar from Justy.

"Have a seat, my friends." He tipped his cowboy hat.

The children settled on the bench, Justy in the middle. Kyle sat on the bed and tuned the guitar, his long fingers more graceful than Jake's. He strummed and grinned wide. "Any requests?"

"How about 'Tennessee Stud'?" Lacee asked.

"What a fine choice," he said, and began to play, singing about two horses that brought a couple together. Micah and Lacee sang the chorus with him, and Justy wondered how they fell so easily into song with this man she still considered a stranger. She was used to feeling the ache to know Jake and Dale before she was born, but now she wanted to see Lacee on a horse with Kyle. And to see Kyle guiding Micah to the dark spots in the pond where the catfish lurked. They sang and she listened, hoping for clues in the songs.

Lacee curled an arm around Justy, closing her eyes and letting the words pour out. She had some of Dale's voice in her and was beginning to realize it, but she kept it guarded. Heat from the stove started cutting into the chill, and their voices made Jake's return ease down in Justy. The children clapped when the song ended, and Kyle beamed. "Jake's been doing his work, I see."

"We really don't sing with him," Micah said, looking at his tennis shoes.

"But we still know all the songs," Lacee said.

"A family should have its songs," Kyle said. "And its stories." He adjusted the cowboy hat. "Okay, Mike. Lay a choice on me."

Micah squirmed, causing the bench to rock forward. He tossed his brown bangs. "I don't know the title."

"Say the words, boy."

"You know, the one about the storm across the valley."

Kyle said, "Another good one." He sang about the clouds rolling in and ain't it good to be back home again.

Jake had just hit the dirt road leading to the house. Dale was making dumplings to go along with the venison stew, hands grateful for a task as she heard Jake's truck.

The song finished as Jake pulled the Willys up next to Kyle's Chevy. They all heard the quiet after he turned off the truck.

"Sounds like Dad's home," Lacee said. She got up and added wood to the fire. Kyle set the guitar on the bed, stood, then sat back down. "Well, string bean. We didn't play you a tune."

Justy stared at Kyle, whose face remained calm.

Jake walked into the house, greeted Dale and asked after the children.

"What's your pick?" Kyle placed the guitar back on his lap and held his hands ready. Justy closed her eyes and tried to push back Jake and Dale. She wanted a soothing song, one that would bring them all together. Lacee bumped Justy's head forward with an elbow.

"Answer him."

Justy wished for a song to swim toward her. Whenever Jake sang, Dale hummed before she realized it was a pagan tune, and then she'd whisper a prayer to herself.

Kyle said, "How about this one?" He began to sing "On the Wings of a Dove," stretching his deep voice and singing about pure sweet love. All of it a sign from above.

Again, Lacee and Micah joined in on the chorus. Jake walked up the plank to the cabin and Justy wondered if the feeling that flooded her would be similar when Armageddon happened. Jake opened the door, and Lacee and Micah stopped singing. A cold draft filled the room while Jake stood there, his jeans and flannel shirt mud-splattered. Kyle nodded but kept singing.

Jake pushed his glasses back when Lacee joined Kyle again on the chorus. Her sweet voice hit him sideways, distracting him from his old anger. Lacee saw his look and closed her eyes, her voice growing stronger. Kyle kept his voice down, giving Lacee room. When the song ended, she tossed her hair, her neck and face painted with a deep blush. Micah reached across Justy to pat Lacee on the knee. Kyle beamed. Jake shook his head, wondering where she'd learned to sing like that.

"Listen, Kyle." Jake pointed his index finger. "We're gonna have some rules."

Kyle nodded and said, "I reckoned."

The tide of Jake's anger faded, leaving him with a pointing finger and his father and children waiting. He realized how much he'd missed Kyle, even though he'd sworn to keep him at a distance. The creek rolled under the plank, and time seemed to crawl. Jake dropped his finger.

"How about rosining up the bow, son?" Kyle tapped the body of the guitar. Jake gently closed the door behind himself. "Whew," Lacee said.

"What do you say? Is he coming back?" Kyle's eyebrows raised.

"I bet you a motorcycle ride he is." Lacee walked to Kyle with her hand extended.

"Lacee," Micah hissed. "We ain't supposed to bet. You know it's worldly."

She shrugged and said, "It's not gonna hurt anybody, so you keep quiet."

"All right," Kyle said to Lacee, and they shook. "We got us a bet." While they waited, Kyle tinkered on the guitar, making up a song about a grandfather being too long gone, his grandchildren growing up like trees in the forest. He even sang about his tomboy granddaughters, wearing pants. Justy smiled and looked down at her and Lacee's jeans, thinking about that prissy Sky Harris who wore dresses every day; she and Lacee wore them only to meeting.

Jake came in with his fiddle case. He stood next to the children and pulled out the instrument. Kyle watched him draw the bow across the amber rosin, and Justy thought she saw tears in Kyle's eyes. Jake began playing "I Am a Man of Constant Sorrow." Jake slid the bow through the somber melody. The song was one of his favorites—it had seemed sad in a beautiful sort of way, just like the Eel seemed lonely in the early mornings with its curtain of fog. Now Jake seemed to be making a statement to Kyle, and the room filled with the power of it, how it carried Jake away from the confines of his body and soothed his hands. As he swayed with the melody, his glasses caught the candlelight and hid his eyes.

The song ended and Kyle strummed a few chords, and said, "'Sing Me Back Home.'" Jake started the song, and the two of them were off, playing and singing about a prisoner's final request before dying. Kyle sang the story part of the song, and Jake joined on the chorus. Justy knew she wasn't supposed to think such things, but it felt like magic, their voices combining in that way. It was hard to imagine that these two men hadn't spoken in years, but maybe that's what the music did for them—let them glide next to each other. Justy watched Jake's fingers on the fiddle and wondered what other Colby hands had played it.

Kyle started a Cajun waltz, opening with a dance of fingers. Jake smiled and the children watched them trading licks and playing across the years. Dale caught the strands of music coming from the cabin while she plopped the last of the dumpling dough on top of the stew, then washed her hands. Through the kitchen window she saw the smoke curl from the cabin roof and the candlelight glowing through the windows. She went to the back door and drew aside the curtain, smiling.

The night air raised her bare arms in gooseflesh. She glanced at the moonless sky and saw hundreds of stars. The work of Jehovah constantly amazed her, and she thanked Him again for the chance to live in such country, even though surviving felt like a daily miracle.

***

Sweat dotted both the men's foreheads, yet they kept playing, talking through the songs. They paused for a moment and Kyle winked at Jake.

"Let's go down to the river, boy."

Jake nodded and Justy sat straighter. Kyle said to the children, "You can help us on this one."

Lacee leaned forward and Micah smiled. Kyle taught them the refrain and said, "That's the basic song. Ready?"

Kyle began, "As I went down in the river to pray, studying about that good old way." Jake eased in the fiddle. If the sound of all their voices joined together was anything near to love, Justy wanted in. The harmony pushed up against her promise—it felt like two kinds of hunger wrestling inside her, pulling her stomach apart. She jiggled the penny in her shoe, trying to remind herself that someone had to tend Jake and Dale's words and their silences, and Justy knew she was the one. She let the song wash over her and felt Dale outside, also aching to join. Dale swayed with the harmony, closing her eyes and remembering back when her voice had been the pillar for this song, when she hadn't made her own kind of sacrifices to Jehovah. It made her think of her baptism, not in a river but in a tank of warm water at a Witness convention. Her heart surged at the memory, how she'd made the strange promise never to sing the pagan songs again, not with Kyle hitting Jake and then leaving. Her hand went to her chest to keep from reaching out toward the cabin.

J usty sat outside the classroom on a wooden bench, listening to the sounds of Jennifer Sloan's birthday party. The afternoon sun sat an inch above the western mountains, and she could tell there was an hour of school left. She kicked her legs and the bench rocked. The snow had completely melted, but cold air stung her eyes. Three small chickadees pecked in the dirt of the baseball field, and a crow flew overhead. Kyle had been with them about two weeks now, but Gaines had found some excuse for the grave job not to start. Kyle had dropped the children off at the bus stop that morning, heading south to the sawmill in Madrone to maybe pick up a couple days of work. Jake still dug ditch for Gaines, helping create a waterline on the property where a hot tub and sauna would go. Dale was out in service with Joella Mills, knocking on doors in the Madrone area, spreading Jesus' word. Justy didn't understand how Dale could find the courage to speak to strangers about her faith, but it was part of the commitment to witness to Jehovah's Truth, and Dale tried to make good on it at least once a month.

Ms. Long had told the students to move their desks for the board games and jacks. When the students began, she walked to Justy, squatted and smiled gently. The flowers in her hair had wilted like they did every day by this time.

"Justy. Go ahead and wait outside." Ms. Long laid a warm hand on Justy's.

Justy walked to the door, trying not to notice how the room seemed to pause and inspect her. Ochre watched, his blue eyes intense. Justy frowned, knowing that even though she wanted to stay, she was doing the right thing by leaving the room. When the four riders came, she'd be on the right side of things, even if there were no sign of Jehovah in her heart. The copy of the birthday calendar Ms. Long had sent home at the beginning of the year didn't have Justy's name on it. Dale had transferred the dates to the Tucker's Logging Supply calendar. Under pictures of horses and beaches and redwood trees, Dale drew small X's in the right-hand corner of the days her children should be sent out of their classrooms. Halloween, Christmas-decoration days, any birthday.

The children inside sang "Happy Birthday" to Jennifer and then clapped. Justy waited outside and thought about Ochre and his strange name. The other kids didn't talk to him, except to call him okra or ogre. He still sat by her at lunch without comment, and he'd begun to smell good to her, like fallen leaves in the autumn.

The empty playground was quiet. Uptown, a quarter mile away, an occasional pickup drove by, leaving the store or the post office, maybe stopping at the gas station for cigarettes or a fill-up. It seemed only tourists ate at the two diners, their long cars or RVs seeming out of place. Justy walked to the pole in the center of the playground, where the flags danced in the slight breeze. The red, white and blue flag folded in on itself, and the state bear on the other one walked up into the sky. She loved the California flag, though she knew she shouldn't love anything to do with man's government. She liked how the brown of the bear contrasted with the white background. She wished she could see one someday.

Justy walked to the swings, the penny's slide a comfort, and sat facing the baseball field and the old mill farther on. Almost all the kids she'd watched from the bench looked toward the school while they flew higher and higher from the ground. Her legs found a rhythm, and she felt the glorious pull of gravity and motion. It reminded her of her dreams, how she felt swimming, free and without a body.

Her view of the sawmill came and went, and she remembered the pictures in Jake's yearbooks. So many more children played in the school-yard then, and stacks and stacks of logs waited in the background. In some of the photos, smoke poured from the domed mill, its white plume seeming to drift from the tops of the children's heads. Justy saw the gutted mill yard, the orange-red rust of the dome, and thought about the soil that the mining company wanted. The trees and the soil and the mill were different shades of red, and she wondered about the Indian blood running her body. Her hands seemed as pale as any of her classmates'.

A piece of glass glimmered, and she knew it was a broken beer bottle. A few of the remaining high school students and their dropout friends would gather at the mill yard on the weekends, drinking and throwing bottles at the dome, a circle of smashed glass ringing the rusted structure.

The chill forced tears from her eyes. She heard a door open and she stopped pumping, turning gently to see Ochre walking toward her. She twisted the swing so she could face him. He wore black corduroy overalls and the denim jacket with all the bright colors. His face widened into a deep smile. Justy liked how his eyes crinkled at the corners. She tried to look fierce, telling this boy to go away. He sat on the swing next to her, facing away from the school. She slowly turned back around and sat as still as any stone she'd ever watched.

"The cupcakes were burnt on the bottom," he said. She wanted to laugh, since this was the first thing he'd ever said to her, but she kept her eyes on the mill dome. The chains of his swing creaked. "My mom, she doesn't want me to eat any refined sugar." His boots were covered in mud. "We eat things made with honey and carob."

Justy knew he was scrunching up his face. She wondered what it was like to live in a tipi, the way some real Indians used to. Helen from Hilltop had said these people were from Berkeley, and Justy had looked on a map to see where it was. It seemed so far, but then she'd looked to see where Arkansas was and realized it was worlds away, and that was where Kyle and Lila had both come from. The only thing Justy knew about Berkeley was that it had a university, a place Colbys didn't go. She wanted to know if Ochre had lived in a tipi in Berkeley, but she pulled her gaze away and he began to swing. Justy watched his shadow kiss his feet and then release him back to the sky. After a few minutes, he stopped swinging and stared at her.

"And my mom," Ochre said, "she believes in a true separation of church and state, like it's written in the Constitution, so that's why I don't participate in all that holiday stuff."

Justy didn't understand what he was saying, but she knew he was giving her some clues. She realized he'd be ready whenever she decided to talk to him. She felt it all well up inside her, the nights without food and praying the hunger would end, hoping to find a way to fill the silences between Jake and Dale. Ochre would listen with that wide-eyed look and that would be enough.

She pushed off and they were swinging, their rhythms out of sync, and then they were evenly matched. Justy leaned back, letting her head and hair hang so that the world was upside down, the sky a generous patch of cloudless blue. Ochre leaned back, too, and they both gradually came to a stop, her loose hair and the tip of his braid brushing the dirt beneath them.

He stood and Justy sat up, looking at his calm face.

"I got to go walking." He smiled and started to move away, then turned. "Come swim sometime," he said.

She didn't know what he meant but she liked that he asked her, that her circle of people could maybe grow to include someone like him, a boy with color who seemed to understand her lack of speech. The peace sign flashed as he walked on beyond the baseball field and disappeared in the tall grass by the creek.

She swung gently and wanted to walk with him the farther distance to the Drive-Thru Tree a half mile past the mill yard. She'd show him the color of the Tree, see if he understood that the innards of a sequoia might be red. Men told stories in the bars—pretending she wasn't there—about how they liked to take their dates to the Tree because the women couldn't open the doors. Justy imagined her and Ochre standing free in the cut-out, running their hands over the names and dates carved into the Tree. They'd stand the wintry shade of the tunnel, and Justy would be in the place Jake and Dale had first come together.

She wondered if Dale had sung for Jake that night, sixteen and hopeful at his interest. Dale's voice must have been beautiful, filling the truck and the night and the Tree. Justy guessed Dale probably sang for all she was worth, using the one thing she had in this world to call her own, after her adoptive mother put her back in the foster-care system.

Ochre's blond hair bobbed up and he waved. He started walking back at the same time the bell rang for the last recess. Children flooded out of the classrooms, and as they did, he walked to her and opened his fist. The five other swings filled with eager bodies and Justy took the tiny, smooth green rock he held out to her.

**

Lacee sat in the last seat of the bus, reading away while Micah sat again near the Harris twins, keeping his spirit safe from worldly influence. Justy remembered the scripture that the Witnesses quoted often, "Bad association spoils useful habits," and she wondered what would become of her since she spent so much time in bars with Jake. She sat by herself and looked out the window as the rest of the children took seats. The boxy blue car sat near the bus and Sunshine waited, twirling the beads hanging from the rearview mirror. Ochre walked over and she got out of the car and they hugged a long time. When they pulled apart, he touched her green scarf as he told her something that made her laugh. Justy turned the stone over and watched them drive away, and she saw the car's name, Volvo.

The ride was long, the yellow metal bending through the curves of the old highway. The Colby children got off the bus, and Emmet headed south to drop off the Harris twins and one other kid, a hippie type named Forest. A hundred feet from their bus stop, a silver sedan waited in the shade of the freeway overpass. Micah ran to the car, becoming a silhouette as he entered the dark shadows of the concrete structure. Lacee and Justy walked up and stood behind Micah.

Lucas Mills sat in the car, his brown hair slicked back, a smile lurking on his pale face. His slim body seemed hidden in the folds of his blue suit. A Bible lay open in front of him, and on the seat sat a pad with neatly printed notes.

"Come on, kids. I'll take you home." His smooth words filled the afternoon.

Micah ran around and climbed in while Lacee and Justy slid into the backseat. Lucas handed Micah his Bible and started the car. Micah traced his fingers over the gilded letters. Lucas glanced every few seconds at Micah and he smiled back, his brown eyes full of shine.

It had been Lucas's wife, Joella, who had first knocked on the door before Justy was born. Joella was the one with the quiet voice who spoke some kind of sense to Dale and helped open up a river of faith between Dale and Jehovah. Joella had the kindest eyes of anyone Justy had ever seen.

Lucas drove to the house for Jake's monthly Bible study, the same way Joella had studied with Dale. Sometimes Jake didn't show up, and Justy couldn't remember when she'd last seen Brother Mills at their house.

He didn't talk, his hands loose on the steering wheel. When they reached the house, Lucas turned to Lacee and Justy. "You girls been good?"

His right arm lined the seat behind Micah, almost pulling him closer to his presence. Lacee and Justy nodded, and Justy wanted to know why he never asked Micah. She tried to see her brother as Lucas did, and she felt a stab of jealousy fill her. She didn't understand how it was Micah who got to be the boy and the one to feel Jehovah so solidly in his heart.

"Glad to hear that," Lucas said, and then Lacee and Justy went in the house. Justy looked back and saw Lucas and Micah talking. She knew Micah's name was in the Bible—maybe that was why he was connected to Jehovah. Dale had picked his name even before she'd heard of the Jehovah's Witnesses. Justy knew that Jake had picked her name while Dale was at a congregation meeting, cementing her alliance with Jehovah after Kyle had left, Justy still growing inside her. Jake was so sure Justy would be another boy, he took her name from his favorite pair of cowboy boots. When she'd shown herself to the world as a girl, he changed the name to Justine.

Dale greeted the girls, then walked to her bedroom with an armload of clean clothes. They set the books on the kitchen table and went to help her. The house was spotless, and Justy could smell coffee and something sweet, fresh from the oven. The clothes were stiff having dried out on the line in the crisp spring air. Most of the things were seconds from Mamie or Joella, brought into the house when Jake wasn't home. They folded the clothes in silence, Lacee standing next to Dale, their hair almost opposites.

When the clothes were folded, Dale brushed her hair, making sure Lucas would be able to tell she tried to make this a godly family. Lacee and Justy went to the kitchen table and began their homework. After fifteen minutes, Lucas followed Micah into the house. Lucas carried a black plastic bag in one hand and his book bag in the other. Micah smiled broadly and whispered, "Brother Mills says I can get baptized when I'm ten."

Dale and Lucas said hello and she offered him coffee. He declined, saying he'd wait until Jake arrived. Then he held up the plastic bag. "Sister Harris asked me to pass these along to you."

Dale's face turned scarlet, and she took the bag of more hand-me-down clothes, probably collected by Mamie when she'd gone on a visit to the Santa Rosa congregation where a Harris cousin lived.

"It'll be one of the youngest baptisms," Micah whispered to Justy. He stuck his hands in his faded jeans and rocked on his toes, just like Kyle. Justy blinked at his confidence. She knew the Witnesses were different from most religions because a person had to make a conscious choice to be baptized. The responsibilities that came with it were too large to give to an unknowing child, and most Witness children were baptized at fifteen or sixteen. Justy looked from Micah's sure smile to Lacee, stuck in another book. If any one of them was supposed to get baptized, it should be her.

Lucas walked to the table and laid his Bible down. He cleared his throat and straightened his tie. "See the difference?" he asked. Lacee shrugged. Dale stepped closer, laying her arms across the back of Micah's chair. A long minute passed.

"What I'm talking about is the difference between that homework of yours, the ideas of man, and this Bible, the knowledge of Jehovah God."

Dale nodded, but she frowned slightly.

"I'm not saying your homework isn't important. Schooling is valuable."

Dale's face relaxed and she leaned forward.

"The word of God deserves equal or more time in your lives."

Lucas tilted his head and ran a finger over Lacee's math book, clicking his tongue, and then walked to the couch, where he sat and studied his notes. Justy tumbled the pebble from Ochre in her hand, under the table where no one could see.

***

The last of the day's sunlight slipped over the mountains as Jake walked into the house and stopped just inside the door, his eyes trying to make sense of Lucas. Then he pivoted and placed his muddy hand on the doorknob—all he wanted was a shower, and he'd forgotten that Dale had arranged another monthly study for him. Lucas stood, his feet hitting the rug with a soft thud. His piston-like legs carried him across the room to Jake in a whirl of motion and blue cloth.

"Jacob," Lucas said, drawing out the name.

"Luke." Jake nodded once, and adjusted his glasses. Lucas wrapped an arm around Jake and guided him toward the table. Jake moved as far away as he could within that grasp, his mud-spattered flannel shirt contrasting against Lucas's suit. Lucas waved his free hand and the children stood, leaving the two men to face the table and the Bible.

"How's things been, Jacob?"

"Fine." Jake stole a look at Dale and then studied the mud creased into his jeans. Lucas cleared his throat and said, "Let us pray to begin this study."

He bowed his head. While he spoke, asking for Jehovah's loving spirit to fill the house, Jake looked around, his gaze caged by the angle of his downcast head. He wanted to feel blessed—be connected to the higher order of things—but he was almost sure that what he felt when he was in the woods or playing the fiddle was enough. Justy thought about the song Jake and Kyle had sung a few weeks before, the one about going to the river to pray. It made the most sense to her, the river being the place to talk to God.

She sat on the living room floor and listened to Lucas read from a brown book he held. He told the story of Job, how God allowed Satan to test one of Jehovah's most faithful servants. Lucas's voice was smooth, and the Bible pages rustled as he turned to the Scriptures cited in the brown book. Dale floured meat in the kitchen, and Justy heard the sizzle when Dale placed it in the skillet. The house seemed to grow smaller, the four rooms leading into one another and this moment, anger blooming inside Jake. He sat straighter and listened from a greater and greater distance to this story—God allowing Satan to strip Job of his land and livestock, then his wives, then his children. The knuckles of Jake's hands moved a little closer to one another.

"Wait a minute." Jake pushed back from the table, the chair scraping harshly on the floor.

Lucas looked up from his books and cocked his head. "Yes, Jacob?"

Dale paused in the kitchen, a piece of illegal meat in her hands.

"You mean to tell me God made a bet with the Devil?" Jake asked.

Lucas placed his thin hands over the two books and sighed.

"Well, in a way, he did."

"And Job, he lost it all?"

"If we keep reading, we'll see that Job got everything back, more than he had before." Lucas leaned over the table, his tie dangling on the Bible.

"He got his wives back? His kids?" Jakes legs were flexed, ready to leave.

Lucas cleared his throat. "Jehovah gave him other wives, prettier than the first ones, and his children, he had twice as many."

Jake ran his hands through his hair, took off his glasses and rubbed his eyes.

"And he came to know Jehovah on a deeper, more humble level."

Jake put his glasses back on and looked at Dale, then to the children in the living room. He caught Justy's eyes. His expression—a mixture of love and rage—was too much, and she looked away, reaching for the stone in her pocket. Micah and Lacee watched her slip it in her mouth. She flipped it with her tongue as the moment grew and the house shrank.

"That ain't right."

Jake stood. Lucas followed and reached across the table, his palm soothing the air between them. "If we can talk some more, Jacob, I think you'll see it makes sense, in the big picture. This really is a story we can learn from if we step back from it."

Lucas's hand kept caressing the air. The stone tasted flat, like Justy imagined the bottom of the Eel at Carver's Hole would taste.

She knew the Witnesses didn't believe these were just stories, things to learn from.

"I've been studying with you going on two years, Luke."

Jake looked at Dale, who met his gaze and swallowed. "I been trying to understand what it is Dale sees in this stuff." He turned back to Lucas. "But no more. I won't have any more of your shit. I ain't having no part with a god that'd kill a man's children, his family, just to prove a point."

His voice rose in pitch and volume, and all eyes and ears tensed further. Jake walked into the living room and took one steady look at the children, his brown eyes wild behind his glasses. Justy felt Dale panic, knowing Jake's chances in the New System dwindled as he walked out the door.

***

Dinner was quiet—chicken-fried steak and mashed potatoes. The silence stretched until Justy felt it would flood the house, leaving nothing. Kyle was the only one to find any words. When he walked in the door an hour after Jake had left, he took one look around and then drew a big breath. When they sat at the table, he told them the sawmill had at least three days' work for him and he was pleased, seeing as how the foreman used to be a rodeo buddy of his. Justy ate slowly and imagined what it would be like to chew with Ochre's stone in her mouth, the mashed potatoes easing around the pebble like the stream that had formed it.

Dale tried to pay attention to Kyle and succeeded for a bit, a sad smile pasted to her mouth. But after ten minutes she gave up, her insides turning icy at the thought of what would happen to Jake now, when the End came.

Lacee saved them by asking Kyle for a story. She tossed her black hair out of her eyes, took a breath and moved forward from the afternoon. "What do you remember about me as a baby?"

Kyle laid down his fork and paused. His silence drove back the other one, and when he spoke, the room seemed to grow warmer. Dale took bites of her food rather than just playing with it.

"Well, you was born in the Ukiah hospital in the summer heat. Your mama and dad were living out at the Reese Ranch then, in the very same house your dad and me used to live in. Funny, huh? This was before they got lined up here, caretaking this place."

Kyle indicated Dale with a gentle point of his thumb, and she smiled.

"Your dad and me, we were working a falling job, and one afternoon your dad just lays down his chain saw while he's in the middle of a face cut into a lovely, ancient hemlock. He says to me, 'It's time.'"

Kyle was rolling now, pulling them into that other afternoon with his direct gaze, the way he leaned into his words.

"So, I'm not a man to doubt another most times, especially when it comes to birthing babies. I put down my chain saw, too, and we walk out of the woods and to the truck, and Jake, he's like a man made of rubber, not able to get the door open, losing his glasses in the dust of the landing. I work the handle for him and there's no way he's driving, so I climb in behind the wheel and he says, 'Haul ass,' and I do. We get to the ranch, and there's your mama, seventeen and full with you, and your dad was right. You're about to enter the world and we got to get to the hospital. Now."

Dale laid down her fork and leaned into her hand, carried back. Lacee listened to Kyle, her head slightly cocked, enjoying her story. Justy took in Kyle's words like they were food, letting her body find new places for the story to rest.

"Can we go to the River Fork hospital?" Kyle shook his head.

"Nope, not good enough. How about the Willits hospital? No, we got to go to Ukiah because it's got the best reputation and your mama will not have you enter this world unless it's in the best way. And off we go, Dale in the middle and your dad over by the door, wound tighter than a bantam rooster. The two of them are clinging to each other during the contractions, sweat on all three of our brows, and it ain't 'cause of the June heat, let me tell you. The truck is doing the best it can and I'm just hoping we don't start to hear pistons knocking. A little past Willits, I see the lights from a highway patrol car. I pull over, hoping this ain't going to take too long. Your dad is out of the truck and charging the officer. The guy is so afraid to move we're all stuck, me thinking I shouldn't take off without Jake. But Dale, she starts to singing and her singing gets louder and louder. Her voice is so dazzling, I'm thinking she should be making records while she's in labor if this is what pain does to her voice."

Kyle stopped to take a drink of water, setting it down with a chuckle. Justy noticed again how his eyes looked like the Eel when she wore her fall colors.

"What happened next?" Micah asked. Kyle rubbed his hands together, looked at each child in turn, then he and Dale grinned.

"We left him," Kyle said.

"You left Jake?" Micah and Lacee asked together.

"Yep, I put the Willys in gear and we took off. I figured the two of them would work it out and then we'd have a police escort."

"I turned around, and the look on Jake's face..." Dale held up her hands as if to ward off the look, even now.

Kyle paused for a moment before continuing. "The next time I see Jake, he and the cop are standing outside the nursery pointing and talking about which is the cutest baby." Kyle grinned even wider. "Of course, the darling of the bunch, they both decided, was the black-haired little girl in the left corner." Kyle reached out and tousled Lacee's hair. She crossed her arms and smiled.

"Tell the rest, Kyle," Dale said.

He puzzled a look at her.

"You know, about that lady and her comment."

"Oh. Yeah. While we're standing there admiring you, and your mama is sleeping off the work she's done to bring you here, this couple walks up, not much older than Jake and Dale."

Lacee leaned forward, greedy for her details, Justy understood this hunger.

"And the woman," Kyle said, "she said in this whispering sort of voice, but it ain't any whisper because we can all hear her, plain as day. She says, 'Why, look at that little Indian baby,' pointing right at you."

"At me?" Lacee furrowed her brow.

Kyle and Dale nodded.

"You were a little Indian baby," Micah said.

Lacee laughed a little and threw a glance at Dale.

"Can you believe that?" Dale asked and then looked at her pale hands, feeling lost again because her children looked so much like Jake.

"What about me?" Micah asked. "What happened when I was born? Did I look Indian?"

"I remember that night," Lacee said. A scowl crossed her face.

"It was a crazy one," Kyle said.

"Tell me," Micah almost pleaded.

"Guns and horses, that's what I remember," Lacee said.

"And don't forget the whiskey," Dale said, her voice firm. A moment passed and the good feeling that had been blossoming in Justy wilted.

"Lots of firewater," Kyle finally said. "I'll tell you another time, Mike." He stood and Micah frowned at his empty dinner plate. Kyle placed a hand on his head.

"Your daddy was proud, don't you think different," Kyle said. He took his plate to the sink and then left through the back door after thanking Dale for dinner. They heard his guitar from the cabin while they cleared the table and washed the dishes. Justy tumbled Ochre's stone in her mouth, her stomach eased. Hovering on the edge of this calm was all she felt but couldn't express—Dale's lonesome worry about Jake and Jehovah, Jake's idea of the Witnesses, the distant place she was trying to put Kyle in.

Spring rolled forward and the rain continued to fall, feeding the Eel and the restless places inside Justy. Her favorite part of school came at ten o'clock, when she and Ochre were sent to the sixth-grade classroom for reading. Even though they were second-graders, their book reports and poetry declared them advanced, and daily they walked the short distance to Lacee's room. Justy sat next to her sister for the whole hour. The group took turns reading aloud and whenever it was Justy's turn, Lacee or Ochre would read her part. No teacher supervised the group, and Justy loved how the story spun itself around them and they were taken to other places and other times.

Eleven-o'clock recess came and Justy sat on the bench, the other children whirling in the spring rain. She held the stone tight in her right hand and checked the landscape of her family. Ochre sat next to her, waiting. She was thinking about the four riders again and when the world would end. She knew there was supposed to be a raising of the dead and a chance for the resurrected to learn the Word of Jehovah. Jake and Kyle sat in the Willys at the town cemetery, waiting to begin the unearthing of bodies. She kept listening for the sound of hooves.

***

Jake toyed with the steering wheel while Kyle stared out the windshield. Between them sat a black metal lunch box that Dale had packed with sandwiches, jerky and two apples. Three days before, Jake had finished the waterline trough and Gaines had finally agreed to begin the grave job. Beyond the tree trunks that ringed the cemetery, the roiling Eel moved powerfully, eating at the bank. Headstones scattered the area, most of them gray and canted, a few moss-covered and deep green. Salal and redwood ferns grew in sporadic clumps throughout the gravesite. Redwoods reached tall and dark toward the gray sky. Part of one tree's looping roots jutted out over the water, the soil washed away.

"It doesn't make much sense, does it?" Kyle asked.

"What?"

"How them great big trees got those shallow roots. You'd think Mother Nature would've given them a taproot that went all the way to China."

Jake blinked behind his glasses, amazed anew at the giants. Kyle leaned forward and whistled. Jake shivered inside his denim jacket and glanced into the truck's side mirror. Kyle looked from the ancient trees to the white sky. "Looks like more rain," he said.

Jake used to be able to feel close to this man. "Figures," he said, and turned back to the graying clouds and looked from sky to river—almost a mean-spirited thing in the winter in these high-water years. It seemed like forever ago. In summer, the river was an inviting green, nothing like the brown mass of movement in front of him now.

The rain had fallen for a week, the river rising and finally pushing Gaines to get the job done. The Eel seemed close to its breaking point, like it had in '64, and Jake knew if it kept raining, their work would only be miserable and hard-pressed.

"Damn that Gaines," Jake said. The silence swelled and he shifted in his seat. He rolled down the window. Cool air crept in and he sighed.

"You think the graves are going because they took out all the trees in the middle of this grove?" Kyle asked.

"Probably so," Jake answered. "Just wait until that mine goes through. They'll strip it all down." They both shook their heads.

"How the salmon runs been down here?" Kyle asked.

"Kind of shitty. Not like they used to be."

"One guy I worked with in Washington, Indian fellow from the Puyallup tribe, he liked to tell how the salmon used to be so thick, a person could walk across the river on their backs. He said maybe Jesus wasn't so original."

Jake smiled and rolled his neck against the tension building in his shoulders.

Kyle gestured toward the graves and said, "We've done our part."

Jake considered this. All the trees he'd helped fall rose up in his thoughts and fell again—an earthquake's rumble in his memory. It made him proud and angry and confused all at once.

"I wonder if the bastard'll show," Jake said. He hated that he needed to rely on someone like Gaines to make it through the winter. Depending on the man in the summer was insult enough.

Kyle said, "If I remember old Shelby properly, he'll show all right, but not until he makes us sweat a little, like he's made us sweat for the job in the first place."

Jake studied his hands and wished they were wrapped around the handle of a chain saw. His fingers wanted the vibration of chain cutting solidly into a tree. Kyle looked back to the swirling river. A fat drop of rain landed on the windshield, and they both watched its watery path to the hood. Gaines's shiny white Ford pulled up next to them.

"Here we go," Jake said. They climbed out of the Willys and walked over to Gaines. The hum of a power window revealed his craggy face, and cigarette smoke poured out of the cab. A small white dog sat on Gaines's lap, barking at them until Gaines shoved him back. Gaines squinted against the smoke from the cigarette in his mouth. The dog worked his way back onto Gaines's lap and stuck his head out the window at Jake and Kyle.

"Sorry I'm late, boys, but I had to spend some time with Nigger this morning. She was acting funny, like maybe her stomach was paining her," Gaines said. When he talked, ash fell from his mouth onto the dog's back.

"Isn't that mare getting up in years?" Kyle asked, and Gaines stared at him. Jake shifted his weight and his thumbs danced outside his pockets.

"Been a while since I seen the famous high climber in these parts," Gaines finally said.

"Shelby." Kyle dipped his head toward Gaines.

"If you could've seen the look on her face, you'd of known something was wrong. You used to be horse people." Gaines looked through the windshield. Then he shook his head and said, "You going to sign that petition, Chief?"

Jake shrugged. Gaines talked like it had been weeks instead of hours since he'd seen Jake.

"They going to hire you or anybody else from around here?"

"Don't seem like it." Jake looked at the ground and stepped on a small rock, rolling it underneath his boot.

"They bringing people in?" Gaines sat up straighter, the wrinkles in his forehead doubling as he sucked on the cigarette.

"Probably so. Specialty crews."

"Shit fire if that ain't going to screw this town." Smoke drifted from the cab.

Jake pushed his boot harder against the rock.

"Can't be a caretaker all your life, eh?" Gaines smiled. He petted the dog without paying attention to where his hand landed. "Ready to dig, boys?" He grinned and said, "The vet is coming, so I can't stay long."

"Yes, sir," Jake said, thinking about the falling jobs later in the spring and the way his chain saw would feel. Kyle studied the sky.

"Good." Gaines threw his cigarette butt out the window. He placed a CAT cap on his thick brown hair and opened the door. The dog jumped out and sniffed Jake and Kyle's boots. Gaines started walking the instant his feet hit the ground. His short legs took quick and precise steps, the denim of his jeans making whipping sounds. The little dog trotted beside him. Jake and Kyle followed Gaines to the biggest family plot. The thick humus softened their steps, and the water rushed past noisily.

"This here's my family." Gaines gestured toward the group of headstones separated from the other graves by a decrepit wooden fence, some of the markers dated back to the eighteen hundreds, some were unread-

able, two simply said, "Child." Gaines stopped in front of the most recent headstone, military insignia decorating the corners. It read: "Shelby
Gaines, Jr. 1950–1970. Died an honorable death serving his country."

"He goes first," Gaines said, and coughed. "Then the rest of
my folks."

Jake looked to where the river ate at the bank. Other graves
would slip into the water soon. Gaines coughed again, deep and lung
bruising. He wiped his eyes and tried to grin, but all three men knew
he was in pain. Gaines stared at his son's grave, then pointed to the
plot of his wife, Rose. The dog pushed through the fence, lifted his leg
and sent a stream of urine on her headstone. Gaines moved like he
was going to kick the dog but stopped short. The dog slinked behind
a redwood tree.

"Damn mutt," Gaines said. Jake didn't know whether he wanted to
laugh or cry.

"Where do they go?" Kyle asked, hands deep in the pockets of his
jacket. He could see Gaines reflected in Jake's glasses. Jake closed his eyes
and listened to the river, thinking about how far away it could take him.
He heard movement and opened his eyes to see Gaines leave the plot and
walk to the bank, where he stood at the edge, hands on his blocky hips, as
if daring the water to move any closer. He turned to them after a minute
and raised his voice a notch.

"They go up by the Grange. The town has agreed to use the land
behind the hall," Gaines said, and gestured with his left hand. "All these
dead folks won't be my worry anymore, and they'll have a nice view of
the river from up there." He laughed and started into another raspy fit,
turning back to the water, his body heaving.

Jake and Kyle exchanged a look, and Kyle mimed smoking a cigarette. Gaines walked back to them, quiet tremors rippling his chest.

"The way this is going to work," he said, "is that you two dig up the
graves, sift through the dirt, find the bones and put them in labeled boxes." Gaines paused and looked at his family's headstones. "Not that I give a
good goddamn whether you throw all the bones in one box. Excepting my

kin, of course." He grinned and started back to the truck, seeming almost to run. The dog darted after him. Jake and Kyle followed, and when they reached the truck, Gaines climbed in and lit up a cigarette. The dog jumped in. "Move your ass, Shirley," Gaines said as he closed the door.

"You can unload the stuff," he said to them, and picked up a Zane Grey novel from the dashboard. The dog watched Jake and Kyle, sometimes pausing at Gaines's cough, tail stopped in midwag. When the bed of the truck was emptied, Jake and Kyle waited. Gaines used a book of matches to mark his place.

"I expect you to be here at eight every morning." Gaines coughed shallow and grinned. "Handle my family careful, especially Junior."

Jake and Kyle nodded as Gaines started the truck and shifted into reverse.

"I'll bring some more boxes come Wednesday." He pushed the dog off his lap and said, "Gotta go tend my girl." A small motor eased the window upward as he pulled away. The dog watched Jake and Kyle, tiny body quivering, mouth sending out soundless barks.

"He's a warm one, ain't he?" Kyle asked.

"Belongs in the ground with the rest of his bunch."

"Won't be too long."

"No wonder he got motivated to move this thing." Jake indicated the cemetery with an up tilt of his head. He watched the river and Kyle looked the direction Gaines had driven. Not a single vehicle passed on Highway 1 this time of day.

"Let's get after it," Jake said. He moved to the Gaines plot and felt the restless, cagey feeling in his hands. To stop it, he started building the sifter with a careful frenzy.

As Jake finished hammering one side of the chicken wire to the box frame he'd built, Kyle walked past him with a shovel. Drops of rain hit the backs of their necks and they both looked to the sky. They flipped up the collars of their jackets. Kyle sank a shovel slowly into the son's grave, as though he might feel something creep up through the soil, into the metal, into his leg.

The river rushed past and the sky lowered itself, the canopy pushing more water at the earth. Kyle continued to dig and Jake finished making the sifter. The redwoods around them leaned up to the sky, and when he wasn't looking, Jake knew for sure that the treetops had disappeared into the fog. The waterlogged earth gave easily under Kyle's shovel.

Jake stretched his back. He walked to the pile of supplies just outside the plot and grabbed a shovel. He roamed, shovel perched on his shoulder—a gesture he felt was too casual. But he didn't know how to carry himself. He didn't look at Kyle, digging up a boy Jake had gone to school with, killed in another forest. He stopped at Rose's grave and stood where he thought her feet had been.

"Begging your pardon," he said, and pushed the shovel into the ground. Kyle paid Jake's words no mind, only worked deeper into the son's grave. The sky released more rain and the dirt soon became mud. The shovels pulled away with sucking sounds. Jake tried to think of something funny to say, but his mind yielded nothing of the like, and so they worked in silence, the river full and hungry, the trees bridging the distance from earth to sky.

***

Justy sat in class, waiting for Ochre and then the rest of the students to finish their spelling papers. Ms. Long watched the new aquarium she'd brought in the week before, the tropical fish flashing their brilliant colors as they swam. Justy liked to watch them, too—how their tiny bodies flowed through the water, like she did in her dreams. Ms. Long's brown dress pooled at her ankles as she sat in front of the fish; the yellow flowers in her hair were beginning to wilt again. She turned from the tank to look at Justy. They held each other's gaze and then Ms. Long crooked a finger.

Justy stood and felt Jake growing angrier as the rain heckled his back. Dale sat at the kitchen table, studying the week's *Watchtower*, marking answers to the magazine questions. The meeting clothes she'd ironed still hung on the edge of the ironing board, and the love she felt from Jehovah softened her day.

Justy walked to Ms. Long, who placed an arm around her slight shoulders and smiled at her. She still smelled like vanilla. The teacher led Justy outside and squatted in front of her. The rain pounded on the breezeway roof and out of the corner of her eye, Justy saw the rain as if it were a curtain she could walk through.

"Now, Justine. I've put up with your not talking for months now." Ms. Long cleared her throat and rubbed at the rose tattoo on her hand. Justy thought she might even have tears in her hazel eyes.

"I'm trying to be understanding, but I'm beginning to worry." She cleared her throat again. "I don't know how to say this next part, so I'll just tell you. I've heard talk about your dad—that he, he has a temper. I just want to make sure everything is okay at home."

Justy closed her eyes and wanted to scream.

Ms. Long shifted her weight on her bent knees. "You can tell me, Justine. You really can. I used to volunteer in a shelter."

Justy blinked, wondering what a shelter was. Ms. Long sighed and patted Justy's arm, then stood. "I'm here if you ever want to talk."

Justy nodded and turned from the teacher, needing to pay attention to what was happening in Jake.

***

Kyle slowed as he and Jake approached the coffins. His skin felt dry and wet at the same time, and it was something he didn't feel comfortable wearing. Jake tried not to think about the coming mine and how it'd be a similar thing, a digging into the earth that somehow shouldn't happen. But not thinking about the mine was like not breathing. He couldn't do it—couldn't keep back images of the mountain assaulted. When the company had turned the land Jake loved into a raw hill, where would he be? Things started to slide around in his head—Dale's distance, Kyle's coming back after so many years. Jake stopped and spat at the base of the nearest tree. It felt like his guts would burst with his burden.

"Damn this," he said, wiping rain off his glasses on his wet sleeve. The caged feeling grew and he wished he'd brought his fiddle. Kyle paused and took off his jacket. He tried to toss it at the headstone between the two graves he and Jake worked on, but it landed at Jake's feet. Kyle grinned and Jake reached down, winter blood starting to fill his body. He picked up the jacket, glared at Kyle and said, "Watch it."

He tossed the jacket then and it landed on the rickety plot fence. Kyle went back to working the soggy soil until his shovel finally hit Shelby Jr.'s coffin with a thud. He shivered and began scraping the mud away. "Thanks for the shit job," he said.

Jake dropped his shovel, walked through the gate and to the edge of the cemetery, where the water churned past. He put his arm against a redwood and tested his weight on the roots. They were slippery, but he stepped out farther, watching the river lap at the bank.

Kyle eyed Jake and held his breath. The coffin seemed to leer at him, and he attacked the remaining mud with his shovel.

Jake closed his eyes and tried to let the sound of the water ease the knot building inside him. His boots were only inches above the torrent, and he looked to the gray sky, rain hitting him square in the face. He let go of the tree and his arms shot out for balance so that he felt like a ridiculous bird, equipped with useless wings that could take him nowhere, even if he knew where he wanted to go.

He walked back and glanced at Kyle, more in than out of the hole. It made him furious to see his father soaking and muddy in a buddy's grave.

Kyle ran a hand over the top of the coffin. Jake began to dig haphazardly. Pictures flashed through his mind, tricky images that captured a place and time he could no longer access. He dug faster, wanting to forget everything that ballooned inside him. His muscles burned cold and the rain fell harder, and he remembered the last fight with Kyle, how Dale had looked so swollen in her pregnancy, how it was Kyle who'd stepped in and stopped Jake's hands from losing themselves on her again. Kyle had moved in between them and slugged Jake for all he was worth, and Dale had stopped singing. Jake dug even faster, and his thoughts ran back to the first time Kyle had hit him. It made him want to leave his skin, how Kyle had judged him for hitting Dale. Jake hadn't wanted to. He stopped digging and felt his jawbone, still able to remember the way the pain had knifed through his head. Then he dropped into his body fully, tired of memories, tired already of this job, tired in general. The mud seemed to rise up around his ankles, and he fought his way out of the grave.

Kyle looked to the trees, then turned to see Jake's fist come at his face. He slipped the blow, and Jake lost his balance and fell into the grave. He recovered and came at Kyle again. But Kyle threw a punch before Jake had time to land one himself. Jake paused at the pain in his jaw, and in that moment, Kyle took a step back and dropped his hands.

"I'm tired, son." He shrugged, though his chest heaved in the old way, reminding him that he knew how to do this. Kyle wiped at his eyes and at the gritty soil on his lips. Jake shook his head and then pulled himself out of the grave, heart knocking against his ribs. He muttered to his hands and willed them to pick up the shovel again.

***

Justy looked at the fish tank, prepared to see the fish swimming backward or looping through the water as if crazed. She'd seen it before—how animals acted strangely before an earthquake. But the fish floated serenely, and she wondered if only she could feel the world shattering and the raising of the dead.

O n Sunday morning, Dale gently shook the children awake and told them to get dressed for meeting. Justy blinked and couldn't believe that seconds before, she'd been in the Eel again, swimming away. She could hear the sound of rain and of the shower running. Ochre's stone remained tight in her fist, where she'd willed it to stay before she fell off to sleep. Lacee crawled over her and headed toward the bathroom, but the door was locked and the shower muffled the sounds of Kyle singing. She came back to the bed and stood over Justy. Dale was cooking pancakes, and the smell of warm syrup filled the house. Jake still slept a dreamless sleep, last night's whiskey carrying him away from the bruises he and Kyle still wore. Micah rolled over and mumbled.

"Get up," Lacee said, and poked Justy in the ribs through the blankets. Justy blinked once more, then emerged from the covers, feeling the cool air hit her skin. Lacee walked to the closet and rolled aside one of the two doors. She felt the different dresses and sneered. Justy understood this feeling—dresses didn't allow a girl to be prepared for anything, except being reliant on someone else. Justy joined Lacee and picked out an orange and cream dress that reminded her of Creamsicles. She pulled off her T-shirt and stepped into the dress, feeling trapped and exposed at the same time by the loose fabric around her legs. Lacee sighed and grabbed a red-and-white gingham dress that other girls had worn on Sunday mornings.

The shower stopped and Kyle emerged a few minutes later fully dressed, with his brown hair slicked back. He stuck his head in the children's bedroom and grinned, taking stock of the dresses, then whistled. "Well, aren't you two pretty little things?"

Micah sat up and said, "Today is meeting." His voice rang with enthusiasm and Lacee rolled her eyes.

"We know already. Get up." She flopped on the bed and pulled on the brown dress shoes that had come in a bag of things from Mamie. Kyle watched her and hummed. Then he bowed out of the room, and Justy wondered how he could be so merry with a swollen lip.

They all gathered at the kitchen table, except for Jake. Dale had curled the ends of her blond hair, and it bounced around her face when she moved. She sat in her usual spot, just left of the head of the table, where Jake usually hunkered and where no one else ever sat.

"Do you mind?" Dale asked Kyle, and he shook his head. The children followed Dale and bowed their heads. She led them in a prayer, feeling uncomfortable; since there was a male present, he should be saying the words. She made it quick, and they began eating the hot pancakes.

"Mighty fine grub," Kyle said, affecting an old man's toothless speech. The children laughed and Dale smiled. She cleared her throat and said, "Kyle, would you be interested in coming with us this morning?" Then she looked back to her plate.

Kyle sighed deep and shook his head, "I appreciate the offer, but I been to just about every church there is, and nothing I heard there ever made me want to go back."

Dale winced and wished she hadn't asked him in front of the children. She struggled to remember how she was supposed to handle this. Maybe if she could attend all three weekly meetings instead of just Sundays, she might be better equipped to help Kyle—and maybe even Jake.

Kyle shook a loaded fork at the children and said, "Yup, I been to most every Sunday gathering people can have, excepting maybe for Jews and Arabs. All I can say is that the Baptists feed you the best."

He waved the fork and then swooped the food into his mouth. Justy and Lacee smiled and Micah looked confused; a smile danced in his eyes, but he frowned.

"Now, Kyle," Dale said, standing up from the table. She leaned toward him, grinning. "You've never been to a Witness meeting, have you?"

Kyle shrugged and a blush spread over his wrinkled face. "I don't need to know about them, Dale. I see you every day." He sat up straighter.

Lacee looked at her dress and said, "Yeah, Granpa, you should go. Just to check it out."

"That's right," Micah said. "Come with us."

Kyle shook his head and laughed. "Now, now. I don't need all of you to gang up on me." He turned to Dale. "You expect me to go, looking like this?" He indicated the black eye and the fat lip. He stuck out his lip, making it fatter. "What will the good people think if I walk in there with you and this ugly mug?"

Dale walked to the sink. Kyle's words had struck a buried memory and he shook his head at himself. The smile faded from his face.

"I still think you should go," Lacee said. "If Justy and I can go wearing these things, then you can wear a black eye."

Kyle looked at her and closed his eyes for a minute.

"All right," he said, "I'll go to your meeting and I'll wear a smile. I've made enough mistakes this trip already."

Dale turned to him and said, "It'd mean so much."

***

Dale called Joella Mills to say they didn't need a ride that morning, and Joella gently asked Dale if she was still coming.

"Oh, yes," Dale said, surprised at how much like a little girl she felt.

They piled into Kyle's truck—Dale on the outside, as usual—and drove through the heavy rain the twenty miles to the Kingdom Hall. On the way, Dale explained that most Witnesses had better meeting places than the Madrone congregation and that the members were saving up for what the Witnesses called a quick-build. Kyle seemed interested in this idea, that a group of people could construct a new Kingdom Hall essentially in one day. Justy watched him from Dale's lap, realizing he didn't have his cowboy hat on like he had every other time he left the house. She looked to the flooded landscape blurring past, wishing Jake were with them, too.

They pulled into the open space near the beauty parlor and the Kingdom Hall. Sullivan's waited a few feet away. They climbed out of Kyle's truck and walked past the mud-covered white Volkswagen that Mamie Harris drove. Dark green curtains hung in the side windows, and a bumper sticker said "Arms Are for Hugging."

Dale led the way up the narrow stairs and they saw light pouring from the open door. They moved down the dark hallway, toward the light. When they entered, Lucas Mills glanced at them from the front of the room, saw Kyle and left the conversation he was having with Brother McLean. Lucas approached and extended his hand to Kyle. While they exchanged awkward hellos, Justy saw that the members of the congregation were turned backward in their seats, looking at Kyle. She saw Mamie and the twins up in the front row; Caleb waved at Micah and he waved back. The room smelled stale to Justy, and she pulled at her Creamsicle dress, already tired.

Lucas directed them to a seat and the old record player began the music—the members sang the words from the brown songbooks *Sing Praises to Jehovah*. Justy didn't even mouth the words like she had in the months since she'd stopped talking, but just slipped Ochre's stone into her mouth.

When the hymn ended, Lucas led them in a prayer and then they sat. Justy tried to pay attention, but she wandered in her thoughts. Kyle kept shifting in his seat and Justy looked beyond him, out the small window. Lucas began speaking about the shelter available through Jehovah's love, and Justy remembered the concerned look on Ms. Long's face and her volunteering at a shelter. Justy knew the meanings were different, but she didn't know how.

***

After the public talk, the *Watchtower* study began. Kyle looked at the magazine in Dale's lap as the discussion went on. She had all the answers underlined, but she kept her hand down when the conducting brother asked the appropriate questions. When Micah raised his hand to answer, she smiled at him, then at Kyle, as if proving a point. Lacee and Justy shared a magazine and both tried to pay attention. Every few minutes Justy closed her eyes, hoping Jehovah had found a way into her murky waters. She supposed it would happen someday, maybe when Jake and Dale and Kyle left her alone and became their own people again.

The congregation stood again to sing, and Dale's voice began to fill the room without her seeming to be aware of it. Justy saw that people around Dale, including Kyle, only pretended to sing, listening to Dale's voice grow in force. Lacee sang, too, but her voice seemed small—nothing like the day Kyle arrived. The song finished, Lucas said a closing prayer, and the meeting was over. Justy wanted to go home and get out of the dress and watch the rain through the living room windows. A few men introduced themselves to Kyle, and he shook hands and smiled like he'd be back.

The twins approached with Mamie, who reached out a hand to Dale. Mamie smelled strongly of cinnamon and her stringy blond hair reminded Justy of Sunshine's. Her dress was tie-dyed, and she wore socks with her sandals. Justy noticed none of the other women in the congregation wore similar shoes. Dale thanked her for the most recent bag of clothes, and Mamie waved her hand.

"It's nothing, Dale. I'm just glad to see you can use them." Justy went out into the hall, looking for Micah and the twins. They were sitting at the head of the stairs, talking about when they would get baptized. Sky Harris looked at Justy and then turned her red hair and green eyes away.

***

They rode back in silence, a Sunday newspaper from San Francisco on Justy's lap. On the outside were comics that didn't make sense to Justy; she flipped through the pages until she reached the front one. The headline said the Vietnamese government had returned the bodies of two American men. She thought of Paco and wondered where his body was.

She looked to the blond fields filled with rain. If she understood it right, bodies should remain in the ground until after Armageddon.

She held the paper so Micah and Lacee could see the headline, but neither of them seemed to notice. Lacee held another book, *Watership Down*, and Micah looked to be in a daze, as he usually did after meeting. She handed him the comics and he took them, coming back into his body. Justy looked to Kyle, but he just stared at the road, lost in his own thoughts. The Witnesses believed there were seven signs until the end of the world, and she thought the dead being unearthed was one of them. It didn't make sense—how life was going to stop at any moment but everyone around her seemed to carry on as if these were ordinary times.

The road curved up a hill, and at the top, she could see the Eel again. It made her relax, but still she wanted to yell at her family because they didn't know a thing about what was going on. It started with Jake and Dale and how they thought they didn't love each other anymore. If she could make it right between them again, the other things would fall in place. The mine wouldn't go through and they'd have a place to live forever until Jehovah's New Kingdom. The trees would grow back and the forests would sing again. She sighed and Dale adjusted her on her lap. The road turned into a four-lane highway until Kyle took the off-ramp that led to their dirt road, then home.

***

Jake sat at the kitchen table, eating the pancakes Dale had left warming on the woodstove. His jaw still hurt from where Kyle's fist had caught him, so he chewed carefully, thinking about how his fists flew out from his body sometimes before he was even aware of them. Jake had heard of blackout alcoholics, and he knew he might fall into that category, but what scared him more was that he was something different and that he had no words for it. When the anger came on, all his thinking just left him. He looked at his hands, saw again the limbless trees bending over his knuckles, and he cursed them. The fork looked like a weapon, so he set it down and turned over his hands to study his palms. Calluses lined the pads and his fingers curled toward him. Sometimes it felt like all he had in the world were these two hands, his strong back and the deep ache for land. Maybe in the end, these wouldn't be enough.

Jake and Kyle fell into a rhythm as they dug up the cemetery, rising early and leaving before the children were fully awake. The men didn't talk during the day, sifting through the earth and finding ashy bones. In one grave there were only two finger bones, a button and a ring. It got to Jake. As he dug each day, he wanted to know what had happened to the rest of the skeleton. The nearly empty box sat with the others under the tarp near the entrance to the cemetery, and he paused each time he walked past the pile. He thought about his own wedding ring, lost in the woods on a job, before he knew it wasn't smart to wear it when he was working, back when even if he'd known the danger, he still would have worn it.

Justy remained quiet, and Ms. Long kept an eye on her but stopped asking her to speak in the story circle, stopped asking what was wrong. Justy did her work, did it well and fast, and often sat with her eyes closed, aware of the sound of Ochre's pencil hitting the desk, aware of Dale's lonely wanderings in the house and Jake's smoldering anger. Rain fell from the gray skies, and Justy wished for it to stop. She wanted the smell of spring and heat to coax the trees to form new buds.

***

Dale pulled the lemon meringue pie from the oven, and it dazzled the children from where they sat eating a lunch of split pea soup. Jake and Kyle were already in town, helping to set up the senior class trapshoot.

The browned tips of the meringue reminded Justy of the Pacific and the storms that stirred up whitecaps. The kitchen smelled deeply of lemon and crust. Dale smiled at the pie as she set it on the counter.

"Looks good, Mama," Micah said, between slurps of soup. Lacee nodded and Justy wished her stringy hair would braid as nicely as Lacee's did. Lacee had learned to French-braid, and that's how she'd worn her long hair for six days now.

"Thanks," Dale said, and washed her hands. She went into the bedroom she and Jake shared and changed into warmer clothes. When the kids had washed their bowls, they walked to the Willys, a cardboard box holding the pie. Lacee arranged it on her legs. Dale changed the truck's gears with authority, and they curved onto the old road. The Eel was calming down a little, the letup in the rain the past two days helping to clear her out, and the color of the trees leading down to the river was almost like the color of the water.

Dale guided the truck onto the road that led back to the shooting range. Cars and trucks lined the dirt parking lot, and Justy was disappointed not to see the Volvo. Harris's red Toyota sat next to Kyle's tired-looking Chevy. She didn't know some of the vehicles and realized that people from River Fork and Madrone must have come. A gray Chevy had a small bumper sticker in the window that read, "Insured by Smith & Wesson," and Justy wondered who they were.

She looked for Jake and Kyle but couldn't see them. The family climbed out, Dale carrying the pie and heading toward the knot of people gathered around the two tables with donated cakes, pies and frozen turkeys. The senior class—all fifteen of them—were trying to raise enough money to take a trip to Disneyland. Dale handed the pie to Lacee, who boldly walked through the people and offered it to the two women in charge of the trapshoot prizes. Justy gazed at the food while the women talked, wishing she could take all of the prizes home and fill up the empty spaces.

"This looks lovely," said Connie Fry, who was Jordan's mother and also had a son in the senior class. Lacee nodded and turned to seek Dale, who approached with a slight blush budding on her fair face. The other woman at the table was the school cook, Sally Ferris. Her husband, Fred, was a faller, too.

"Thanks," Dale said, and smiled. The two women knew Dale only from the stories told about Jake and her appearance at their doors on infrequent Sunday afternoons, holding the *Watchtower* and *Awake!* in her hands while Joella Mills spoke to them. Justy had seen Connie at Hilltop, laughing and drinking. She looked better in the sunlight, her red hair curled and her makeup all in place. Dale and her girls walked toward the cement strip where the shooters would stand. Micah had disappeared, and Justy was torn between looking for him and studying the shotguns lined up in a row, leaning against a low wooden barrier. The guns were all oiled and shined, and their barrels reflected the spring sun. Gil Walker sat in a wheelchair at the edge of the strip. He couldn't read or write, but he carried a whole different kind of knowledge in his old body. Jake always said he was the best faller in the state, even though he spent most of his time these days in the wheelchair.

Justy closed her eyes and sensed Jake in the small cement building that was half buried in the ground forty feet in front of the rifles. When she opened her eyes, she saw Jake, Kyle, Micah and Jeff Harris walking back to the crowd. Jake held an orange disk in his hand and tossed it as he walked. He stopped in front of Dale and said, "Glad to see you made it." Harris kept walking, not acknowledging Dale or the girls, his left foot leaving a slight trail behind him.

Jake and Kyle had had no trace of the fight in their faces for weeks now. But Dale still looked for it, grateful it was not her own skin that purpled, then yellowed, then betrayed by returning to its normal tone. Jake held the orange disk out to Micah, told him he could have the pigeon and followed Harris to sign up for the first shoot.

Mark Sloan, another faller and Jennifer's grandfather, stepped forward and called for the first round to begin. He told the men to make sure they'd paid and to check their guns. Six men stepped from the crowd and picked shotguns from the row. Dale pulled her children back from the cement strip onto the dirt where the majority of the crowd stood. Shelby Gaines readied himself first, cigarette hanging from his lip. He brought the gun to his shoulder and sighted just above the cement building. He yelled "Pull," and a clay pigeon flew from the building off to the right, and Gaines fired, blowing it to pieces. Justy's head hurt from the gun's blast, and she worked her way back through the crowd, plugging her ears. She saw Ms. Long's green Subaru pull into the parking lot, and Justy stepped next to Gaines's white Ford to avoid her.

The teacher climbed out, a clipboard and a pen in one hand, a brown folding chair in the other. Another shotgun fired, and Justy could tell from the crowd's reaction that the shooter had missed. Ms. Long flinched as she walked toward the crowd, and Justy smiled at her faded jeans, white turtleneck and green vest. Her flowerless hair frizzed more wildly than on a school day, and she wore heavy hiking boots. She walked past Justy to the tables where the prizes waited.

A third man yelled "Pull" and Justy plugged her ears again, starting to understand the rhythm of the gunfire. The image of Ochre's denim jacket with the bright circle and the four spokes inside glimmered through her mind. Maybe that's why the Ravens weren't here, because of the peace sign. She felt her pocket for the stone, knowing if she wanted to speak, she could place it in her mouth. After the shot, she stepped forward to see Ms. Long talking to Sally Ferris. Justy moved along the front end of the trucks and kneeled when she got within earshot. Ms. Long thumped the clipboard and said something about the community taking a stand. Sally Ferris told her she didn't think this was the best place to introduce the petition, and Ms. Long responded with facts about erosion and salmon habitat. Sally looked at Connie, who sucked on a cigarette and looked at Ms. Long as if she weren't human.

Justy heard Kyle yell, "Pull" and plugged her ears. She could tell from the crowd that he'd hit the pigeon. Connie whispered to Sally, and Ms. Long smiled at them. It was her circle-time smile, her exasperated but patient look. When Connie pulled away from Sally, Ms. Long opened her mouth, paused and then closed it.

"If you want to cook your own goose, go ahead," Sally said and picked at the ice on a thawing turkey. Connie snorted and took another pull on her cigarette.

"Thanks," Ms. Long said and set her chair up at the other table, pushing back baked goods to make room for the clipboard and her elbows. Justy watched the men take turns shooting and Mark Sloan tabulating scores on a piece of paper he held in his wrinkled hands. Jenny tapped her grandfather on the leg, but he waved her away. On cue, Justy plugged her ears again as Jake trained Kyle's shotgun on the flying clay pigeon. She felt the recoil of the shotgun on his shoulder and rubbed at her arm. He also hit the target, Dale and Lacee stood on the outskirts of the crowd, off to the left. Ms. Long flinched each time a gun went off, and Connie smirked at her.

The round ended and Gaines won, his prize a ten-pound turkey. He lit up a cigarette and swaggered over to the tables. Ms. Long sat up straighter and tried to catch his eye, but he ignored her and stopped in front of Connie and Sally.

"Nice work, Gaines," Sally said.

"Thanks, there." He and Connie puffed on their cigarettes while he looked over the three turkeys, examining each dead, thawing bird as if it would be his first and last meal. Justy's legs grew tired from crouching, and she stood, getting ready to walk back to the Willys and wait out the gunfire. Gaines finally chose a bird and Sally wrote his name on the list of prizes. He turned away.

Ms. Long took a deep breath. "Sir," she called, but he kept on walking. "Sir?" He paused and walked back, smoke drifting from his nostrils.

"What is it?" He shifted the turkey in his arms.

"Would you be interested in signing this petition against the coming mine?"

Justy smiled at the way she talked, just like she did to the students, calm but with eagerness lacing her voice.

"Why should I?" Gaines suppressed a cough.

"Well, it will radically change the environment of Red Mountain, dump soil into the streams and affect the salmon runs." Ms. Long tapped the clipboard.

"Do you know who I am? What I do for a living?" Gaines shifted the turkey again and spat out his cigarette. People turned at his raised voice. Connie poked Sally, but she was watching Ms. Long with a serious look.

"No disrespect, sir, but this mine doesn't care who you are. This company, Pacific Mining, does not care one bit about any of us. They're just about profits."

Gaines laughed his raspy laugh and said, "My kind of people." He coughed and held out his free hand. When he finished coughing, he said, "Hold on." He walked through the crowd with his turkey and stopped in front of Jake. "Come here, Chief."

Jake handed Kyle's shotgun to him and moved after Gaines. They both walked back to Ms. Long. She clenched her right fist, took a deep breath.

"Mr. Colby," she said, and gave Jake a curt nod. Dale moved to stand two people back.

"You know Jake?" Gaines set the turkey on the table and lit another cigarette. The entire group watched. Gil Walker yelled at people to get out of his way as he rolled the wheelchair over the rough dirt. His eyes darted back and forth between Ms. Long and Gaines, his toothless mouth gaping open. Lefty Fry came to stand behind Gil, resting his hands on the back of the chair.

"Mr. Colby's daughter is in my class," Ms. Long said. Justy hoped the teacher wouldn't start discussing what she thought were Justy's problems.

"Right," Gaines said, and put an arm around Jake's shoulder. Jake pulled at his collar. "This lady here, she's got a petition and she's trying to get me to sign it. She says the mining company doesn't give a rat's ass about anybody in this town. What do you say to that?"

Ms. Long opened her mouth and her chest heaved a little, but she just tilted her head. Jake looked at her, actually seeing her face for the first time, even though she'd lived in the town for over six months. Kyle walked up and stepped near Gaines and Jake. Jake felt trapped by all the eyes, and he twisted his boot toe into the still-wet earth. He didn't know what he thought about the mine or the petition; he just knew that living where he did out on Red Mountain made it so he could survive.

"That company ain't ever done one thing wrong to me and mine," he said.

Gaines smiled at the teacher and sucked on his cigarette. She slumped in her seat but kept her lips curved upward. Jake made as if to move away, but Gaines held tight to Jake's shoulders.

"Whoa, there. I need some advice. You figure I should sign the petition? Should I join the nice hippie woman's cause? She ain't got but five signatures so far."

Ms. Long stood and Jake shrugged. Kyle stepped forward and said to her in a soft voice, "Don't worry about these two. They're just fooling."

Justy gripped Ochre's stone as Lefty stepped from behind Gil's chair and bowed to Ms. Long. She nodded at him and smiled. Lefty cleared his throat and said in a voice that the whole crowd could hear, "I'll sign the petition." He stood straight, adjusted the collar of his sky-blue button-down shirt and soothed his lengthy gray beard.

"You've already signed it, Lefty," Gaines said, releasing Jake and taking a step back. Ms. Long nodded but watched Lefty with a generous smile on her face. Gil Walker waved a hand at Lefty, as if dismissing him.

"How about I sign it again?" Lefty turned and asked the crowd, his arms in an exaggerated shrug. A few people smiled and Justy felt a wave of relief pass through both Jake and Dale. Lefty picked up a pen and signed his name with a flourish. Gaines grumbled under his breath, moving in his distinctive run-walk back to his truck, the frozen turkey jiggling in his arms.

Mark Sloan called the next round of shooting and people moved away from the tables. Ms. Long straightened her clipboard and for the rest of the afternoon sat alone. Justy climbed into the back of the truck she was kneeling near and watched the few clouds. She pretended the sky was another kind of river, one she could tumble into if suddenly the law of gravity released her. The gunshots and the smell of the gunpowder held her in place, and she felt the different pulls of Jake and Dale. One of the clouds looked like a doe, and she thought that maybe she needed to keep her ears open for the sound of both horse and deer hooves.

On April twentieth, Justy rode to school and tried to tell if she was somehow different. She had entered this world seven years before, and she wanted to feel altered. If she'd been in another family, a celebration with a song and a cake would acknowledge her birth. She traced shapes on the fogged window beside her. She knew she wasn't supposed to want those things, but she couldn't remember why they were bad. It made her think that maybe Jehovah's Witnesses were started by people who didn't have any money and had found a way to make their children feel better by telling them it was God's wish for a pure life that they weren't supposed to celebrate holidays.

The tops of the western mountains were held again in the misty paw of the coast fog. It made her feel good to know spring had arrived and that summer was gathering close. She wanted the heat so she could find relief in the Eel. In less than two months, school would be out and Dale would find ways to take the children to Carver's Hole and let the water ease them all. And maybe Sunshine would take Ochre to Carver's and Justy would still get to see him, even if only once in a while.

She held the assigned book for the sixth-graders, *Animal Farm*. She'd read it and decided the pigs were like the people who first came to the United States—people with good intentions until other people got in their way, such as the Indians. In her shoe, the penny rode safe, and she decided it'd be a good thing to give it to Ochre, even though the Folgers can still sat in a kitchen cupboard.

Jake and Kyle continued to dig up bodies, and each time Jake walked past the growing pile of labeled boxes, he felt a pull to look into the one with only the finger bones, the button and the ring. Dale spent more and more time at the meetings, attending two or three a week now, getting rides from Mamie or Joella. Micah often went with her to the Kingdom Hall. Lacee took to sitting out by the pond and filling the twilight with her voice, singing cowboy songs. Justy explored the trees, the barns, the awakening of the blackberry vines, never straying from the sound of Lacee's voice floating out across the water. She would return in the dusk, singing silently along with Lacee, the words woven into the caves of her mind. This was what Dale did—hovering near the melodies she knew, sometimes not even aware of what her mind was doing. On the nights Dale wasn't at meeting, Lacee simply sat by the pond, reading or watching the water. Justy found a rock in the trees opposite the pond where she could sit and watch the dark settle. The bats flitting through the evening made her think of musical notes, zipping above the pond, eating insects. She knew a song hung in the changing shapes and she wished she could read the music.

***

Justy's birthday passed unmarked at school, and she watched Ochre closer to see if he saw anything different about her. He treated her as usual. Justy thought maybe he was a birthday present that spread itself out over time, and this pleased her. A small part of her wished Dale would suddenly show up with cupcakes and a smile, and the ache to be like the others welled up inside her.

At the end of the day, she took the penny from her shoe and rinsed it off. Before Ochre walked to the Volvo, Justy tapped him on the arm and held out the coin. He smiled instantly and she breathed a sigh of relief. He tucked the penny into his pocket, nodded and then moved over to the car.

Justy rode the bus home and walked with Lacee and Micah up the hill. Her hands paused often on the dry skin of the trees; she liked to look up through their branches, seeing how they framed the sky. Something was eating at Dale, and Justy was torn between getting home quickly and lingering with the trees. She decided to walk as fast as she could. When the children arrived home, Dale stood from the kitchen table, the week's *Watchtower* in her hands. The house was spotless and Justy studied her, trying to ferret out what was going on. Dale offered them hot chocolate, and Justy thought maybe the rare treat was Dale's way of celebrating her birth.

After the children settled themselves, Dale joined them, sitting at the head of the table, flipping through the pages of the *Watchtower*. Micah drank his chocolate in three swallows and had a brown mustache. Lacee didn't drink, her arms crossed, waiting. "Why are you in Dad's chair?"

So many thoughts raced through Dale's mind that Justy held the mug to her lips, not drinking, trying to understand what was going on.

Dale finally stopped fiddling with the magazine. "What more do you hear about the petition?"

Lacee shrugged. "A few more people have signed since the trapshoot, even Sally Ferris."

"But are most of the people those hippie teachers?" Dale asked.

"Seems like. If you mean those women who don't shave their legs."

Dale looked to the wall of the windows in the living room. Justy struggled to let the smell of the chocolate fill her mind and not the nervous thoughts running through Dale.

"Mr. Walters is coming," Dale said.

"When?" Lacee asked, and stood.

"Anytime. Do you think you can call Gaines so he could tell Jake?"

Lacee flipped through the thin phone book and found Gaines's name. She turned the dial and they all waited.

"There's no answer," Lacee said, and gently replaced the receiver. Dale had sat here for hours, afraid to pick up the phone, but she could still walk up to a stranger's house and knock on the door.

"Well," Dale said. "Can you three go outside and take a look around? Straighten up a bit? I've done some, but more would help."

Lacee pulled the rubber band from her French braid, releasing her black hair like rapids in the Eel. Micah and Justy followed her outside and looked at the fence separating the yard from the surrounding field. Over by the deserted chicken coop, wood and scrap metal lingered in haphazard piles. On the far side of the Doug fir where the illegal deer had hung, five or six old batteries waited. It was all stuff that could be used in one way or another but never was. Lacee rebraided her hair and then began to pick up sticks and dump them in the kindling box on the porch. Micah walked over and pushed the batteries into straight rows with his feet.

Justy's hands remained on a piece of madrone in the woodpile. She tried to see things as if for the first time. What she saw was the makings of a life in the middle of nowhere. She looked out at the valley they lived in—a grassy field tucked into the tree-covered mountains. It made her think about the first people who had tried to live on the land—the Maurers. A sudden hatred toward Mr. Walters filled her, even though she knew hate was the work of Satan. She didn't want that man to tell them they had to leave.

Ms. Long had said the river might die if the mine happened. Justy didn't know how a river could die, but she knew it would be the end of everything she knew.

Lacee dumped another load in the kindling box and prodded Justy. "Hey, help out, will ya?"

Justy went through the house to the small back porch and grabbed the broom. As she returned, she saw that Dale had left the mugs on the table and was standing in the living room, staring out the windows, her bones pressing closer together as she prayed and prayed. Justy swept the wood chips, thinking about the trees that Jake fed into the stove.

Lacee stopped in the yard and shrugged. "Good enough," she said, and the three of them went into the house. Justy returned the broom to the back porch, and they sat at the table to finish the hot chocolate and do homework. The clock's hands said it was four-thirty, and when half an hour had passed, Dale stirred herself from the window and went into the kitchen. Before she had a chance to unwrap the venison, the sound of a vehicle vibrated through the afternoon quiet, a brown pickup appeared, then drove out of view as it curved its way to the house.

"It's a company truck," Micah said. Dale went into the bathroom, checked her scant makeup and brushed her hair. Lacee and Micah walked out the front door, and Justy waited for Dale. They went to stand behind Micah and Lacee at the east edge of the porch. Mr. Walters leaned over to the passenger side and flipped through a stack of papers. Dale placed her hand on Justy's shoulder and squeezed. Mr. Walters fell out of the truck, almost crumbling to his knees but recovering in time. His tie was loose, and one of his pant legs was partially tucked into a black sock. He looked up and saw the Colbys watching him, and his pale face turned a deep pink. He coughed and smiled. "Mrs. Colby."

He half waved, lurching forward. "Oh," he said. He shut the truck door and then struggled to open it again. He pulled out a foil-wrapped package from a cooler and Justy wondered if it was illegal venison. The logo on the truck read "Pacific Mining Company" and showed a stream running between two trees. It looked nothing like the stories Justy had heard about mines and the destruction they could do. Mr. Walters walked toward them, leaving the truck door open. He extended his hand to Dale, and shook hers, long and earnestly.

"How are you, Lollie?" He leaned toward Lacee and grinned. His tie hung forward and Justy realized that the only people she ever saw in ties were Witnesses and mine people.

"I'm fine, Mr. Walters. But my name is Lacee."

Dale squeezed Justy's shoulder again while Walters slapped his forehead. "Right, right. Lacee. How could I forget? And you, you're Mike?"

Micah smiled and said, "Close enough, sir."

Mr. Walters winked at Justy and held the package out to Dale. She just looked at it.

"Gayle, my wife, as you know, she thought you all might like some of the marlin we caught when we were down in Mexico." Walters wiped his forehead with the back of his hand, the package sweeping through the air.

"That was nice of her," Dale said in an even voice.

"I hope you like it, and Gayle, she figured you guys probably wouldn't ever get a chance to have some marlin…"

Dale stiffened and Micah said, "No, we haven't tried it. Tell her thanks."

Walters's grin broadened. "I think grilling is the best way to eat it." He pulled the tie's knot at his throat tighter. They watched him roll his white shirtsleeves in the diluting light. "Jake around?"

Dale softly said, "No."

"My secretary did call?" Walters studied their faces.

"Yes, but only about two hours ago," Dale said. "I wasn't able to get ahold of Jacob."

"He's got some work, then?"

"Digging up graves." Lacee said this as if it were a challenge, like she did at school when anyone mocked Justy or Jake.

"Oh, I see." He scratched at his neck. "What's this petition about?" He pulled a white handkerchief from his pants pocket.

"We don't know much about it, Mr. Walters," Dale said.

"Some teachers at the school started it," Micah said. Walters nodded and looked to the pond. Justy followed his gaze and saw the quick blurs that were the bats.

"You haven't signed it, have you, Dale?"

"No, Mr. Walters," Dale said, and sighed. "Even if I did sign it, which I won't, it wouldn't mean anything because I'm not registered to vote."

"She doesn't vote," Micah said. Walters wiped his forehead again and then looked down, seeing his pant leg tucked into his sock.

"What about Jake? Does he vote?"

"Most of the time, no. He doesn't make it in time."

The twilight deepened and quiet reigned for a moment.

"He hasn't signed the petition, Mr. Walters. Not that I know of."

"Good, good."

Walters asked if he could have a moment alone with Dale. She reluctantly let go of Justy's shoulder, and Lacee led Justy and Micah into the house, taking the marlin. Justy stood at the window, studying where the creek disappeared into the trees at the bottom of the field. Walters asked Dale about the rumors he'd been hearing about marijuana. He wanted to be sure that Jake kept an eye out for people who might try and grow on the company's property. Nothing illegal was to be done on the land, especially with the mining proposal undergoing such close scrutiny by the Environmental Protection Agency.

Dale assured Walters that nothing unlawful was happening, and Justy knew her mind gently curved away from the night of the hunt, months back. Dale focused herself down and let her words come from the place of truth regarding the marijuana.

Walters talked on and Justy thought he was like an overgrown guard dog, anxious to please. She wondered whether he ever considered what it would be like for them when they had to find somewhere else to live. Walters and Dale finished talking, and Justy wondered whether he'd take a Polaroid like he usually did.

He told Dale he'd be staying at a motel in Madrone. He'd drive the back roads of the property the next day, taking soil samples and tying yellow ribbons to trees, marking spots for preliminary digging. Dale walked into the house and sat on the couch. Justy felt Dale's worries surge, and they both wondered how Walters could be so nice when they knew that one day soon he'd bring the orders for them to leave.

Justy went outside and watched the night come and seal itself down on the valley. They began the evening wait for Jake and Kyle to return while stars filled the sky.

***

They ate dinner in suspension, listening for the sound of Kyle's truck. Every time a big rig rumbled by on the freeway, they sat up straighter. Micah's and Lacee's faces echoed Dale's as they each reached out toward the sound. They all knew how to divide themselves, letting half of their bodies eat the venison stew Dale had cooked, while the other half stayed tuned for Jake's arrival, wondering what kind of mood he'd come home in. Justy didn't know if Micah and Lacee did the same with their eating half but she spun out different possibilities while waiting. She imagined Jake coming home with fistfuls of dollars and, more importantly, gentle and calm, how he was when he played certain slow songs on his fiddle. Jake and Kyle had stopped at Hilltop, and she could feel them slide away from the bones they'd dealt with all day.

After half an hour, Dale laid down her fork. Justy could feel her fracturing as she leaned her head into her fist. Lacee started talking about a paper on democracy she was supposed to write, but her words couldn't bring Dale back to the table. She looked at her plate and Justy felt like crying. The stone in Justy's pocket seemed to pulse.

Dale picked up Kyle's and Jake's empty plates and carried them to the sink. She slammed the plates on the counter and pieces flew. No one said anything while she stood over the broken plates, trying not to cry. She wrapped a bleeding finger in a kitchen towel. Lacee opened the back door to grab the broom and dustpan.

"I'm sorry," Dale said. The children nodded, not surprised by the small violences she allowed herself. Walters's visits always set her on edge, never knowing when he'd bring the orders for them to leave. Walters and his bumbling kindness seemed to home in on the terror underlying the bare sense of security Dale felt.

"It's just…" She heaved a sigh and let the tears fall. She played with the ends of her hair. "He's never here when we need him…and…" Dale stopped—what she had to say was too huge for words. She stared out the kitchen window while Lacee finished sweeping. Then she returned to the table and the three of them tried to continue eating, but the food was cold, the stew lumping in Justy's mouth. Dale finally walked to the head of the table. Strands of her hair had come out of her ponytail, small wisps curling near her cheeks.

"That's enough," she said quietly, and made herself stop crying. She sniffled and then fixed each child for a brief instant in her distant gaze. "If he isn't home by midnight, we leave."

Justy shivered.

"Do your chores, finish your homework and get some things ready."

When she spoke, Dale looked over the children's heads. She went into the bathroom and the shower started.

"I don't see why we should do our homework when we probably won't go to school tomorrow anyway," Lacee said.

"Maybe we should pray," Micah said. Lacee laughed and carried her plate to the sink.

***

They went to bed early, Dale clearing them out of her view. Micah murmured prayers until he started snoring lightly. Lacee slept instantly—maybe because she knew she'd be woken at any time. Justy listened to Dale pacing and watching the clock. Dale tried not to remember how she'd been awakened in the night so many times as a child, pulled from one city to another by her adoptive parents, people who didn't know how to live a steady life. The old question about how those people had been seen fit to raise children held her for a moment and she paused. The night dragged on and Dale felt it again—the promise she made to herself each time. Never, Dale had told herself, never will I do this to my children. I will find a way for them to sleep the night through.

She didn't want to think about it, how she did it the first time, responding to a call from Helen at Hilltop, telling her Jake had left the bar talking mean. It frightened her how easy it came, how she knew to gather her children to her in the darkness, wake them with shaking hands, tell them to dress. It had become too familiar, finding themselves running down the dirt road, trying to get away before Jake got home. The reasons were different for her now, but the running was the same—the pounding of her heart blocking out the possible sound of the Willys driving drunkenly toward her. That first time they made it to the old post office on the far side of the freeway and huddled into the shadows of the ghostly building. Jake had driven by, missing the off-ramp, the truck limping along with a flat tire. Dale had closed her eyes then, not wanting to see his truck weave on the freeway, not wanting to see him finally make the other off-ramp, not wanting to see what had become of her life. This is how you do it, then, she thought, feeling a strange kinship with her adoptive mother as Dale held her eyes shut, arms around her children, waiting for the light of day so she could return home.

And then, when they'd walked in the door, Jake had woken from the couch and crawled to them, so sorry for scaring them. His hands had found Dale's face and cradled her chin, his bloodshot eyes full of every kind of sorry there was. It was addicting—that touch—and she hated that she had to leave in the middle of the night to receive it.

Dale walked back and forth in the living room, struggling not to remember what she could never forget. Justy lay in bed until the sound of Dale's pacing lulled her to sleep.

***

"Justy." Dale shook her and she sat up, knowing Dale wanted the children to move fast, before Jake returned or she changed her mind.

"Here." Dale handed Justy her jacket. The hall light lit the room fairly well. Lacee sat on the floor, putting on her tennis shoes. Micah sat sleepily next to her, fumbling with his socks. He leaned into Lacee and she smoothed his hair, then pushed him up, telling him to hurry. Dale wore a green plaid shirt of Jake's and a baseball cap, her hair pulled through the opening in the back. She stuffed some clothes into a pillowcase.

"Justy. Put these on." Lacee handed Justy her tennis shoes and Justy pulled them over bare feet.

"Okay," Dale said. She watched her children and winced at how they knew the ritual of running so well. The silent clock in her head ticked away the time until Jake could reach the house. It wasn't like that first time, but she still didn't want him to catch her running away, not when he'd been drinking. "Let's go."

They walked through the living room, and the clock by the kitchen table read one-fifteen—Dale must have wavered in her deadline. The almost full moon lit the night like it was an ashen day. Tree shadows distinctly lined the valley floor. Warm spring air cloaked them as they moved away from the house.

Dale drove through the bleached night, leaving the headlights off. The cab jammed them together and Justy was glad for the warmth, even though it wasn't cold. A dancing moon wavered at them from the surface of the pond. The dashboard dials glowed and cast an odd sheen to their skin. Dale's profile was rigid as she bit her bottom lip, looking out from under the low brim of her hat. Torn from the river of sleep, Justy kept her eyes open wide. It was easy to remember that first time—something about that night lay dormant until the next time they ran, and even though the danger wasn't as present tonight, Justy knew in her stomach that it was still possible.

Dale coasted to a halt at the stop sign where the children caught the bus. She kept the motor running and they waited, looking for headlights on the freeway. Lacee and Micah breathed heavy and it seemed they'd fallen asleep.

"Fifty cars," Dale said.

"North and south?" Lacee asked, and Dale chased down an answer. If she really wanted to go, they counted cars in both directions. If she were unsure, she chose one direction. While she decided, Justy relaxed her grip on Ochre's stone and began tumbling it. Sunshine probably never woke Ochre up in the night, walking across the floor of the tipi to shake him from his dreams.

"Both," Dale said. She pulled the cap lower and sighed. She sent out a silent prayer. Justy felt the sky open up and her edges slip away. The moon hovered behind, sending shadows through the landscape. A wave of Dale came at her; she took a deep breath and plunged into the marrow of those thoughts.

Dale never knew how to change the way things were between her and Jake. It had seemed so clear seven years before, when she dedicated her voice to Jehovah, when she'd been dipped into the waters of redemption. The anger in Jake confused her and she tried to keep it at bay with her faith. Sometimes, on nights like tonight, when the drinking had been going on for months and the loneliness leaped inside her like madness, she had to leave—make a statement. At certain moments, an inexplicable exhaustion welled up inside her and she struggled to not go under the surface of it. It would carry her away completely, and who would be left for her children? What guarantee did she have that Jake's hands would not find their enraged way to them? She kept her head above water by remembering that an unknown woman had given her up for adoption. That and the small hope that something might change. And in the meantime, Jehovah watched over her, guarding her voice and her future.

Dale squeezed the steering wheel, Justy squeezed the stone and lights loomed in front of them from the north. Dale and Justy watched, a simultaneous desire pulling at them. The lights continued, not taking the southbound off-ramp on the other side of the freeway. The car drove on and the night returned to shadowy paleness.

"One," Lacee said. She trusted her closed eyes to the counting, something Justy wouldn't do. Only more darkness waited behind her eyes, more ways to slide out of herself and possibly for Satan to enter. Micah slept, leaning up against Lacee. Justy believed he could sleep so easily because he could carry himself away with prayer, dreaming of the New System in which the only living people would be perfect, the earth would have its paradise restored and Micah would live forever. Justy returned her gaze to Dale, knew she did not think of the future, even the one promised by the religion. She remained stuck in this vivid present, unable to imagine what the next moment might hold.

Justy placed the stone in her mouth, knocked it gently against her teeth, liking the sound, watching the moon shadows around them.

***

They counted the passing of twenty-seven vehicles, each set of headlights searing the night. Most of them were big rigs, carrying paper products or trees up and down the north coast. When the twenty-eighth pair appeared, they watched and waited. The truck behind those lights slowed and widened off the road. The vehicle was taking the off-ramp, dipping down from the freeway. Justy felt Jake's presence rise up in the strong stream of Dale, and Lacee opened her eyes. Dale sat up straight, pushed in the clutch and slipped the Willys into gear. The lights disappeared, the freeway overpass cutting off their view as the other truck rolled toward the corresponding southbound stop sign, kitty-corner from the Willys. Dale turned the truck left, going south, the wrong way up the off-ramp, away from the approaching vehicle. She kept the lights off and they rolled in moonlight.

Justy turned to see lights beam out from the underpass, then Kyle's truck appeared. It drove past and headed up the dirt road to the house. Dale touched the brakes and they sat pointed in the wrong direction, a red glow behind them. She took a deep breath and put the truck into reverse, driving backward to the spot where they had been.

They waited, not counting cars anymore, just watching the night. Dale pulled off her hat, put the truck into gear and started down the old road toward town. When she could, Justy caught sight of the Eel, dark and winding below them. Dale drove through the main part of Sequoia, past the entrance to the Drive-Thru Tree, past the two filling stations, the Redwood Diner, the post office and general store, past the few houses. Dale turned right onto the dirt road that led to Carver's Hole. Justy felt the confusion mount in Dale as she guided the truck over the rough ruts to the Eel. It was too early in the spring for Judge Carver to have the road graded, and the winter rains had created grooves. The Scotch broom lining the road reached out to the Willys, slapping the hood and sides with sharp twangs.

Micah continued to sleep, and Justy and Lacee waited while Dale brought the truck to a halt, climbed out and closed the door. The headlights reached out to the river walls, illuminating gray crevasses. Justy and Lacee exchanged a look and then Lacee shrugged. Dale opened the driver's door and shut off the headlights, leaving them in moon shadow.

"I'll be back," Dale said. Justy scooted behind the steering wheel and looked at the few stars bright enough to shine alongside the moon. She smelled the river's clean movement and rolled down the window so she could draw it in deeper. The water moved fast, talking to Justy as Dale undressed in the dark. She left her clothes at the edge and stepped into the river with a deep intake of breath. Her skin seemed to drink in the night, free and goose-pimpled. She could feel the current pull at her ankles. The moon behind her shed pale light on the river wall opposite her, and she marked off in her mind the places her children loved to jump from. Pebbles underneath her feet urged her forward to the sand she knew lay a few feet deeper.

"This is crazy," Lacee said. As Dale dove into the darkness, Justy slid from the truck and walked to the pile of clothes. Dale's blond hair broke the surface, and Justy felt her heart gallop at the cold water. Dale swam upriver, her strokes silent, feeling the anger and confusion wash from her. Asking for Jehovah's guidance, she pulled her naked body through the water, stretching each pale arm in front of her, carrying herself against the current.

Justy's moon shadow wavered in front of her, already swimming, and she wondered if she was dreaming. The skin on the back of her neck rose and she looked for the doe, expecting to see her mournful eyes. But there was no deer, so she squatted and put her hand in the water, her fingers floating. She wanted to follow Dale, but it seemed too wild—to step into the night river and let the darkness consume her. An image of the beer sign from Hilltop came to Justy, and she thought about how water could keep a person in place or carry her away.

After twenty minutes, Dale walked from the river, her naked body shining in the moonlight. Justy moved back from the clothes and tried not to look at Dale dressing, but she was still fascinated with the woman's body Dale carried beneath her clothes. Dale tied her tennis shoes, wrung water from her hair and turned. Her head was framed by the white moon in the indigo sky as she prayed hard.

"Let's go home," she said, finally, and started to the Willys. Justy followed her with only a slight understanding of what had just happened.

***

"Your dad and me, we used to go to the river." Dale guided the truck through town, the smell of water still on her skin. Justy sat up straight next to her and saw that Lacee was listening also, but Micah continued to sleep. Dale hardly ever spoke about her and Jake, and Justy yearned to travel in time and know them then.

"Sometimes, when we still went on dates, when there was the money," Dale said, "after dinner or whatnot, I'd talk him into going to Carver's Hole and we'd park. He wouldn't get out of the truck. I'd dive into that water and he'd just watch with the headlights on while I swam for a half an hour or so."

Her voice was soft and Justy could feel that Dale was barely in the truck with them.

"It's so amazing, to have the water surround you and have it be so dark. I love it."

Justy leaned toward Dale, the words about the river echoing her dreams. Justy took a deep breath and reached to the place where Jake lived inside her. He was sleeping, bathed in another kind of river—the one that lives inside a whiskey bottle. She pondered how things would have been different between Jake and Dale if he'd left the safety of the truck and followed her into the river, if swimming together in the dark might have given them something they lacked now.

When they hit the dirt road that led to the house, Dale turned off the headlights and relied on the moon again. She stopped the Willys next to Kyle's Chevy. "Let's go to sleep," she said, her voice one notch above a whisper.

Lacee climbed out while Justy gently shook Micah awake. Dale walked to the passenger side and helped Micah down.

"Wake up, buddy." Dale had her arms on his shoulders, holding him until he gained his bearings.

"Where are we?" he asked.

"Home," Lacee said.

Micah rubbed his eyes. "We didn't make fifty?"

"Mom changed the rules again," Lacee said. Justy could tell her teeth were clenched.

"Take hands," Dale said.

Justy reached out her fingers, finding Lacee's in front of her and Micah's behind. Dale held Micah's other hand.

"Be extra quiet."

The voice was Dale's, but any one of them could've uttered the caution. None of them wanted to wake Jake—not in the night, after they'd tried to leave. Together they inched forward, Dale leading. They climbed into the shadows of the porch. The wood creaked, and Justy tried not to put any weight on the boards. Dale fell forward with a soft thud. The chain of movement stopped, and Jake's logging boots scraped against the wood as Dale untangled from them. She brushed her pants, stood and reached out for Micah's hand again. She arrived at the door, and then they were inside. The house was darker than the night, and Dale guided them forward through the smell of smoke from the bar, brought into the house on Jake's clothes. In their room, the children slid under the covers after soundlessly taking off their shoes and jackets. Dale tucked them in, lingering in the doorway. She waited until Micah's and Lacee's breathing indicated sleep, then she walked to the living room couch.

From where Justy lay, she could see moonlight streaming through the living room windows. Dale sat on the edge, fingers folded together under her chin. She rocked slightly, as though the river still took her weight and made her feel light. Justy felt the tidal split again and knew Dale wouldn't go to sleep next to Jake, not after she'd wanted to run away, not after she'd visited the Eel. Her faith filled in the cracks between her and Jake, the same cracks that ate away at Jake. Justy turned over and tried again to find any trace of Jehovah, but all she felt that was real was the stone in her hand and the very different ways Jake and Dale moved through the world.

Dale stood up and walked out onto the porch, where she waited, considering. It didn't work to try and tell Jake how she felt when he didn't come home, or how she felt so small when Walters came with his fancy gifts. Dale wanted to tell Jake she was tired of it—all of it. She picked up the logging boots and moved through the night to the pond, where the moon continued to tremble on the water. The night pushed up against her there, and she wondered if this was normal, standing at the dark edge of a body of water.

Words couldn't take her where she wanted to go with Jake, and so she flung one boot, then the other, out and away from her, loving each instant of release. The rich moment after the weight left her hands filled her, making her think of her body in the river.

The boots floated on the surface of the water, dark blobs breaking the moon's reflection. Dale brushed her hands together and returned to the house, to the couch, to the Bible and maybe sleep.

When he woke, Jake's head hurt and he groaned. His stomach lurched at the smell of potatoes cooking. He pulled on his jeans and moved through the house to the porch, where he closed his eyes and let the morning sun pierce the pain. Drawing in a deep breath, he pictured the valley as it would be when he opened his eyes. Mist would be rising from the pond, the wooded mountains would stand tall around him and apple blossoms would dot the ground underneath the tree just outside the yard. It soothed him, the steady image of the land.

He blinked and realized something was wrong with his picture. He didn't understand at first, but as the fuzz cleared, he realized Dale was out by the pond, a tree branch in her hands as she tried to hook an object in the water. She leaned out and tried again and again to snare the floating thing. Jake blinked one more time and the night came back to him—how he and Kyle had stopped off at Hilltop for a Friday drink and how it had turned into a playing session, he and Kyle filling the bar with their music. Dale and the kids had been gone and he remembered the flat space in the bed next to him.

Dale held a dripping boot. Jake didn't recall anything in the evening that might've included boot throwing, but what he didn't need was to find his logging boots floating in the pond this morning. He went back into the house and sat at the kitchen table, commanding his twitchy hands to remain still. Jake cradled his head and didn't hear Justy slip past him. She went out the door, through the gate and climbed into the apple tree, lodging herself in tight so she could soothe the stirring ache rising between Jake and Dale. Her hands felt the woodpecker-scarred surface of the tree as Dale walked beneath her, set the boots on the porch where the sun could find them and moved inside.

The fight began with small sentences, words that veered near the aged hurt between them. Justy wanted to know what Jake and Dale were really saying to each other when Dale offered him coffee and breakfast, when he waited a full minute before answering. Justy hugged herself against the chill in their prefight conversation and wished she could be asleep like Lacee and Micah, wished she hadn't woken when Dale had slipped from under the blanket on the couch. Justy looked at the water-logged boots with their spiky claws on the bottom and guessed they'd be forever tight on Jake's working feet.

Kyle walked from his cabin whistling a tune, glanced at the fresh crop of weeds in the garden, then turned to the mounting fight inside. Justy wanted him to step in and make them stop, but he continued on, walking past the porch and the apple tree and out through the front gate. He walked to the Doug fir tree, and Justy tried to push away her anger at him for not guiding Jake home sooner each night, for being the one to teach Jake to use his hands in anger. But she didn't have the time or space to pay attention to him right now, not with Jake and Dale slinging words.

Justy focused her gaze back on the house, thinking about the birds that got dazed in the winter storms, sometimes striking the hard wall of windows of the living room with a thump. She willed herself to be a net, one she could throw over the house so she could catch the words before they left their world and gained power or fell dead at Jake's and Dale's feet.

Kyle tried to toss a rope over a branch and Justy tried not to be distracted by him. On his fourth try, the rope fell as he wanted. He walked to the bed of his truck and pulled out a small board with a drilled hole that he worked the rope through. Justy could see he was making a swing, and it made her smile before she remembered she shouldn't be watching him. She moved so she couldn't see him and listened to the silence coming from the house.

A half-eaten plate of potatoes sat in front of Jake, and the eggs he'd just swallowed left an odd taste in his mouth. Dale washed the dishes, and the air in the house changed as something dangerous rose up between them. Justy held tight to the tree as Kyle walked over to her, leaving the swing swaying from the Doug fir. He tapped his finger on the wood, imitating the noisy woodpeckers in their quests for tree grubs. But his tapping was too soft to sound like the birds, and Justy felt annoyance creep into her stomach. He was part of the problem. She looked at his cowboy boots, their tired blackness framed by the white apple blossoms, and she realized their sweet smell.

Kyle stood quiet, his hands now stilled on the tree. A rush of questions filled Justy and she reached for the stone in her pocket. She wanted to know exactly what had happened during Dale's pregnancy and why Dale had decided to stop singing with Jake. Justy pushed the stone against her teeth and sighed. The creases in Kyle's face told stories she could never know, ones she could only imagine.

Dale didn't mean to, but she screamed, her formless words carrying out over Justy's head where she couldn't catch them. Justy willed herself to live in this instant, in how the apple blossoms sang their scent, how Kyle felt the rough surface of the tree, how the tip of the western mountains were still held in the final traces of coastal fog. She felt so completely split by the feelings of Jake and Dale that she had no room for herself or even a shadow of Jehovah. The house was full of murmurings she couldn't understand, but she stretched toward the sound of their voices. She heard a thump and Kyle paused; she knew Jake had thrown Dale's Bible books across the room, cursing the day the Witnesses arrived and stole his wife.

"A tree is a good thing," Kyle said. He looked at the pond's rippling surface, and Justy wasn't sure if he was speaking to her. Blue sky and occasional clouds mottled the water.

"Before we came west, those few times your great-granddad and mom got into it, I'd go out to this old cottonwood and lean back. I'd watch the sky and the dirt road and wonder where it'd take me if I just took off left, them and my sisters. But I couldn't. Not after the twins died."

Kyle half closed his eyes. Justy loved the sound of his voice, the way its deep tones made the world seem logical and easy. She hadn't decided what she liked better, his singing voice or his speaking voice. Another thump came from the house and Kyle turned so he could keep an eye on the front door. His fingers looped over the bark and Justy thought maybe he talked to keep himself from going to the house and stepping into Jake and Dale's business again.

"You see," Kyle said, "Mama and Daddy were fighting. 'Discussing,' Mama called it, the move to California." He kept his eyes on the house, and Justy decided to dedicate one ear to him and one ear to the fight, hoping Kyle might say something that would help her. "So many families were going, had gone. Daddy wanted to go, but Mama, she thought it was better to stay and keep working what was left of the land. Ever since the twins died, she hadn't left the county, afraid for some reason that their graves wouldn't be safe. She told Daddy that things just had to get better, and me and Essie and Jewell? Well, we didn't even have one pair of shoes between the three of us to walk to school, so we sort of sided with Daddy. We heard talk, you know, that California had more jobs than people, and we wanted to go, all of us teenaged and able-bodied. In Clifty, we couldn't do a thing but stare at the walls and play music. Mama thought it'd be worse, heading out to a place where we didn't have any family, any know-how of life."

Kyle shook his head and said, "But there wasn't a thing left in the soil, not a damn thing. Thirty-four. That was a year."

A bird squawked and Kyle searched the surrounding trees. "That's a scrub jay. You can tell by the call." The world slowed with the silence coming from the house. Kyle returned to his story, "And Daddy won out, piling us into a Model T and driving us, with all of our fool stuff, and when we arrived in southern California, all those families, it made a person sick. And it was hard on both of them, but Daddy grew quiet. Seeing all that hunger. After a while, he even stopped playing the fiddle, and one day he just handed it to me without a word."

Justy felt something big stirring within Kyle, and she sensed she didn't want to know what he would say next. Kyle closed his eyes and Justy wished she were swimming—somewhere different than where she was.

Kyle stood up straight, said the words fast: "The next night and with the help of too much whiskey and the family shotgun, he left."

Kyle shook his head again and remained silent for a few minutes. Justy thought of the graves, how Jake and Kyle moved the bodies of people who probably never imagined they'd be rootless, especially in death. A small spider distracted her and she watched its quick little legs take it on a journey.

"I missed that cottonwood," Kyle finally said. Justy shut her eyes and tried to imagine it. A lone house with a simple wooden porch came to her, a single tree standing trusty guard. A clear stream ran near the Cottonwood, cattails and reeds growing along the water. The picture seemed empty, and she realized she'd given the house no family. She had them already moved to California.

A wry smile gathered in the left side of Kyle's mouth. "I met your grandmother in Arkansas, right before Daddy piled us into the truck. Kind of funny if you think about it, the two of us meeting up again."

Kyle pushed away from the tree, winked at her and then moved. He went back toward the road, then on down to the barn, going either to visit the pictures or oil his saddle. Justy thought about him meeting Jake's mother when he was so young, about the chances of Lila and Kyle meeting again in California. It seemed to Justy that they should've stayed together, life pushing them at each other after traveling all those miles.

She turned back to the house and knew that the fight was over. Dale stood on the porch, her eyes red-rimmed. Her hair was half falling out of its braid, and she held a towel in her hands that she wrung tight. Justy could tell Dale saw the distant future in God's kingdom, when she would be perfect. Dale looked down and saw the drying boots. She slowly brought her right foot forward and pushed them off the porch.

***

Even though the next day was Sunday, Joella didn't come to take them to the Kingdom Hall. Dale woke the children an hour later than usual and told them to get dressed in outside clothes. Lacee and Justy looked at each other and smiled. No dresses on Sunday meant something special. The house smelled of syrup and French toast, and Justy walked sleepy-eyed to the kitchen table where Jake and Kyle already sat. Kyle patted the seat next to him, said, "Here, string bean."

She sat down, smelling his crisp aftershave. He wrapped a warm arm around her and pulled her to his side. She closed her eyes, feeling the strength of his body, and wondered if he felt closer to her because he'd told her stories yesterday or because he'd waited out Jake and Dale's fight with her. When everyone sat at the table, Jake cleared his throat and said, "Today, we go see a tree cut." He took a bite.

"Your mother here"—he pointed with his fork—"she says we don't spend enough time together as a family. So, we're having a family day."

"Finally," Dale said under her breath, "What is it, Dad?" Micah asked. His brown hair stood up in sleep-worn tufts. Jake pretended not to hear Micah, who wiggled in his seat and looked at Kyle and then Dale to see if they would tell him. Finally, Jake swallowed and grinned at Micah.

"We're going to see one of the last giants fall." Jake took another bite of French toast and smiled. "I think it's a good thing you kids get a look at this tree, seeing as how there aren't going to be too many more." Jake looked at Kyle, who cupped his own chin with his hand and said, "So."

Dale went to the kitchen counter to make peanut-butter-and-jelly sandwiches. The rest of the family waited and then Kyle nodded. He rubbed his long fingers together. "There's the time I decide to teach your dad here to be a high climber."

Jake stabbed at another piece of French toast with his fork.

"We was working a job near Myers Flat, some private property tucked in among all them state parks. And Jake, he's been pestering me for weeks to let him top a tree and I haven't wanted to let him, it being more dangerous than falling or choker setting, and it being a job on the outs. But the boy is persistent." Kyle looked across the table and smiled.

"Jake, he's all of seventeen, working with me in the woods during the summers, and he thinks he's some hot stuff."

"You know them fallers said I was better than most old-timers," Jake said, the slightest urgency in his voice.

Kyle nodded. "I didn't say you weren't good, boy. But high climbing, it's a whole other ball game."

Jake accepted this and went back to his French toast.

"It's about the beginning of August, and all summer long Jake's been hounding me to teach him to climb the big trees. I give in on one of those mornings you can barely feel that somewhere down the road, winter is packing its bags, headed your way. It ain't much. Just the tiniest shiver running up your spine that don't last longer than a second, but all the same it makes you think about the rain, and the long, dark days, and you wonder how you'll survive one more rainy season. I get one of them shivers and I think to myself, Self, it's as good as any other day to show your boy the thing he wants so much he acts like a rabid dog.

"I go to wake Jake and he's already outside the cabin, brewing coffee over the camp stove. Eager about another day of work. I stand and watch him for a minute, him not knowing I'm there, and I see him eye the camp cat sleeping on the hood of the crummy. The thing about the cat is that she and Jake hate each other, more than is reasonable, and all for some unknown reason. The other guys in the camp make a point to bring Jake and the cat together in all kinds of situations, like stuffing the poor animal in Jake's sleeping bag in the middle of the night when he's stepped out to take a leak. Places where Jake and the cat are bound to continue their relationship." Kyle chuckled, and took a sip of coffee.

"While Jake is eyeballing the cat and I'm eyeballing Jake, I step forward and tell him that today's the day. Jake jumps up, spilling coffee all over the front of his hickory shirt, and a shit-eating grin covers his face. The cat? She sees Jake jump up and hightails it out of there, thinking he's coming after her. We go on about the day and then around eleven, I call

Jake over and show him how to hook himself into the lanyard, how to dig the spikes of his caulk boots into the tree as he starts to loop himself upward. Of course, Jake waves my instructions away, having studied my moves for years. I give him a few more pointers and then Johnny Jones steps forward…Remember him, Jake?"

Jake nodded and Kyle continued, "Well, Johnny, he hands Jake a pack, and then Jake is off running up the tree like he's a born natural. He looks good, and I get this feeling of pride start to fill my chest as I watch him scramble up the tree, chain saw hanging down his back. You can just tell he can't wait to get to that first branch a hundred feet up the redwood and go at it with the saw. And then he reaches the branch…"

Kyle started laughing and had to clear his throat. "I don't know how Johnny did it, but somehow he got that cat into the pack he'd handed Jake. And that cat, she must've been too scared to move until Jake reached back for the chain saw and started it up. I'm craning my neck backwards to watch him, holding my breath. Then I see Jake coming down, down, down that tree, seven times faster than he went up, and when he gets near the bottom, I can hear the cat screaming, and the back of Jake's neck is covered with scratches. Johnny Jones is on the ground laughing his fool head off and I'm trying not to laugh, not when it could've caused Jake to fall. But there's Jake, trying to wriggle out of that pack and trying at the same time to keep as far as he can from the cat, who has absolutely lost her mind. I think it took Jake about as long to get out of that pack as it did to convince me to let him try climbing."

Lacee and Micah laughed and Jake stood and moved away from the table.

"Let's leave in twenty minutes," he said at the front door. Dale cleared his plate without looking anyone in the eye.

***

The children climbed into the bed of the Willys, and Dale handed them two sleeping bags. Lacee placed one up against the cab and then the children sat, using the second sleeping bag as a cover. Warm air—full of the promise of summer—surrounded them, but that promise would last only until the truck started moving. Jake climbed in and started the engine. Dale placed a Styrofoam ice chest in the bed of the truck and looked at the children as if to secure each one in place for the ride.

They hit the highway and the world seemed wide open to Justy, with the wind blowing and the fresh air filling her senses. The pale blue sky rolled overhead. Tree-lined mountains edged the view, and she imagined climbing those hills, back into country that hardly ever had a human visitor, walking through the trees and shivering in the shade as she headed west. Over the lip of the mountains, she'd gain a view of the grand Pacific. She'd see waves crashing against the rocky north coast. Lacee's teacher, one of the ones who had helped start the petition and didn't shave her legs, had told the reading group that she'd been to Ireland. Ms. Parsons said the cliffs over by the towns of Westport and Fort Bragg reminded her of the Irish coastal country. Jake said the Colbys were part Irish, part Indian, part something else—all people who'd been given the runaround.

As the truck traveled toward the big tree, Justy thought about Dale sitting up front between Jake and Kyle, like in the old days before Justy had arrived.

They drove under the second overpass, the one that fed the old highway into downtown Sequoia. Justy had heard talk that used to be hundreds of people living in the area, and she wondered where they had gone, what kind of stories they were living now. And this new wave of people, direct from the cities, bringing art and a love of the land that seemed different from Jake's feelings. Sunshine and Nolan and Ochre were people Justy was drawn to, despite what Jake and Dale said about how they must earn their money. Ochre never smelled like the kids whose parents grew what Dale called the pot.

Lacee started singing a song, the wind whipping her voice away, almost before Micah and Justy had a chance to hear it. They continued on the freeway that took them past River Fork, and when Jake took an off-ramp, Justy leaned forward and saw the sign that said "Avenue of the Giants." The truck entered the shade of the redwood grove, and they curved on the road in between the trees. Justy loved the incredible height of the trees and how the damp world beneath them kept all the plants so green. The Eel was off to her right, and she caught glimpses of it every few minutes.

In an open area, Jake brought the truck to a stop. The children stood and looked over the cab. Jake, Dale and Kyle climbed out of the truck, and Jake pointed to a pole in front of them with a small sign at the very top that said "High-Water Mark, 1964."

"See that?" he said. "That's how high the Eel got the year the bridge washed out at the Reese Ranch. That tiny little sign tells you why your mother didn't graduate from high school." He walked forward until he stood directly under the marker. More than thirty feet of pole rose above him. Justy looked at Dale and saw her stare up at the sign. Justy tried to imagine the river rising that high and saw herself swimming under tons of water, unable to see the sun. She'd heard the story about the bridge washing out—how Dale had been newly married to Jake, four months pregnant and six months shy of her high school diploma. How they'd had to use the old box-pulley system, the size of a coffin, hanging from cables across the expanse of Hollow Tree Creek Canyon. How Jake and Dale had climbed inside the box and how when they got to the other side, that platform was washed away also, so that Jake had to lower Dale to the ground by a rope tied beneath her arms. Justy didn't know when she hadn't known this story, but it took on another meaning for her as she looked at the sign. What Jake and Dale hadn't talked about was the water raging underneath them. But maybe that wasn't a thing a person could put into words.

"Thought you guys should see it," Jake said, and climbed back into the truck. Dale stood a moment more and Justy thought about her swimming in the middle of the night. Maybe Dale felt like she was constantly surrounded by things that wanted to carry her away and felt that by swimming the Eel, she stayed strong. Dale nodded at the sign, went to the passenger side of the truck and climbed in while Kyle held the door for her. Jake headed the truck south to the logging site.

Lacee arranged the sleeping bags around them again. "What he doesn't tell you," she said, "is that a few miles farther on, he rolled a car once."

Justy sat up and looked at Lacee, wanting to know the whole story.

"He did not," Micah said.

"You can ask Kyle. They went to his high school reunion and Dad drank too much. You wouldn't remember because you were just a baby."

Micah blew his bangs from his eyes. Justy could tell he wasn't sure whether to believe Lacee.

"Dad had to get twenty-four stitches in his head," Lacee told him.

"How come he doesn't have any scars?" Micah smiled, thinking he'd caught Lacee in a fib.

"Because the scar is under his hair." She hit him on the arm.

The truck eased onto a dirt road and the children covered their heads with the top sleeping bag, trying to keep out the dust. Justy peeked out and saw redwood ferns and trees covered in an ashy layer. She ducked back under the cover and knew from the dust that this was a route many logging trucks had taken, their weight turning the dirt road into a fine powder. The children huddled under their dark canopy, and Lacee started laughing at the way Micah kept filling his lungs with air, trying not to breathe, turning red, then finally exhaling to take in another, equally dusty breath. Justy wanted to know how Lacee could tell such a scary story and then laugh so soon after.

The road became rougher and Jake shifted into second gear. Justy pulled the sleeping bag down, and the three children looked at the patches of empty forest. They had to hang on to one another when the Willys crossed the water bars, rattling their teeth. The engine whined as they climbed a small incline and then they were in a clearing, the earth raw with human and machine movement. Stumps dotted the landing, and six trucks were parked in a line by one of them. The area seemed nude, completely different from the redwood grove they'd just passed through. Jake pulled up next to Harris's red Toyota, and Justy recognized Lefty Fry's battered green Ford. Another new white foreign truck with fog lights and a roll bar waited on the other side of Harris's truck. When Jake cut the Willys's engine, they all could hear a chain saw and the deep rumbling of a Caterpillar tractor. Jake climbed out of the cab.

"Okay, kids." He had to raise his voice to be heard. "We're here to see that tree fall." He pointed at a redwood tree looming at the left edge of the landing. It stood more than a hundred feet from the truck. Justy leaned forward, eyes searching for the top of the tree. Dale and Kyle got out of the truck. Jake indicated the new white pickup with a nod. "Looks like we got more than one grower here."

Dale and Kyle both looked at the shiny vehicle, standing out among the dirty collection of trucks even with its layer of new dust. Kyle shrugged and Dale shook her head.

"If Gaines knew we were here, with the kids…" Jake looked at Dale.

"I'll keep them close," she half shouted back to him.

"Good idea," Jake said, and walked to the group of men gathered around a cooler on the tailgate of the truck that was farthest away. Dale watched him go, then turned to the tree marked for falling. Kyle leaned against the side of the truck, following her gaze. The chain saw stopped. He whistled.

"What's Juan doing with the Cat, Granpa?" Lacee asked. They all looked from the tree to the yellow D8 tractor pushing dirt into a pile.

"He's making a bed for the tree. See, if you don't make a bed, a redwood will shatter when it hits the ground, and then none of the timber is any good. There's no money in a shattered tree, no matter how many board feet it has."

"And that thing over there?" Micah asked, pointing to another yellow machine sitting idle at the far end of the landing.

"That's a loader. It's what we use to get the cut trees onto the logging trucks."

Justy didn't like the way it looked, with its sharp, pointy arms jutting in the air. She remembered the pictures she'd seen in a book about logging, how the men had such tiny saws and how tremendously huge the trees were.

"Figure I'll go say hello to the guys," Kyle said to Dale. He walked away and Lacee asked if the children could follow. Dale studied the enormity of the tree, then the tractor pushing its way across the dirt.

"Yes," she finally said, still not looking at the children. "But don't go too far." She turned her gaze to the knot of men. No other women were present. The children each swung a leg over the tailgate, notched a foot on the bumper, brought the other leg over and jumped. Their feet thudded into the dust, and puffs of dirt rose in the air around their shoes.

"Keep an eye on each other," Dale said, and they all nodded. Justy felt like they automatically watched out for each other, that maybe they were a tribe of three. A heavy trail in the dust next to one boot print showed where Harris had walked. Justy also noticed Gil Walker's wheelchair marks.

"Look, I'm Bigfoot," Micah said. His footprints were much bigger than his tennis shoes. Justy started walking, trying to be Bigfoot also. She searched the trees. The metal tread of the Cat clanked as Juan pushed dirt from in between the stumps. Young, pale redwood ferns grew at the edges of the landing, their lacy leaves gracing the red-ochre of the stumps. The earth was dry and small roots twisted in the soil as the maw of the Cat bulldozed forward. Justy noted the dirt was brown, not like the deep orange of the land the mining company owned and wanted.

Along with the dust, she smelled the fresh-cut redwood and breathed in its honeyed smell. Lacee linked arms with her and headed them in the direction of the men. When they approached, Lacee let go of Justy and stood next to Jake. Micah joined the girls, and the children waited to be noticed. They watched Mark Sloan lay his chain saw into the redwood trunk. A crescent of sawdust arced behind him. Sam Sloan and his brother, Frank, stood off to the side, watching their father's progress. Frank held a Budweiser in his free hand. They all wore the same uniform—striped hickory shirts, loose-fitting Ben Davis jeans ripped off above the ankles, red suspenders, gloves, hard hats and the spiky black caulk boots.

Justy looked back at Dale and thought about her flowing in the Eel the other night. Dale gazed off in the distance, her lean body supported by the truck. Mark pulled the chain saw away from the tree and shut off the engine. The clank of the Cat didn't seem so loud now and Lacee coughed. Jake put an arm around her shoulders. Justy tried to remember the last time Jake had touched any of them. Lacee stood straighter into her years, apparently forgiving Jake for not coming home earlier two nights before. Kyle winked at the girls and drank deeply from a beer. Next to him stood a clean-cut man with a camera hanging from his neck. The Cat stopped and the men shifted in the quiet.

"Too bad you can't top it, Kyle," Lefty said, saluting Kyle with his beer.

Kyle turned and gauged the tree again. "Once this one goes, there won't be much call for my line of work."

"Biggest tree I ever seen," Jeff Harris said, his bushy beard twitching with his words.

"Gonna bring lots of widow makers with it," Lefty said. He smiled at Justy and she looked away from him to the T-shirt Harris wore. It said "This bud's for you," and huge leaves filled the white space under the words. She wondered whose new white pickup was parked by Harris's. All the men in the circle except the one with the camera were people she recognized from town and Hilltop, but she couldn't guess which one had crossed over from logging.

"I seen bigger," Gil Walker said from his wheelchair. Justy studied his face again, trying to see any changes in the lines since she'd watched him the day of the trapshoot.

"Hell, Gil. You seen everything," Jake said. The group laughed.

Gil adjusted his Peterbilt cap and spat into the dust. "I've worked harder than any of you, climbed more trees than you'll ever dream about." He took a gulp of his beer and wiped his mouth. The men waited a minute and Justy assumed it was out of respect.

"Yeah, yeah. And screwed more women than there are stars in the sky," Harris said.

The men laughed. When Kyle stopped, he pointed with his index finger from the side of his beer toward the children. Jake removed his arm from Lacee and said, "You kids go sit with your mother."

They walked back to Dale and stopped in front of her. She returned from her thoughts and lowered the tailgate. The children climbed up and she handed them each a sandwich from the cooler. While Justy tasted the sweet blackberry jam, she looked at the sky, saw the tops of the trees hovering in a circle around the clearing. The doomed tree stood so tall and immobile, it was hard for her to imagine it falling. The trunk was clean of branches, much like the Drive-Thru Tree, broken only by the deep grooves in the bark. She watched Mark and his sons wedge metal pieces into the cut Mark had made.

"Mama," Micah said, "will there be logging in the New System?"

"I don't know," Dale said, "but it seems that since the Bible says the earth will be restored, like how it was in the Garden of Eden, I figure not."

Micah thought about this and then asked, "Since we'll be perfect human beings, will I know how to play all musical instruments?"

Dale shrugged and said, "Maybe you should ask Brother Lucas next time you see him."

"Okay," he said, and went back to his sandwich. Justy felt closer to Micah than she had in months; she sometimes wondered what the New System would be like, and if maybe that was why Jehovah didn't show up.

Jake and Kyle returned and Dale handed them sandwiches.

"That tree ain't going to fall on us, is it?" Lacee asked Jake from her perch on the edge of the truck. Jake walked over and stood in front of her, facing away.

"No, girl. These guys know what they're doing. See how they're putting those wedges in?" Jake gestured with his beer and took a bite of his sandwich. "Those are to make sure the tree won't twist while Mark does his next cut, what they call the face cut." Jake watched the men with a certain kind of reverence Justy hadn't seen outside the Kingdom Hall.

"Tree fallers in the Pacific Northwest, they're better than all the rest in the world because the trees are so big. They even came up with something that's called the Humboldt cut. It's a special way to deal with the huge bases of the redwoods."

"What's a widow maker?" Micah asked. Jake pointed to the top of the tree. "See those limbs? When a tree is cut, those guys come flying off and can end up anywhere. I know of men who've had their head snapped off by one of them limbs."

"A widow is a wife with a dead husband," Dale said.

"Who's the guy with the camera?" Lacee asked.

"He's from the Eureka logging museum," Kyle said. He shook his head. "That tree is thousands of years old."

"Older than Jesus?" Micah asked, and Kyle nodded. The family remained quiet and Justy thought about the trip the elementary school had taken last year to the museum. In the entrance sat a slab of an old growth, showing how the years could be counted by the tree's growth rings. Small markers indicated where major historical events correlated to the tree's years, things such as when Columbus had landed in America, when the Constitution was written. The tree before them now was older than this country, Justy thought. A sadness tugged at the currents running in her.

"He's beginning the face cut now," Kyle said. Mark started the saw again and they watched him brace his leg before laying the blade into the tree.

"This will be the one that makes it fall," Kyle said. Justy didn't like the sound of a face cut or a widow maker. And the blade was so tiny compared to the tree—it seemed like a trick to her. She didn't understand how that little machine could cut down all that history. And it didn't make sense, how the Drive-Thru Tree continued to stand with its middle cut out. She'd seen pictures of the old logging days, when two men and one tiny saw took days to fall one redwood. Her favorite picture from the logging museum was the one where two men each sat on a horse in the cut of a redwood. Another one she liked was an elementary school photo with about fifty children sitting on the stump of a tree.

They watched Mark cut for thirty more minutes, then he yelled "Timber" above the sound of the running chain saw. He and his sons ran from the tree and stopped about forty yards away. Dale made sure each of the children was in the bed of the truck. The top of the tree swayed a little. Mark killed the chain saw and the landing became still except for a faint breeze in the treetops. The wind stopped and Justy heard a cracking sound. She looked at the men gathered around the beer cooler and saw that they all stood with their mouths open and hats off. Mark yelled "Timber" again. The cracking sound grew. The tree was cut all the way through but wasn't falling. Maybe habit or memory held it in place.

Mark watched the tree, the quiet chain saw in his hand. He and his sons kept their hard hats on. A pop, pop, pop came from the trunk and Mark yelled "Timber" once more, as if the sound of his voice could topple the tree. Time slowed, leaving the people and the tree in a void where things forgot to move forward. The redwood swayed and Justy heard its branches scratching other branches, other trees. Micah sneezed. A low, slow creak came from the trunk and then stopped. Jake looked at Mark, then back at the tree, yelled "Timber" a fourth time, the certainty in his voice diminished. The top of the old growth seemed like it was moving, but Justy wasn't sure, just like she wasn't sure if she really swam the Eel in her dreams. The creaking grew louder and the whole tree began to sway, barely moving, holding on to its severed trunk. Then it groaned again from deep within and began to drop toward the earth, a swath of red hovering in the sky. Then it picked up speed and fell fast, as if it had given up. It crashed its way downward, graceful even in its hugeness, taking and breaking the limbs of other trees with quick snaps of sound. Finally, it hit the bed Juan had made for it dead-on, and a powerful thud echoed when it landed. The Willys rocked with the impact, making Justy think of an earthquake. Two branches, the ones Jake had called widow makers, impaled the earth, and to Justy, it looked like God had thrown them there.

The afternoon felt split open, and a trancelike quiet filled the space the redwood had left behind. Dust filled the air, and occasional creaks of protest came from the tree as it settled into the earth. But for that noise, Justy could hear no other. Everyone remained still, as if frozen by what they'd seen. The forest itself seemed to be in shock, watching in inarticulate protest. She remembered this was a family day, and the sadness she'd felt earlier threatened to overtake her and shake her body with sobs. She placed Ochre's stone on her tongue. The tree's history seemed to press down on her, and she couldn't look at the raw place in the sky where it had been. The image of the high-water sign in the middle of the other redwood grove came to her, and she was grateful that those trees were protected from these men and their machines, even though she knew that the fewer there were, the angrier Jake would become because he'd have no work. She wanted to know what would happen to the tree now that its grand stretch of time was over. The men looked confused, like maybe this power they'd been granted was both a blessing and a curse. Maybe she knew how they felt.

Warm May air swirled into the cab as the miles passed. Dale and the children counted the signs for the Mountain Folk Festival. Justy wanted to know how to compose her feelings, but Dale's face was hard to read. Justy closed her eyes and sensed that Dale was balled up tight, waiting to see what the day would bring. Jake and Kyle were already at the festival, helping to set up for the Bull of the Woods contest. They'd be competing today, a father-and-son team trying to bring back the old days.

Dale took the first off-ramp and drove past Hilltop and then entered the shade of the redwoods. Goose bumps covered Justy's arms. She leaned forward, trying to see the treetops. If she concentrated, she could still feel the earth shaking from when Mark's old growth had hit the ground two weeks before.

The truck burst into sunlight as they left the Drive-Thru Tree Park behind and continued on through the Sequoia Valley. The single road leading through town was filled with cars and trucks—the festival brought in more people than the rest of the year total. A quarter mile off to her left, Justy saw the letters painted on top of the school gym, "Sequoia Valley Panthers." A banner stretched over the main road: "6th Annual Mountain Folk Festival." Inside the O's, someone had painted mountains and trees. As Dale drove under the banner, Justy held her breath for good luck and knew she wasn't supposed to.

Dale parked behind a new truck that said "Toyota" across the tailgate. When she cut the engine, amplified guitar and banjo music echoed from the festival grounds. She pulled a brush from her purse and smoothed her hair. She turned the brush on Justy and then Micah, but he pressed up against Lacee, out of Dale's reach.

"Do I have to stay with you?" Lacee asked. She had her hand on the door, ready to be free and fourteen. Dale looked at the people walking to the grounds, some with beer in their hands. "Not even eleven o'clock," Dale said. She sighed and turned to Lacee. "Just check in with me every once in a while."

Lacee nodded and then was gone, Micah quick to follow.

"Let's go, Justy." Dale patted her arm in a way that told Justy she was glad for the company. They walked toward a hazy cloud of dust, the earth dry and powdery with the movement of feet. It reminded Justy of the logging roads ground to dust by the loaded trucks. They walked past an old blue Ford with a brand-new yellow bumper sticker: "This Family Supported by Timber Dollars." It wasn't a truck she recognized; it could have been from any number of neighboring towns. They continued on and Justy recognized Mamie's VW van.

The dirt road that led to Carver's Hole was the dividing line for the festival. Vendor booths and children's activities filled the left-hand side. Crystals, earrings, colorful windsocks, coin tosses, water dunk, pony rides. On the right side stood the wooden stage where a three-man band played for no one and everyone. This side also had the food booths, near the highway, and the beer booth. Toward the back of the right side, the competition area waited, within plain view of the stage.

Dale paused, and Justy waited for her to decide which way to go. People walked past them in small herds, a few nodding hello, but it seemed to Justy that most folks widened their way around Dale, maybe afraid she carried a *Watchtower* or two in her purse. Dale scanned the crowd and Justy scanned Dale, both looking for signs of Jake or Kyle. Dale spotted an empty place on a log and headed for it. Thirty or so people were already gathered, waiting for the ax-throwing contest. Jake walked through the crowd and approached a small knot of men from the Sloan family. He held a beer and said something that made them all laugh.

Pale wood chips covered the area, and the smell of fresh-cut wood collected in Justy's nose. The music stopped and people turned to face the stage. Mark Sloan fumbled with the microphone, seeming more afraid of it than he'd been of the huge redwood tree. He announced the beginning of the Bull of the Woods competition, then asked everyone to please get off their duffs for the pledge of allegiance. People not already standing rose, and conversations stopped. Faces turned toward the flag at the left of the stage. Dale and Justy stood slowly. Mark led the pledge while Justy looked around for Ochre or Sunshine. Her hand stayed at her side. The people near her and Dale sneaked glances at them. Justy turned her gaze forward, not meeting anyone's eye. She knew Jake's hand lay on his chest, and that he spoke loudly and firmly, as if trying to make up for his pledgeless family.

Dale and Jake confused Justy anew, and she knew they confused each other. Dale insisted that they live by the law but without showing any outright loyalty to the country. Jake wanted to live by his own rules but voiced his allegiance to the same system of government he claimed held him down. Their different worlds swirled in Justy and made her want to gasp for air.

The crowd finished and Justy was sure she heard them say, "And Justine for all." She looked to see if anyone else had heard the same or if people were coming at her, but faces remained turned toward the stage. Mark began announcing the participants for the woodsmen's title. When he read Jake's and Kyle's names, he paused and said, "You got to watch out for those family teams. I should know."

The crowd laughed and Jake raised his beer to Mark in a salute. Mark continued on with the list and thanked one and all for coming out to show their support for timber dollars and the Sequoia volunteer fire department. Then he cleared his throat, swallowed and added, "I'd like to take a moment to mourn the loss of our friend C.C. Davis."

People nodded their heads and murmured. Mark continued, saying there was a collection box at the beer booth for C.C.'s wife and two kids, and if anyone could help out, his family would sure appreciate it.

After Mark stepped down from the stage, Dale and Justy sat down at the ax-throwing contest, and the first contestant stepped forward and took three measured swings before throwing. He hit high on the wooden mark with a solid thunk and kicked sawdust as Martin Fry, Jordan's father, moved forward. He winked at Connie sitting a few people down from Dale and Justy, then he squinted down the blade. In a fluid motion of tool and arm, he flung the ax.

It bounced off the target and fell to the ground. The crowd groaned and someone yelled, "Nice work, Paul Bunyan." Connie stood, spilling her beer, and yelled, "Shut up."

Jake stepped up and adjusted his glasses. He eyed the target, took one practice swing and threw. The ax whizzed and hit the bull's-eye dead on, puncturing the can of Coors shoved into the middle of the target. The beer sprayed out with a hiss, easing off into a drizzle. A few people clapped and a woman whistled. Justy thought about Jake's hands—how they brought both beauty and violence into the world.

"Not bad for an Injun," a voice called. Shelby Gaines stood behind the seated people, cigarette dangling from his lips. The little dog wagged its tail at his ankle. Jake gave Gaines a quick look. Gil Walker stood up on wobbly legs and turned to face Gaines.

"You shut your horse-loving trap," Gil called. Gaines waved a hand as if he were a fly. Sam Sloan walked to Gil and patted him on the shoulder before stepping up to take his turn. Frank Sloan appeared and replaced the beer can. Sam nailed the can also, and his father yelled approval from the back of the crowd. Kyle was next, and after Frank replaced the beer can, Kyle hit the target dead center, beer spraying to the ground a third time.

Kyle came to sit down in the open spot on the other side of Justy. He patted her bare knee and pulled on a string from her jean cutoffs. He looked over her head to Dale. "How's my favorite daughter-in-law today?"

She smiled at him. "Not too bad."

Kyle wrapped an arm around Justy's shoulders and squeezed. She wanted to know how this warmth came pouring out of him toward her and Lacee and Micah and Dale when what filled the space between him and Jake was anger. Kyle reached down to the wood chips and picked one up.

"This here is incense cedar. Smell it?" He held his hand in front of Justy. Her nose filled with the sweet scent. Kyle stood, dropping the chip. "I'm going to find me a beer. Either of you want anything?"

Dale and Justy shook their heads and he moved off through the crowd.

"Look at that," Dale said, nodding at the next contestant. A young man with a full beard, long hair, ripped jeans and no shirt swung an ax, getting ready for his turn. A tattoo of a peace sign covered most of his back. Seeing him made Justy realize how clean-cut all the other loggers were. The man seemed spaced out, but when his turn came, he hit the target squarely in the center.

An older man Justy didn't recognize walked up to Shelby Gaines, standing a few feet behind Justy and Dale. The man asked Gaines how his mare was, and Gaines chuckled and said, "Nigger? That girl is just fine. Did have a stomach spell a while back, but the vet said it was some kind of worms. Got them out of her and she's as good as ever."

The two men kept talking and Justy wondered about the name of Gaines's horse. She'd heard that word in the bar and knew from the way it came out of the men's mouths that it meant something bad.

***

Dale and Justy watched the rest of the events in the beating sun. Lacee and Micah joined them periodically but always disappeared quickly into the crowd after a few minutes. For the handsaw contest, Juan stepped forward with a wedge and a can of oil as Jake and Kyle began pulling and pushing the saw through the wood. Juan slipped the wedge in the groove and poured oil on the saw. Beads of sweat formed on Kyle's and Jake's foreheads as they tried to keep the blade flat, knowing its balanced edge cut better. The blade bit into the redwood log, metal teeth sliding back and forth. The layers of red faded into one another.

The slab fell off and people cheered. Jake and Kyle walked to Dale and Justy, breathing heavy but with smiles on their shiny faces. Someone handed Jake another beer. Both men's white T-shirts were covered in a fine layer of pale sawdust. Behind his glasses, Jake's black eyelashes were also powdered. Mark announced their time: four minutes and thirty-three seconds.

"That wasn't half bad," Kyle said. He stuck out his hand, but Jake gulped down the beer. Kyle continued holding out his hand until Jake finally yielded. They shook for a long minute, fingers squeezing together. Dale stood, and the men stepped back from each other.

"There he is again," she said. Jake and Kyle turned to see the tattooed man paired with another longhair. They settled into position and Harris was with them, climbing up on the log to place the wedges and oil their efforts.

"What's Harris doing?" Jake grumbled. Kyle shrugged, and Dale looked around for Mamie.

"He ain't done an honest day of work in years," Jake said, and started to walk away. The longhaired men began and they were good, moving smoothly through the log. Harris looked funny to Justy, straddling the log, his bad foot hanging awkwardly. Jake stopped and watched the fluid motion of the men. They beat Jake and Kyle's time by almost a full minute, and Justy felt Jake will his hands to be calm. Dale and Kyle moved over to where Jake stood.

"I should get the kids home," she said.

Jake drank from his beer. "Okay." He waved at Gil Walker rolling slowly past.

"Should I expect you two for dinner?" Dale tried to catch Jake's eyes, but he was staring at the hippie men. Kyle glanced at Jake and then back at Dale. He nodded.

"I just don't know," Jake said. Dale began to walk away. Justy took a step, stopped and looked at Jake.

"Dale," Jake called. She turned.

"Want to walk around for a bit? See the booths?" Jake took off his glasses and rubbed his eyes. She smiled in the corner of her mouth and walked back to his side. He handed Justy the beer and hooked his arm around Dale's shoulders. Kyle fell in beside Justy, and the four of them walked from the contest area, crossed the dirt road that led to the swimming hole and looked at the vendor booths. While they walked, Justy turned the can upside down, letting the beer sputter onto the dirt.

The first booth held an array of stained glass and crystals hanging from strings. The crystals caught the afternoon light and sent prismed rainbows into the air. A man with pale skin, long brown hair and an immense beard sat in a folding chair, a pink-and-white tie-dyed shirt covering his skinny torso. He smiled, but they didn't stop. The path became crowded and they had to collapse into single file, Jake leading the way as they walked past jewelry, windsocks and wicker furniture. At one booth, Justy saw Ochre, Nolan and Sunshine sitting cross-legged on pillows in the back corner. On the walls and on two easels were paintings of flowers—huge, colorful flowers that seemed alive, maybe even dancing in a slight breeze. Justy stared at the painting on the nearest easel. It was an Indian paintbrush, full of reds bleeding into oranges at the base of each flower. Justy wanted to reach out, see if it felt as fuzzy and soft as it looked, nothing like the empty beer can in her hand.

"Hey," Ochre said and stood.

"Hey," Sunshine said, her voice gentle and inviting. Her many-colored skirt whirled around as she walked to Justy and knelt. Ochre followed, his bare chest tanned deep brown. His hair was in its usual braid, and Justy thought about what it would feel like to savor the feel of her own hair on her skin. Sunshine wore a green scarf on her head.

Under their feet lay a thick red carpet with white fringes and yellowish flowers. Baskets of different sizes held various dried plants, and Justy remembered the sign at the post office with Sunshine's name and the mention of herbs. Bolts of cloth hung from the makeshift ceiling of the booth. Justy felt like she'd entered a new world—one full of color.

"How are you, Justy?" Nolan asked from his pillow. He was barefoot and held on to his trimmed beard with his left hand. A rich, heady smell came from a tiny smoking stick tucked into the pole nearest Nolan. Sunshine reached toward the paintbrush painting and said, "You like this one?"

Justy nodded.

"Nolan paints them," Ochre said. "He uses watercolors." He smiled and Justy felt soothed. She loved the idea that water and color could create something so beautiful.

"Ochre paints with me sometimes," Nolan said.

"Justy."

Dale walked up and placed a hand on Justy's shoulders, pulling her close. She wouldn't look at the Ravens.

"Mrs. Colby," Sunshine said, holding out her hand. Dale positioned Justy in between herself and Sunshine.

"Our son is a friend of your daughter," Nolan said. Ochre smiled at Dale.

"Oh," Dale said. It pained Justy to think of how Dale saw Ochre, with his long braided hair and his patch-covered shorts.

"It must be hard to be friends with someone who doesn't say a word," Dale said. Justy looked away from Ochre, almost embarrassed by the tone of Dale's voice and the lack of understanding in it.

"I don't mind," Ochre said, words quiet. He tried to catch Justy's eye. Nolan came over to Dale and Justy and started talking about the painting. Justy could see he was trying to pull Dale in. But she stiffened and Nolan paused.

"We don't have money for things like this," Dale said. It was the same way she'd told Lacee there was nothing for frills, magazines included.

"Your daughter seemed very interested in the painting, and I just wanted to tell her how it was done."

"Well, thank you, but we have to be moving on," Dale said, and started to pull at Justy. Kyle walked up and looked at the painting Justy was so drawn to. He whistled and squatted by her side. Dale stopped trying to force Justy away and stepped back, watching. Justy knew it was because Kyle was male; the Witnesses taught that women needed to be in submission to the men. He reached out a finger and followed a line of color through the painting. Justy saw the sawdust in his hair, on his eyelashes, even in his wrinkles. She also saw that he really did like the painting.

"Thank you," Nolan said, and held out his hand for Kyle, who stood and shook hands with all three Ravens. Sunshine started telling him about her herbs when he asked what the weeds in the baskets were all about. Ochre turned and smiled at Justy at the same time Dale stepped up and steered her away. After they passed a couple of booths, Dale stopped.

"Justy. I don't like the looks of those people. You need to stay away from them. They're probably doing pot." Dale turned Justy around and kept her moving until they caught up with Jake. He stood in the shade of a booth, talking to Ms. Long and a male high school teacher. The teachers sat behind a long folding table. A banner hung from the table: "Save Red Mountain." Ms. Long waved at Justy and seemed less timid with Jake. She and Jake were talking about how the petition was faring. Justy could see Ms. Long had gained some signatures and gotten more organized. She had T-shirts for sale, and the banner looked to Justy like Nolan had painted it. The man with Ms. Long watched her talk as if in a daze until Jake said that the land was private property and he didn't see how a few names could stop what somebody wanted to do on his own land. Then the man sat up straight, his short red hair standing away from his scalp as if it wanted to escape.

"Man, it doesn't matter if it's private property, since what they want to do will affect the entire ecosystem of this area."

"If we get enough signatures," Ms. Long said, "we can stop them."

"If I sign it, what am I asking to be done?" Jake took a step forward, images of the land roaming through his head. Dale gripped Justy's shoulders tighter, but Justy didn't think Dale was aware of it.

"Well," the man said. Justy knew he taught science, math and PE— all the high school teachers taught three or four subjects. His T-shirt said, "Remember the Land."

"Nobody that I know from around here wants to see the mountain mined," the man said, and pointed his index finger at photographs lying on the table. Justy strained forward, and she and Dale moved so they could see the pictures. They were taken from the air, before and after. The first picture showed the green-on-green of a forested mountain. The next ones revealed a bald and blocky pyramid.

"You know what they use nickel for?" Ms. Long asked. Jake nodded and the man answered, "They usc it in missiles and shit. Like we need more of those. As if 'Nam wasn't enough." The man sat back with a jerk, throwing his hands in the air.

"What the petition is for," Ms. Long said, giving the man a sideways glance, "is to ask that further studies be done so we have a better understanding of the mine's impact, how it affects the streams and the salmon runs. That sort of thing."

Jake stepped back and glanced at Dale. "If I sign it, will the mine people see my name?"

"You got to take a stand," the man said, leaning forward. Jake looked at him, opened his mouth and closed it. Justy felt his ache for the land they lived on well up in him again. If the mine was stopped, there might be a way to make the land his.

"If they really want to see the names, they can find them," Ms. Long said.

"I don't know, Jacob," Dale said.

Jake studied his boots and then said, "Can I think it over?"

The man shook his head and Ms. Long said, "Of course. But we want to have this in by the end of June."

"We have another petition if you're interested," the man said. "It's to protest the proposed search-and-seizure laws." He talked fast, trying to jam in the information. "Did you know that if you get busted growing dope, they're trying to make it so they can take your land, your vehicles, everything? It's unconstitutional."

He was yelling the last part. Ms. Long patted him on the arm. He took a breath and said in a calmer voice, "It's the war on drugs, man. Money is being pumped into this area for CAMP. Guns, ammunition, helicopters, the whole shebang. It's like another Vietnam, and where does the government think people learned to start smoking herb in the first place? To get away from their trumped-up war."

He stood and Dale took a step back, letting go of Justy.

"That's enough, Roger," Ms. Long said.

"It makes me sick," he said, and walked through the back of the booth. Justy stepped forward to look at the petition. Lefty's beautiful writing was the only indication that a local had signed it. Justy wondered if, because he'd signed it twice, he'd canceled himself out. She saw that Sunshine's and Nolan's names were numbers 18 and 19, last on the list.

Ms. Long smiled at Justy and looked back at Jake. "I can understand your position. But...your name on the list could swing a lot of people in this town."

Jake studied his boots again. "I'll think it over," he said finally. He gave a curt nod and walked away, Justy and Dale following. They moved through the crowd and then Dale stopped. She leaned down to Justy, "Smell that?"

Justy sniffed something sharp and sweet, like the tarweed that grew on the ranch. Some of the kids at school smelled similar in the fall, when it was harvest time.

"Somebody's doing pot," Dale said. "Probably those painter people."

Then Dale stood and walked fast to catch up with Jake. He joined Kyle in the last booth. Photos of the past century covered seven make-shift walls. From left to right, the pictures showed the passage of time in the logging world. An elderly man sat in a wheelchair; Justy recognized him from the mining museum in Eureka. Gil Walker sat next to him, and the two men didn't seem to notice the world around them as they talked about the old days, when loggers had been real men and the trees bigger than anyone could imagine. Justy wondered what the words next to the pictures looked like to Gil, whether the letters he couldn't read appeared like twisted little trees that he might want to cut down.

The pictures progressed through time, showing men and mules, rivers of logs, handsaws standing three times taller than the loggers holding them. Then came pictures of steam engines known as donkeys, then chain saws, tractors and men in hard hats. Justy wondered where the women were, if the wives living somewhere else thought about their husbands, who risked their lives on a daily basis. She wanted to know what the women dreamt about at night.

In the last panel, the redwood they'd seen fall last month lay on the ground, Mark and his sons in front of it. Even on its side, it still towered over them. Juan walked up and clapped his hands on Kyle's and Jake's backs.

"Nice work back there, Colbys." Juan winked at Dale.

"You did your part," Kyle said. Juan waved his hand and the men started walking, slightly in front of Dale and Justy. They talked bar talk: what was happening in the woods, the thinness of the work compared to years past, about C.C. Davis's death last week—a redwood had slabbed, and the part of the tree that had kicked back had pinned him to another tree, killing him. The funeral would be held the next Saturday at the cemetery in Madrone. Juan stopped and put his brown hands in his jeans. "You know, Helen's turning fifty next Sunday. We're having a big barbecue, and she'd love it if you all came and played in her honor."

Jake pointed a thumb at Dale. "She can't make it, Johnny. But me and Kyle, I bet we'd be able to make some time to sing her a song or two."

Dale looked away and Juan nodded. "That'd be great," he said. They fell quiet and then the tattooed man walked past, smelling like tarweed. Juan leaned in closer. "There's more and more of those kind these days."

They all watched the man continue through the crowd, the peace tattoo on his back shining in the sun. Justy liked how the symbol made the cliffs of his shoulder blades stand out sharper against his sun-browned skin.

"Probably down from River Fork," Dale said.

"You're right," Juan said. "Lots of them there. Harris sells property to them."

"They're buying up too much land," Jake said, and Justy felt a far idea play in the corner of his mind.

"It isn't legal money," Dale said.

"I know what you're saying, Dale. Helen, she feels the same way. It's hard, though, when they bring in all that cash, ready to pay. You don't really want to take their money, but sometimes it helps us make it through the month."

"Helen is a good woman," Dale said, and Justy wondered if Jake or Juan knew about the night calls she made to Dale.

"It gets to be so confusing," Juan said. "You get all these city types going back to the land, or whatever they call it." He pulled at the corner of his black mustache.

"It don't feel right," Kyle said, "seeing the land go to people who ain't even lived here a winter, lived through the rain."

They walked away from the logging pictures and back toward the contest area. Country music came from the speakers near the stage, and a woman in a thin blue dress danced, her hands caressing the air. Her bare feet stirred up a small cloud of dust while six men sitting at a picnic table wearing cowboy hats watched her.

Where the ax contest had been, a tiny man with a gigantic beard was checking the oil in his chain saw. He started the engine and laid the blade into a redwood log, making small cuts into the upended chunk of wood. A hand-carved sign leaned against another log: "Chainsaws for Jesus." Jeff and Mamie walked toward the Colbys, and Mamie and Dale said hello.

Harris leaned toward Jake, beer in hand, and said over the sound of the saw, "Get a load of this guy." He shook his head, a smirk riding the top of his beard. He smelled heavily of the tarweed odor. Dale took a step back, and Kyle cocked his head at Harris. Jake kept his face blank.

"He comes from Oregon. Says he was out falling one day when he gets this vision, light through the trees and everything." While Harris talked, Mamie played with her stringy brown hair and seemed to be watching something in the distance.

"Says Jesus came to him in the woods and told him to become a chain-saw artist. The guy falls to his knees and asks Jesus what he should carve, and Jesus? He tells him to make fish and bears and Indian heads.

I figure he'll be carving your mug sometime soon." Harris indicated Jake with his finger and laughed.

"What a crock," Jake said. Dale and Mamie met each other's eyes for an instant. The man continued, the chain whirring. A small group of people gathered to watch him. Within a few minutes, a tree began to emerge from the wood, a redwood, complete in miniature.

The Colbys and Juan started to walk away, and the Harrises followed them. Harris kept laughing and said, "You know, Jesus was a carpenter."

Lacee and Micah joined the group, Caleb and Sky Harris behind them, all of their skin pink with the day's sun. The tattooed man walked past and said hello to Harris. Then the Harrises headed together toward the beer booth.

"What you been up to?" Jake asked Micah and Lacee.

"I went swimming," Lacee said, and Justy ached for the river.

"I've been hanging out with Caleb and Sky," Micah said.

"Harris's kids?" Jake asked. "That guy," he went on, talking to Juan and watching Harris. "He's got that JW wife, and everyone in this county knows he's a grower."

"I know, I know," Juan said, shrugging.

"Sky and Caleb are nice," Micah said.

Dale patted him on the shoulder. "We better head home," she said, not looking at Jake. Juan took stock of the silence and said his good-byes. Dale started walking to the Willys.

"We'll be home after a while," Jake called. Dale didn't look back.

***

"Justy. Wake up." Dale shook her from rivered sleep and she sat up, blinking. The deer had been standing at the mouth of the Eel again, watching Justy and wanting her to do something she didn't understand. Ochre's stone had rolled from her hand and she slid her fingers along the sheets, searching for it.

"Come on," Dale whispered. Justy followed her into the living room. She squinted against the kitchen light and saw that it was eleven-thirty. Dale wore a long-sleeve shirt and held out pants and a lightweight sweater for Justy, who slipped into the clothes. Justy could hear the truck running. Outside, the moonless night wore its darkness like a dream, and they entered it.

Dale turned on the headlights. Justy watched the road roll in front of them as if it were a map to all the confusion. The truck hit the asphalt and Dale took the old road. Justy sensed the Eel on their left, far below them. Somewhere down there at the place called the Hermitage, Ochre was sleeping in his tipi, probably dreaming of how colors came alive with water. The old road took them through the curved night until they reached the first houses of South Sequoia.

Dale slowed and Justy began searching for Kyle's truck in any of the driveways. She wanted to see into those houses, see what love meant in those squares. Many of the buildings were boarded up, the logging families having moved on in search of other work.

Justy scanned the night, her eyes rays of hope for Jake and Kyle. She wished for Ochre's stone and felt undone because she hadn't found it. Dale drove through the south part of town, on past the full parking lot at Hilltop. The Willys rolled on, down through the redwoods, through the tall darknesses lining the road, past the Drive-Thru Tree entrance, on through town and the fairgrounds. Dale drove into the now-dormant festival and turned off the headlights and the engine. The night loomed closer while their eyes adjusted. The engine clicked and cooled. In front of them, cables led from the top of a fifty-foot pole to the ground, holding it in place.

In the morning, the tree-climbing contest would take place and men would scramble up the pole, looping their way upward, chain saws dangling down their backs. Justy was sure Kyle would be the fastest, even at his age, hugging the tree to his body, digging his caulk boots into the wood. High climbing was a dying art, he'd told Justy, and she thought he'd be able to shine tomorrow, even if the contest wasn't the real thing.

The tree before her stood lonely, and the cables holding it in place seemed the work of a magnificent wood spider, come to spin a giant web for the unknowing. Dale got out and walked to the pole. She placed her palms against the fuzzy cedar, leaned her forehead on the bark and breathed in the scent of the tree. Justy felt Dale draw in the things that drove the men, and maybe even try to bring back some of that original night with Jake so many years before. Dale took breath after lung-filling breath until Justy felt dizzy with her indecision. The river called to Dale, but she wanted to make sure Jake was all right.

The sharp, sweet cedar incense filled the cab as Dale drove north on Highway 101 for a mile and then took the dirt road to the Grange hall. The Willys rounded a corner and the headlights revealed a full parking area. Dale pulled in next to the truck farthest from the hall and cut the engine. They sat in the relative dark and listened to music coming from the building. Dale rolled down her window, and Jake's fiddle courted the night. The song burst out as someone left the hall, the sound carrying sharp and twangy through the open door.

"Please go look," Dale said. Justy walked toward the hall. After a few steps, she looked back and saw Dale hanging her head out the truck window, face open to the sky and Jehovah beyond. Justy walked to the back of the building, feeling strange, knowing that the bones Jake and Kyle had dug up and repositioned were a few feet farther back in the darkness. People sat on benches, smoking and talking. Justy smelled the distinct odor of tarweed and knew some people were doing pot. No one noticed her as she moved to the picture window and looked into the hall. Jake and Kyle played with a group of musicians, all of them clean-cut and pale-skinned. Juan and Helen danced gracefully to the two-step, smiling into each other. Sunshine and Nolan were tucked into the corner of the room, and Justy saw Ochre standing next to them, talking to a kid his age Justy didn't know. When the song ended, Jake laid his fiddle down and headed to the kitchen-bar area at the back of the room. She saw him talk to D.J. for a minute before Harris tapped Jake on the shoulder.

When Justy saw Jake and Harris walking toward the back door with beers, she headed down the steps into the redwoods that separated the Grange hall from the new cemetery. She slid into the tree shadows and waited. A few headstones caught rays of light. Jake and Harris stopped near the closest grave. Justy could barely see them, so she closed her eyes and listened.

"What is it that you want, Jeff?"

"Well, I've been thinking. You got all that land you watch over, and hardly anyone ever comes to look at it."

"Your point being?" Jake took a long drink.

"If you were to let somebody grow out there, you could take a cut without even lifting a finger."

Justy didn't like Harris's voice. It was too slow for her, as if he were talking from the dream world.

"It ain't my land, Harris. You know that."

"Ay, that's the beauty, Jake. If a bust ever happened, you just say you don't know who's been growing."

Jake remained silent and Justy could tell Harris was shifting his weight from one leg to another.

"I know you could use the money, man."

"I ain't interested." Jake's voice had a tinge of razor in it.

"It's cool, Jake. But why don't you think it over?"

Harris clunked past Justy back to the hall, and she pressed closer to the tree. Jake sat, leaning against one of the headstones. He drank, long, deep swallows, and then leaned his head into his hands.

Two songs wafted into the night, and Justy listened to Jake drink, feeling him tumble over what Harris had said. The grave of Rose Gaines sat underneath Jake, and he didn't want to do work next winter that involved people in her condition. The earth smelled newly disturbed and Justy leaned forward. Jake's face was open to the sky, just like Dale's in the truck. The beer bottle sparkled in a ray of light from the hall.

The music humped around them, and Justy thought she heard Jake talking. She took quiet steps closer but only enough to hear his voice, not the words themselves. She sensed it was a sort of a prayer, the alcohol allowing Jake's tongue to loosen. The part of her that was him ached, wanting him to be so much more than what he was, wanting a piece of the world that was his own. Jake wanted to stick his hands into the earth and know the dirt that collected under his fingernails meant home and not just hard work.

"Jake," a woman's voice called from the porch. Jake stopped his murmuring and remained motionless.

"Jake. You promised me a dance." Her words blurred through the night. "Jake."

Justy heard her walk back into the hall. Jake looked at the bottle in his hand and then flung it into the further darkness. The glass broke against a tree, clattering to the ground. The arc of its flight reminded Justy of the pennies and the day she'd stopped talking. Jake stood, and Justy again pressed herself to a redwood, feeling the shaggy bark on her palms as he walked past her, up the steps and inside.

She looked around to the dark trees reaching higher, the pale headstones sinking eventually under. Her mouth opened and she felt a surge to let it all fall away from her, every single word and phrase she carried for them. But they refused to leave her, and she thought about a Christmas tree with ornaments that couldn't be removed. Someday, she promised herself the words would swim from her, spiraling away, bone outward.

Two Saturdays later Joella called and asked if Dale wanted to go out in service that afternoon. Dale said yes and felt the nerve birds fly in her stomach. It was easier to try talking to someone outside of Sequoia about God's Truth. Speaking to people she knew only somewhat made her even more shy. Micah sat on the couch beside Lacee, who was reading *Catch-22*. Occasionally he glanced down at the *Watchtower* in front of him. Dale went into the kitchen and began cutting flour into a cube of butter. She was making crust for a pie and Justy's stomach gurgled at the thought. Jake was down at the barn, playing music for the photographs. Justy didn't know where Kyle was, but she hadn't heard either his motorcycle or his truck. He might be out taking a walk, "soaking in more nature," as he called it. Justy wanted to go with him; she wanted to know as much as she could.

Lacee turned a page and Justy wondered why Dale didn't pay attention to what the girls read. She imagined that books like *Catch-22* were telling Lacee something different from what the Witnesses thought. But she knew that the books, like the river, could take Lacee away from the unpredictability of Jake's hands, the uncertainty of Dale's days. She thought again of Gil Walker and how he couldn't read. Justy wanted to swim inside his head for a day and feel what that was like, to live in a world where words slid away.

***

After lunch Dale herded the children into the bedroom and helped them pick out clothes to wear. Lacee made such a face that Dale said they might go swimming after service, if she could talk Joella into it. Justy put on her green bathing suit under a skirt. Then they tamed their hair and were ready when Joella and Lucas's silver Ford crawled up the dirt road.

Dale sat up front beside Joella and fiddled with her Bible, thinking about the Scriptures she was supposed to quote. Justy's red corduroy skirt scratched her legs, and she wished for pants or to be already in the river. She looked out the window and turned Ochre's stone, feeling how it was smoother—her constant attention polishing it like water. One more week of school and summer vacation would arrive. Justy wondered again if she would get to see Ochre. She rolled down the window and stuck her head out, letting the warm wind caress her face.

"Justy," Joella said. Justy pulled in her head. Dale turned to look at her and said, "You'll get all mussed up, doing that."

"We need to remember that we are Jehovah's representatives," Joella said. "At all times we must remember this." As she spoke, Joella's thin wrists hung over the steering wheel. Justy studied her eyes in the mirror. Micah elbowed Justy and nodded. Lacee raised her eyebrows. A drawn-out quiet filled the car, and then they turned off the old road and headed downhill to the Hermitage. Their descent brought them almost level with the Eel, and Justy could see the deep green of the river fifty feet away. She looked for the Ravens' parked car but didn't see it. Joella stopped the sedan and got out, then stuck her head back in through the open window and smiled. "Who wants to go first?"

"Me," Micah said. He, Dale and Joella walked to the first house, a black book bag hooked over Joella's arm. Dale looked stiff in her yellow cotton dress, not ready to convert people. Justy stared at the river, wanting to look for pebbles and listen to the water's song.

"Hey, look," Lacee said. She pointed to the top of the tipi tucked behind a stand of bay trees. Justy and Lacee stood in the afternoon sun, simply studying the poles interlinked at the top. Lacee leaned against the trunk of the car and lifted her face to the sun. Justy looked toward Joella, Dale and Micah, who were talking to a woman standing behind a screen door. She waited one more minute and then was walking, sandals slapping against the dirt road. She looked back once. Dale and Joella weren't watching, but Lacee gave her a thumbs-up.

Justy entered the shade of the bay trees, smelling their sharp tang, and followed a path. Her steps quieted on the thick carpet of damp leaves. She stopped when the tipi was in full sight. It sat in a small, grassy clearing. She expected to see symbols or patterns painted on the side, like the ones she'd seen in books, but the canvas walls were a dull white, clear of any design. Flowers bloomed around the base. The boxy Volvo with the beads and leaves sat next to the tipi, and beyond the car was another, smaller tipi. A chicken coop stood farther back in the trees, and nine brown hens and one white rooster scratched in the dirt of the pen. A small goat was staked to a pole, eating the grass in the clearing, the radius around the pole shorn clean. A worn path between the two tipis revealed dry earth, and a less-worn path led back into the trees on the far side of the clearing. Justy could see the green plastic on the roof of what she thought was a greenhouse.

She didn't hear anything except the river and the occasional clicks of grasshoppers. The goat lifted its head and looked at her, chewing. It stared at her with big brown eyes and then let out a soft baa. The tipi flapped open and Sunshine's clear voice lilted through the air. "What is it, Yarrow?"

The goat looked at the tipi, then at Justy. Its little beard made her think it was a hippie, and she smiled. Sunshine stepped out, her head free of any scarf. She wore jean cutoffs and a deep-green halter top. Her stomach and legs were deeply tanned. She stretched, and when she was at the height of her stretch, arms arched over her head, she saw Justy. Sunshine smiled and dropped her arms.

"Ochre's with Nolan." She indicated the river. Justy nodded.

Sunshine squatted and hooked a tanned arm over the goat. "Come over here, Justy. I won't bite."

Justy took three small steps closer and then looked back, thinking about Dale and Joella, why they had come down here. She squeezed the stone and walked closer. She stopped two feet from Sunshine and reached out and touched the goat's head. Its fur felt scratchy and soft at the same time.

"Goats are great animals," Sunshine said. "They give you milk and everything. Yarrow's been a good buddy, even if some people say goats look like the Devil."

She tugged on the goat's beard, and Justy took a step back. Yarrow reached down to the short grass.

"How about some tea?" Sunshine asked, and stood. Justy looked back again, but she couldn't see anyone. Sunshine waited, watching Justy, who finally nodded, heart racing.

"Can you take your shoes off?" Sunshine pointed at Justy's sandals. Justy's feet felt free as she stepped into a cool darkness. She was standing on a carpeted wood floor, and she was hit with the deep smell of plants. The tipi was much larger inside than she had expected; a loft held a bed eight feet above her head. Sunshine followed Justy's gaze and said, "That's where Nolan and I sleep."

The inside of the tipi was extremely tidy. A wood cook stove stood in the center, and lit candles hung in holders from the outside edges of the loft. Bunches of drying plants also hung upside down from the wooden planks. On the backside of the tipi sat a full bookshelf made from a rough redwood burl. On the floor next to the shelf a bundle of blankets and pillows waited. Justy assumed this was where Ochre slept. Pillows of various sizes and colors dotted the floor. Sunshine sat on one near the entrance and poured a clear brown liquid from a mason jar into a ceramic mug. She held it out to Justy, who sat on a smaller pillow, folding her knees under her because the skirt wouldn't allow her to cross her legs. The tea was strong and cool and Justy tasted it carefully.

"Do you like it?"

Justy nodded and took another sip. It tasted like a shady section of creek. Sunshine poured herself a cup and set it on the ground. She coiled her long hair and tucked it into itself forming a bun. Her thin hand picked up the mug and she took a sip.

"I made this myself with herbs I've grown in the greenhouse. There's licorice root, stinging nettle and raspberry." Sunshine watched Justy over the lip of her mug. Justy liked how Sunshine wasn't surprised by her appearance and that she sat with Justy like she would with an adult. Justy looked from her steady gaze to a colorful circular design hanging from the center pole. Sunshine followed her look, stood and unhooked the design from a nail.

"It's a mandala," she said. Justy frowned at her, and Sunshine repeated the word. She handed the disk to Justy, who studied the colors and the way the designs fit into one another.

"Mandalas are centers, or magic circles," Sunshine said. Justy handed it back, afraid of what she meant by magic. According to the Witnesses, all magic was the work of Satan—his ways to deter people from the path of Truth. Sunshine turned the mandala over. Justy took another sip of tea, wondering if maybe the herbs had been grown with magic.

"Circles have always been sacred," Sunshine said, looking at the mandala. "Mother Nature is the first place you'll see them. Rocks, eggs, our wombs." Sunshine put a hand on her lower belly and went on, "The tipi is a circle, too." She then swiveled her wrist, smiled and continued, "Ancient cultures, African and American Indian cultures. Mandalas can be found almost anywhere in the world. They can include colors, numbers, animals."

Sunshine stood and hung the mandala. She closed her eyes, took what Ms. Long would call a cleansing breath and sat back down.

"If you think about it," she said, "even the seasons move in a circle."

Justy closed her eyes, letting the sound of the river be the only thing in the whole world. She shoved Jake and Dale down deep and listened to the water working its way to the Pacific. All the time she'd remained wordless, she'd become full with the noise of other people and never really let herself be quiet. It surprised Justy that it was here, of all places, with a person who probably meditated and opened herself up to Satan and didn't even know it, that Justy felt calm. She felt Sunshine tuck a strand of Justy's hair behind her ear. Justy opened her eyes to see Sunshine resting her head on her drawn-up knees.

"Ochre is so glad you're his friend. He talks about you all the time, telling us how you pay attention to every little thing." Sunshine sighed. "Nolan picked out his name, wanting our child to be colorful." She laughed and said, "He sure is." She straightened her legs, stretched her arms upward and then grabbed her bare feet with her hands.

They heard voices outside and Sunshine stood. Justy handed her the tea mug.

"Hello?" Joella called from the edge of the trees.

Sunshine gently squeezed Justy's shoulder. "Hello," she said. Justy followed her out of the tipi and stood by her while Joella and Dale walked closer. Justy knew she was standing on the wrong side of the equation from the look on Dale's face. For a split second, she pretended she was Sunshine's child and lived in the tipi at the river's edge with Nolan and Ochre. They grew plants they made into teas, painted with bright colors, ate fresh trout and watched the night sky through the open tipi entrance. They fell asleep lulled by the water's song.

All these thoughts flowed through Justy's mind, and then she took a step away from Sunshine. Joella started talking, explaining why she, Dale and Justy were going door-to-door, spreading Jehovah's message and his plan for an earthly paradise. Joella made sure she didn't enter the goat's circle. She held out an *Awake!* magazine depicting people of different skin colors gathered under a flowering tree. In the foreground, a white boy sat next to a lion and a lamb. Dale crooked a finger at Justy, who grabbed her sandals and walked barefoot over to Dale's side while Joella invited Sunshine to the public talk at the Kingdom Hall in Madrone, any Sunday Sunshine felt curious to learn more about God's true plan. While she talked, Justy could see Dale's eyes run up and down the length of Sunshine's body, taking in all the skin Sunshine showed outside her halter-top and cutoffs.

Sunshine accepted the magazine and said she appreciated the invitation but she pretty much believed she'd found her earthly paradise. Joella smiled sweetly and a slow moment passed, with Yarrow inching his way closer to the hem of her skirt.

"Well," Joella said finally. "We don't want to take up too much of your time." She came back to stand next to Dale and Justy. Sunshine picked a red tulip from the mass of flowers that encircled most of the tipi. She walked over and handed it to Justy, who took it with a small nod. Sunshine whispered to her, "Red is for strength and learning."

"We'll be going now," Joella said loudly, waving her hand at Sunshine and moving toward the trees. Dale and Justy followed. Justy didn't look back, but she could feel Sunshine watching them.

***

Joella drove the car up out of the canyon, going faster than she'd driven down. "I'm not sure, but I think they might be dope growers," she said.

"How else do they survive?" Dale asked.

"You know, Dale, some of the brothers in the congregation have been saying it isn't safe for us women to go out in service by ourselves."

Dale nodded.

"I think it's safe until the fall. That's when people are harvesting," Lacee said.

"How would you know that, Lacee?" Joella searched out Lacee's eyes in the mirror, and Dale twisted to look at her.

"At school, you learn stuff," Lacee said, and shrugged. Micah nodded at Dale.

Justy nibbled on the tulip while Joella guided the car onto the old highway. She and Dale continued to talk about Sunshine, wondering who else but dope growers would choose to live in a tipi. Joella spoke in soft tones about people she thought might be growers and the tons of black plastic pipe that the hippies bought at the hardware store she worked at two days a week.

"Lucas says it's for irrigation purposes," Joella said as she turned into the paved driveway that led to Gaines's house. The area surrounding the house was full of flowers, green grass, antique carriages and wheelbarrows. Fifty feet beyond the house, beside a matching red barn with white trim, a black horse in a wooden corral watched the car.

Joella stopped the sedan in the half-circle drive. In the middle of the green lawn, a painted statue of a black man stood, his lips and eyes white. He wore white pants, high black boots and a red-and-white-checkered jacket and hat. Justy looked away from the statue and saw Dale shake her head.

"I don't want to go to his house," Dale said.

Joella took a breath and turned to Justy. "It's your turn, little one, to go to a door with me." Joella grabbed her book bag. Justy left the tulip on the seat, put on her sandals and then followed Joella to the house. Four flower boxes filled with pansies and daffodils lined the edge of the slate porch. Justy smelled horse and looked around her while Joella rang the doorbell. Chimes deep within the big house boomed, and Justy tried to remember if any of the other houses in Sequoia had doorbells. The little white dog began barking somewhere inside, and Justy looked for the ditch Jake had dug for the sauna and hot tub. Joella looked at her watch and rang the doorbell again.

"His truck is here," she said, and Justy saw the tail end of Gaines's truck poking out from behind a neat stack of wood on the far side of the circle. Barks came closer and then Gaines opened the front door, a cigarette hanging from his mouth and a beer bottle in his hand. He wore a white bathrobe over dirty denim overalls.

"What do you want?" he said around the cigarette. His brown hair stuck out in the back and Justy imagined him when the bell rang, slouched on his couch, watching television alone in his big house.

"Well, hello, I'm not sure if you know who I am, but—"

"I recognize you from the hardware store. Get to it, woman." Gaines did not look at Justy, for which she felt a certain amount of relief. Joella swallowed and smoothed the front of her skirt. Justy studied the white fuzzy slippers Gaines wore over his dirty socks.

"Mr. Gaines, we're here to tell you about Jehovah's Word." Joella held out the magazine with the different-colored people in the restored Eden. Gaines ran a hand through his thick hair and scowled at the cover.

"I ain't interested," he said, and started to close the door. The dog got in the way and Joella took a small step forward. Gaines spilled part of his beer trying to back away from her.

"Mr. Gaines, I think with all that's happened to you, you might be interested in what will transpire when this world ends." Her soft voice seemed to grow in strength as she spoke. The dog licked up the beer that had spilled.

Gaines jerked the door back open. "What's happened to me?" Ash from his cigarette fell on the floor.

Joella smiled and said, "You probably didn't realize you could see your son or your wife again, did you?" She didn't look at him but studied the dog's wagging tail. Justy looked at the car, where Dale, Lacee and Micah were watching. The horse snorted and Justy watched its muscles ripple to shed a fly. Each of the four horses and their riders meant something different, and Justy tried to remember what would ride on the black one. Everyone in town knew that horse named Nigger was the only thing in the world Gaines loved besides turning a profit.

Gaines looked from Joella. The silence between them bloomed and he shifted his weight, unable to close the door because of her foot. He took a drink, and Justy wondered if he was afraid of Joella. She looked back at the horse and tried to remember when Jake used to have horses. The dog moved outside and Gaines saw Justy's gaze.

"You like horses, huh?" Excitement filled his voice and he shoved past them, knocking into Joella without seeming to notice. Gaines moved in his run-walk toward the horse, stopped and said, "Come and see." He beckoned to Justy.

Justy took a step toward him and Joella cleared her throat. "Well," she said, "he might listen to us if we listen to him." Joella folded the *Awake!* under her arm and followed Gaines. They all stopped at the corral. Gaines pushed back a bathrobe sleeve and held out a hand. The mare's black hair shone in the sun, and there were white ribbons braided into her mane. The horse reached out and sniffed Gaines's fingers. He threw the cigarette butt on the ground and stamped it out with his slipper. The dog eased under a corral pole and began sniffing the ground.

"Ain't she a beauty?" Gaines spoke to Justy and rubbed the horse's nose; she pushed against his hand. Justy loved how soft the mare's nostrils looked, and she wanted to reach out and feel the animal's breath. Joella cocked her head while raising her eyebrows. She pulled the *Awake!* from under her arm and waved it in front of Gaines. He scowled again and coughed from deep in his lungs.

"Woman, I don't want no part of an afterlife where there'll be coloreds." He pulled the bathrobe tighter and reached his face toward the horse. Joella took a step back and whispered to Justy, "Come on."

The horse stamped her foot, flicked her tail and nuzzled Gaines under the chin. He smiled and Justy watched how his wrinkles changed their direction. She wasn't sure she'd seen him smile before. Joella turned the magazine to see the cover better, and she opened her mouth and then closed it. Gaines set the beer bottle on the ground and turned his back to Justy and Joella.

"We're all Jehovah's children," Joella said. She placed a light hand on Justy's shoulder and pulled her away from Gaines and the horse. He didn't seem to hear Joella as he continued to nuzzle with the horse. Justy followed Joella and checked her senses for Jake. He'd left the pictures in the barn and gone to the backcountry of the ranch with his chain saw. She felt him step away from a Douglas fir, felt the chain saw hum in his barely Indian hands as he watched the tree fall to the ground, a deep ripping sound filling Jake's afternoon, audible even over the sound of the saw. Joella started the car and again opened her mouth, but her words seemed to fail her and she remained quiet. Justy felt sorry for Joella, who was just beginning to understand that sometimes there are things in life that just leave a person without words. This, she wanted to tell Joella, was where Justy lived.

The second-to-last day of school arrived, and in the afternoon, Ochre and Justy sat on the swings. Jeff Sloan was seven today and his mom was inside, leading the kids in a dancing contest. Ochre and Justy flew away from the school grounds, and she imagined that he led her to the river, where they watched water skippers flit across the water's calm surface. Then Justy imagined taking him to the barn and showing him the pictures and telling him the stories she made up about them.

A vehicle approached and Justy closed her eyes against the noise. She leaned backward and let her hair hang down. The footsteps she sensed were Jake's, and she opened her eyes to see his upside-down figure approaching. She sat up and stopped swinging, then twisted to face him. Ochre also came to a stop.

"Get your things," Jake said. He looked around the playground and walked closer. He grabbed the chains, and Justy watched his hands to make sure they didn't express any of the jitters dancing inside him. She jerked with his movements. He looked at Ochre and said, "That's quite the braid you got there."

Ochre flashed Jake a peace sign. Jake shook his head. "Your mama that one that thinks she's an Indian?"

Ochre shrugged and pushed off again, swinging away from Jake. "Tell her I said being an Indian only means trouble," Jake said.

Ochre watched Jake's face while he continued swinging. Jake smiled at Justy and said, "Let's go, girl." He released the swing and she swung away from him and then back. He caught the chains again and said, "Let's hit it."

Justy jumped off and watched the swing right itself before walking to the wooden bench to get her books. Jake moved to the edge of the playground and called back to Ochre, "See you, little Indian." Ochre waved and flashed his broad smile at Justy. She waved back and followed Jake.

As they drove away from the school, Jake said, "This could be a real shitty day, but some things have changed. I've made a decision." He coasted to a stop on the street along the Sequoia Market, checked both ways for traffic, then headed past the post office and the other town buildings. In the empty space between the Redwood Diner and the Cedar Diner, Justy could make out Ochre's small form, still flying high on the swings.

"Your mother sent me after you since there was a birthday party," Jake said.

Justy knew Dale kept track of each day she shouldn't be in the classroom, but this was the first time she had gone to the trouble to make sure Justy was somewhere else. Justy wondered if Dale knew she spent her holiday time with Ochre.

"I was coming into town to pick up some stuff," Jake said. He pointed with his thumb to the bed of the truck. Justy nodded, knowing that Dale always wanted one of the kids with him whenever Jake came into town. Still, he pulled onto the dirt shoulder at Hilltop that overlooked the yawning river canyon. Justy inhaled sharply as she looked out the Willys's window, thinking about Dale and the flood.

"You can come in," Jake said, and she climbed out after him. Lefty's battered green Ford and two other trucks were parked in front. She followed Jake into the dark room and Helen called hello. The three men at the bar said or nodded their greetings. Lefty got off his stool and bowed to Justy, taking off an imaginary hat. He winked at her and she smiled at him, then climbed onto a stool next to where Jake stood.

"What it'll be, Colby?" Helen asked. She smiled around her cigarette at Justy, while Jake remained standing.

"Just one quick shot, please, *Señora*."

Justy felt confused by Jake's good mood. Underneath the smiles, something was itching to get to the surface. Helen poured him a whiskey and he drank it down and then laid money on the counter.

"How's that coast job?" Lefty asked from the far end of the bar.

"Didn't you hear?" Jake said and smirked. "Gaines has some legal problems, something about a timber harvest plan he didn't file. Damn environmentalists."

Justy didn't understand how Jake could act so happy after only one month of falling work. She closed her eyes and realized it had something to do with the stuff in the back of the truck. When she opened her eyes, the Hamm's beer sign caught her gaze. Again she watched the water fall and fall, and she hoped that for all her dreaming, the Eel would actually take her someplace bigger and not leave her here.

***

They drove in silence and Justy waited for glimpses of the Eel. Jake tumbled figures in his head, long lists of numbers that added up to very little. The truck hit the dirt road and they rolled up to the tired barn.

"Your mother's out knocking on doors with Joella again," Jake said as he climbed out. Dale spent more and more time with the Witnesses, maybe tipping the balance toward Jehovah and away from Jake. But, Jake was wrong today, because Dale was with Mamie Harris, the can of pennies in her lap. Justy followed him into the barn, and the smell of the musty hay and decaying leather hit her like it did every time. She stopped just inside the door, letting her eyes adjust. Jake walked farther into the dark and picked up something. As he walked past Justy, she saw that it was a bag of potting soil.

She moved over to the pictures. Cobwebs and dust still layered over them, leaving no trace of any of her visits. She leaned forward and reexamined the infant pictures of Jake. He wore a fancy baby suit and his black hair was perfectly combed, parted on one side. The woman named Lila held him, her once-straight hair permed and frizzing. Justy touched the picture of Lila and her sisters outside the shack. North Arkansas, Kyle had said.

"What are you looking at?" Jake stood in the doorway, his face in shadow. Justy stepped back and studied the tips of her scuffed tennis shoes. He walked close and peered at the pictures. "That one's your granma." Jake pointed to the picture Justy had been studying. He squinted and said, "They look like a bunch of squaws, don't they?"

Justy looked back and forth between the shack picture and the one of Lila and Jake. There were differences, but Lila had the same eyes, the same careful smile, in both pictures.

"She's only half Indian, but she sure looks full there." Jake sat on an old chest opposite the photos. He rested his elbows on his knees and put his chin in his hands. "She was a good woman." He looked out the barn door to the decrepit corrals. "A hard life, though, beginning to end," he said.

Justy stood in the shadows and held her breath, perched at the exact point where Kyle had started telling stories.

"She saw her dad shot when she was five." Jake closed his eyes. "My granddad was a moonshiner, shot by federal revenuers. The sons of bitches."

Justy stood absolutely still and time creaked by. Jake remained lost somewhere in his memories.

"She had a nervous breakdown after that. After seeing him killed," Jake finally said. He blinked and stood. "Some people can't take the hard stuff." He placed a light hand on Justy's head, reaching across some great distance to bring himself to the present. He walked to the pictures and knelt before them. With his hand, he flattened out himself, Lila and Kyle, dust clinging to his fingers. He stared into the pictures for a long minute. Justy wished she could have said something to comfort him, but she wondered, even if she could talk, what words could possibly make Jake feel better about Lila and her dead father.

Jake dropped his hand and said, "Let's get going." Then he walked to the back of the barn. Justy stared at Lila and her sisters outside the shack and felt as if part of her had been blown open by what Jake had just told her. It had cut short her idea of Lila having a proud mother and father watching the picture being taken. She studied Lila's face and saw that the look on her grandmother's face maybe wasn't determination but sadness.

Jake walked by with another bag of soil. Justy followed him to the bed of the truck and she saw two trays full of seedlings. Each stood about six inches tall, with leaves like the ones on the T-shirt Harris wore on the day of the tree falling.

"You ride back here and make sure the plants stay upright," Jake said. Justy climbed into the bed and Jake raised the tailgate. She sat on the wheel well, her legs on the outside of the trays. Jake guided the truck up the hill, away from the barn, following faint tracks to a grassy clearing. He stopped at the far edge, where trees ringed most of the area. Old tires were evenly placed in a semicircle, right at the point where the trees' canopies stopped and the grass began. By each tire a small mound of dirt waited, and by one tire Justy saw a roll of chicken wire, a shovel and some black plastic bags.

Jake walked to the back of the truck and winked at Justy. She sensed that under his light mood, the memory cloud of his mother brewed. He helped Justy down and she closed her eyes, hearing the creek back in the trees gurgle. Too many of Jake's stories ended in violence.

"Come on, Justy. You can help me." He tapped the side of a tray of plants and tilted his head. She walked behind him to the first tire. A fresh hole lined with the black plastic waited. Jake set the plants down gently and picked up a shovel. He scooped dirt from the pile next to the tire and poured it in. The dirt cascaded against the plastic with a sound like water. He laid the shovel down, pulled his knife from his pocket and slit open a bag of potting soil. He walked to the truck and came back with a third bag. Justy watched him grab a handful of both the potting soil and the third soil and dump them into the hole—three colors of brown.

"As I understand it, this stuff it's the trick." He indicated the third bag. "It's worm castings, which is basically worm shit."

He created a hole in the dirt mixture, then took one of the plants from the tray. He squeezed the sides of the black plastic container and then grasped the seedling at its base. Turning the plant upside down, he pulled it out. It slid easily from the container, its pale roots dangling. Jake held it in place with one hand and filled in the hole with his other. Justy watched his barely brown hand press down the dark soil, making sure the plant could stand on its own. He stood, wiped his hands and smiled. "One down." He wiped his forehead, his fingers traced with dirt. "You see, Justy, the thing about these plants is that they're all female."

Justy looked at the seedlings and tried to see how he could tell their gender.

"You only want the females," he said, "'cause when the males are around, the plants get to doing their business. If we keep these girls by themselves, they get all pissed off and become more potent." Jake walked away and Justy thought about Dale running away in the middle of the night, because Jake had been drinking too much and for too long.

Jake turned and said, "And that's when we make some money." He shrugged and said, "Leastwise, that's what I been told." He grinned and walked the rest of the way to the next tire, then held out the tray. "What I want you to do is plant these babies. I'll keep getting the holes ready and you can set the plants in. You were watching what I was doing?"

Justy nodded.

"I knew you would be." He set down the tray and went back to the two bags of different soils. He prepared the hole and stood back. Justy walked to him and picked up one of the containers and squeezed the sides, crinkling the plastic. She turned it upside down as he'd done, holding the plant's base and gently pulling. She did it all the same way he'd done it, though slower, more carefully.

"These are our future, girl," he said and picked up the soils and shovel and moved to the next tire. Justy sat on her heels and looked at the plant. Its delicate leaves drooped a little. She wondered precisely what moonshining was and how this was different. Town talk about CAMP and guns ran through her thoughts, flooding over the face of Lila, standing outside a shack, her father dead since she was five.

***

They finished planting, then Jake went to the truck and pulled out a bucket. He took it to the creek and brought water to each plant, carefully pouring the liquid into the soft soil. The sun eased toward the ocean, and the shadows lengthened as he carried the water. Justy watched, her hands deep in the upturned soil in front of her. Across the creek, the soil was the distinctive red and different trees and plants grew in those other minerals.

Jake arched his back, stretching. Justy thought of the way certain people talked about pot growers, how it was said they were lazy and good-for-nothing. Jake came to stand next to Justy and they looked at the plants, working their roots into the soil, trying to adjust.

"Tomorrow I'll come put the chicken wire around them so the deer won't get them," Jake said. Justy wondered what would happen if the deer ate the plants. Would the animals act goofy like Dale said people were when they did pot? Maybe the plants were too little and had to grow more to become the valuable things Harris and his kind wanted. People in the cities, men back from Vietnam, people who were radicals, Dale said. Justy wondered whether Caleb and Sky had seen their father plant the dope everyone said he grew. Her gaze went back to the seedlings. They didn't look like money, but neither did the trees that Jake and Kyle fell or the mountain with its nickel.

"A one-man reservation," Jake said. If somehow, the mine was stopped, Jake wanted to be ready to stake a claim.

They climbed into the truck and started the slow descent down the steep road, then past the barn. Jake gripped the steering wheel and flashed himself a smile in the rearview mirror. He looked back to the road, navigating the ruts.

***

When they got to the house, Justy walked to Kyle's cabin. She wanted him to tell her a story that would take her away from the secret thing she and Jake had just done. Kyle sat on the plank, guitar in his arms, playing a song with his eyes closed. Justy listened to him sing about the West Texas town and the cowboy who fell in love with Felina, a young Mexican maiden. Kyle's fingers danced over the strings, spinning out the story-song. The cowboy ended up dying, and Justy sighed at another death.

Kyle finished, opened his eyes and smiled at her.

"Come here, string bean." He patted the plank and she walked to him. He placed the guitar in her arms and positioned her hands on the strings. She felt too small, but he showed her how to hold the guitar comfortably. He taught her two chords, and then took the guitar back and sang "Cool Water," a song about a man and his mule in the desert, dying of thirst and having to watch out for the Devil. Kyle's croon filled the air and Justy shivered. It seemed like Satan was everywhere she turned.

Kyle tuned the guitar differently and placed a glass tube on the ring finger of his left hand. Justy studied his face to see if he knew anything about Jake's new plan. Kyle bent the notes of the guitar like the music was waves of feeling. Justy loved it when he used the slide; it made her feel less alone because the melody reached inside and made her imagine she was in the Eel.

***

School ended the next day. A growing sadness filled Justy as the day progressed, and she stayed close to Ochre. The dry air of summer hovered close. She hoped Sunshine might take Ochre to Carver's Hole sometime in the next three months, but she knew it wasn't likely since the Ravens already lived on the Eel.

She and Ochre flew on the swings again during the last recess, and she tried to find a way to thank him. She wanted to tell him how she loved walking next to him when they went to the sixth-grade classroom, and that she always tried to match her stride to his. Justy wanted to know if his friendship would last over the summer. The motion of the swing comforted her as she tried to free even one word.

The sting of losing Ochre grew because she knew Dale would never let her visit him, not while he lived in the tipi with Sunshine and Nolan, not while his hair grew long and he wasn't a Witness. Dale thought they were pagans. But Justy liked that they lived close to the land and seemed to love one another cleanly. Besides, Jake and Justy had planted the illegal plants and she felt corrupted already.

But even if Justy did talk, Dale wouldn't understand. And Justy didn't think there were the right words to be able to explain this to Ochre.

The final bell rang, and Justy and Ochre stopped swinging. Sunshine appeared from around the building and walked toward them. She knelt and reached out a hand to Justy and Ochre. She held each of their wrists in her slender fingers. The deep red scarf around her head revealed the curve of her skull and highlighted the bones of her temples. She remained quiet and looked' back and forth between the two of them, intently, directly, and Justy felt that somehow it was enough.

***

Come Monday, Dale told Jake she'd be out in service with Mamie Harris. He and Kyle sat on the front porch, watching the day dawn. The woodpile was almost gone, so the two of them had a clear view of the pond. Three turtles crawled out of the water while Jake and Kyle talked over what to do. Kyle thought maybe they should head north and look for work at the Scotia mill. Jake wasn't sure. He thought they should wait for the call from Gaines, telling them the permits were good and the work could start again.

Dale had the kids dress in meeting clothes, and then Mamie was there, driving the dirty white Volkswagen van.

"Well, here comes that commie piece of junk," Jake said.

"I think I'd like to buy one," Kyle said, and Jake leaned his chair forward, letting the legs touch the porch. Dale stopped, too, and Kyle nodded once, slow.

"Yep," he said, "I'd buy me one of them vans and then take it out to the range and use it for target practice."

Jake exploded with laughter and Dale nodded good-bye. The men watched her and the children climb into the van. Mamie waved and then pulled away, humming underneath her breath. She wore cutoffs and a T-shirt, her long brown hair piled on top of her head. Justy noticed that, dressed like she was, Mamie didn't look too different from Sunshine.

"I'm so glad you decided to do this," Mamie said. Dale looked out the van window to the valley, still trying to decide. The inside of the van was strange to Justy, with the curtains on the windows and the fuzzy seat covers. She didn't know what Mamie was talking about, but she knew they weren't going out in service and that it had something to do with the disappeared pennies. Ochre's stone in her mouth tumbled and tumbled. The van puttered along, and Mamie guided it onto the freeway going south, toward her house. Micah seemed lost in the Bible in his lap, and although Lacee's book, *1984*, was open, she had an ear cocked toward the conversation between Dale and Mamie.

"I got such nice beans," Mamie said. "I tasted one, and I have to tell you, they are just delicious." She put a hand out toward Dale and then drew it back. Dale nodded and remained quiet. Justy closed her eyes to try and sense what was going on. She felt Jake rise from his chair on the porch and tell Kyle he'd be back in a little while. Justy felt Jake drawn to the plants growing in a circle, working their magic of root and sun, felt him climb into the Willys and drive to them.

"Did you get tomatoes?" Dale asked.

Mamie nodded vigorously. "Such good ones, too. You wouldn't think so, it being early in the season, but I think they came from southern California."

"Good," Dale said as Mamie pulled off the freeway and moved the van up a dirt road. Justy thought about Los Angeles and how it was Jake's birthplace. She barely remembered the trip they'd taken when Jake's mother had died. What she could recall was miles of cars and houses stacked almost on top of one another. She had wanted to ask where the children played. At home she had a whole valley to explore, and when the house grew too small for the five bodies living in it, and when the storms between Jake and Dale flared, she only had to go outside to find herself.

The van bounced over the ruts and the curtains swayed. Within a few minutes, the home of the Harris family sprawled across their view. Justy knew it was huge, but not tidy and planned like Gaines's place.

"This is a pretty big place," Lacee said, leaning forward.

"Isn't it wild?" Mamie said. "It used to be a stagecoach stop. That's why it juts out like that." She pointed to a stretch of building off to the left. Winding plants grew up the sides of the wooden house, and a pair of ducks dabbled in a tiny pond in the middle of the lawn. Off to the left, two pickups and a Volkswagen Beetle were parked, all of the vehicles rusted and missing at least one tire.

"All set?" Mamie turned to Dale and smiled. Dale nodded and they climbed out. Mamie led the way to the front door, but before she opened it, Dale cleared her throat. "Is Jeff here?"

"Oh no, he's out doing some real estate stuff. Don't worry, Dale."

After taking off their shoes at Mamie's request in a small outer room, they followed her through a large dining room and into an even larger kitchen. The house smelled of cumin and garlic. Large windows overlooked the front lawn, and Justy watched the ducks nibble at the air, collecting insects. A crystal dangled from a string above the sink, reminding Justy of the hippies at the Mountain Folk Festival. Two boxes of tomatoes and a crate of green beans sat on the floor. On the counter above the boxes sat the Folgers can, Justy stepped forward and saw that it was empty. Dale smiled at the boxes.

"Okay," Mamie said, "let's get cranking, shall we?" She moved her bare feet and long legs gracefully on the cool tiles of the floor, placing mason jars in the sink.

"Come here, Lacee," Mamie said. Lacee set her book on the counter and pushed her hands into the sudsy sink water. Micah wiggled his hands and Mamie told him without looking that Caleb and Sky were out back, playing by the creek. Micah went out the door, leaving his shoes inside.

"Try to keep your meeting clothes clean," Dale said, not seeming to notice that he was already gone. She stood watching Mamie, looking awkward in her thin yellow dress, feeling out of place in another woman's kitchen. Mamie stopped her motion and re-coiled her hair into a bun. Dale studied her hands.

"Oh," Mamie said, and moved to her and placed a long arm around her shoulders, guiding her to a counter. "Why don't you get after those beans?" With her free hand, Mamie pulled out two metal bowls and a knife and handed them to Dale.

"Thanks," Dale said, and set down the knife. She snapped off the ends. Mamie busied herself supervising Lacee, who seemed to be enjoying the warm water and suds. Justy didn't know what to do, so she went into the living room. She had never seen a room so large in a house and tried to imagine tired passengers finding seats in the long room while they waited. It was dark, with only one tiny window. Large tapestries hung from the walls, full of scenes of people eating and drinking.

Justy felt drawn to the next room because it had more windows and was lighter. Another door stood at the opposite end, and she realized this had been the main entrance when the building was part of the stagecoach line. She wondered how Caleb and Sky felt about living in a place hundreds of people had passed through. And she wanted to know if the twins ever felt torn by the different directions of their parents. Though the children looked more like their father, they seemed to be following in Mamie's spiritual footsteps. Maybe because Caleb and Sky had each other, they were able to keep their parents out, leaving room for Jehovah.

Justy moved to a window at the back end of the room and pulled the stone from her mouth. She knew Ochre saw the river when he woke. She stretched her tongue and watched the creek run down the hill. Its clear movement pulled at her, the same way Dale and Jake did. She looked for Micah and the twins and saw one red head bobbing fifty feet upstream. Across the creek a circle of tires sat, just like the ones Jake had put the plants inside. Chicken wire encircled each of Harris's tires, and his plants stood about three feet tall. He must have planted much earlier than Jake. Harris probably had a greenhouse where he'd sown the seeds and grown the plants until the ground and the weather cooperated.

Justy put the stone back in her mouth and went outside. Her naked feet took her on a worn path around the house and down to the creek. She sat and listened to the sound of the water, trying to decipher the stream's story. It told her of melting snow in the mountains, of rain falling from the sky, and it whispered about finally reaching the Pacific and joining all that wide water. Justy knew the way and let herself imagine again the bends and curves.

When she heard Micah call to Caleb, she stood. Two rocks jutted out of the creek and she stepped on them. She followed a less worn path up the hill to the circle of tires and stood in the middle of the growing plants, wondering whether they were changing the way people were living, how they regarded one another. The leaves curved away from the stalks, drawing her close. One leaf caressed her fingers, and the smell of tarweed filled her head. She let go, worried that the plant might make her act differently.

"Get away from there." Caleb's voice flew at Justy, and she turned toward the sound. She saw him standing with Sky and Micah on the other side of the creek, watching her.

"You move it, now."

Justy had never heard Caleb speak so forcefully, and she automatically moved away from the circle, back toward the water.

"Dad told us not to go over there, that those plants were poisonous." Caleb stood with his hands on his hips, and Justy could see how he was a smaller version of Harris, without the beard or the injured foot. Sky tossed her hair and placed her hands on her hips, too, as the three of them watched Justy. Micah smiled at her with a frown puzzling across his forehead.

"Why don't you talk?" Sky said. Justy rolled the stone in her mouth and ignored the meanness in Sky's voice. She noticed that the twins were dressed almost alike in short overalls, red shirts over their thin frames. She and Micah seemed out of place in their meeting clothes, stuff given to Dale from Mamie. Micah took a step back; Justy knew he didn't want to gang up on her, but he did want to know why she didn't talk. She used the rocks to cross the creek, her bare feet caressed by the cool water. Moving past the twins as if they weren't there, she stopped in front of Micah. He patted Justy on the arm and she wanted to cry. His gentle touch felt like he was saying good-bye, and this didn't make sense to her. She walked back around the house, keeping her ears open for the sound of approaching hooves. In the kitchen, the tile was cool under her feet. Lacee was still at the sink, but it was now full of tomatoes. Dale was filling mason jars with cooked green beans, and Mamie poured hot water over the ones Dale had filled. The air was humid, and sweat dotted the brows of both women.

"Oh, good," Lacee said when she saw Justy. "You can do this." Lacee pulled her hands from the water, a small paring knife in her hands. She showed Justy how to peel the skin from the boiled tomato, then watched Justy plunge her hands in, the knife in her fingers, Justy grabbed a slippery tomato and tried to pull the skin back with the blade.

"Make sure you don't pierce the tomato. We want the seeds to stay inside." Lacee nodded and turned to face Dale. "Mama?"

Justy felt Dale brace.

"When are you going to tell Dad about this?"

Mamie stopped pouring and shifted out of the room. Maybe that's how she does it, thought Justy, maybe Mamie just slips away from the things she doesn't want to know. Justy guessed there was plenty Mamie didn't want to know about where their money came from. Dale cleared her throat and went on filling the jars with the beans.

"It'll work out," she said. Justy felt a surge of confused strength rise within Dale.

"When?" Lacee said, and Justy turned to look at her, admiring again how she was able to step into the silence and challenge it.

"This winter," Dale said, "when we're out of food again. I'll just have these on hand and—"

"You're going behind his back. He won't like it," Lacee said and walked out of the room. Dale wiped her brow and Justy felt her push away thoughts about winter. If the end came, Dale wouldn't have to worry about feeding her family, wouldn't have to even tell Jake about what she'd done with the pennies.

Mamie moved back into the kitchen, her bare feet slapping on the tile. She began chatting about the upcoming *Watchtower* study, and Dale slipped with her from Lacee's questions. Telling herself the story she needs to hear, Justy thought as she pulled away another piece of tomato skin. She thought about the night she'd fallen into the silence between

Jake and Dale, when Jake had shot the doe and Justy had watched in the middle of the snowing night as the doe's hide tore away from its body with those awful ripping sounds.

A tomato started to slide in her grip, and she slipped the tip of the knife into its body. Yellow seeds spilled out and floated on the surface of the water. She gripped the tomato tighter and began skinning it again, wondering how many secrets she could carry before she, too, split wide open.

J usty dreamt the river again, the water sliding beneath her and around her, the ocean approaching. She slipped out of her girl skin as the huge water grew near and a lightness wavered on the outskirts of her dream. Right when she tasted salt, the deer appeared again, and she fell out of the water into the sky. Part of her wondered if this was how a raindrop felt, separate and connected at the same time. She hovered above the ocean, which had changed into a stew of sorts, full of books and words and chunks of deer flesh and marijuana plants and raw mountains and skinned tomatoes. The doe moved from its steadfast place at the mouth of the river and jumped, joining Justy in the sky.

***

The phone woke her. Morning light peeked through the curtains and she sat up, rubbing her eyes. Micah and Lacee still slept. Jake answered the phone after the third ring. She sensed that Dale was working in the garden, readying the soil for the first batch of seeds. Jake spoke gruffly before hanging up. He stood, rubbing his jaw, watching Dale through the living room windows. Justy felt him curl his hands, felt his fists rising against the phone, the day, the world. She slipped from bed and stood in the doorway as Kyle emerged from the bathroom, freshly shaved and showered. He winked at her and went to stand beside Jake. They both watched Dale work the soil until Kyle finally spoke.

"What is it, son?"

Jake's hands uncurled and he said, "Nothing."

"You sure?"

Jake nodded and then his attention shifted. Justy felt a wave of panic rise within Dale. She moved to the window to watch Dale raise the shovel and drive it at the ground, again and again.

"I think that woman has lost her mind," Jake said, watching Dale as if in a trance. Kyle ran out the door to Dale, who was still ramming the shovel into the soil. Justy and Jake watched Kyle place a hand on her arm and take the shovel from her. Dale's breath galloped through her chest and she stared at the ground. Kyle gave her a one-armed hug and Dale tried to calm herself. Kyle reached down and lifted a headless snake, its body writhing even in death. Blood dripped from the spot where the head had been.

"Rattlesnake," Jake said. Justy watched him struggle to come back into his body, to shove the phone call away. She felt him take a deep breath and go to Dale, his cowboy boots moving slowly. Kyle stepped away from Dale when Jake approached. The snake's five-foot body wriggled in his hand. The men started joking with Dale and she finally smiled, her cheeks flushed. Jake adjusted his glasses and reached for the end of the snake. Justy knew he was counting the buttons on the rattle. Like the rings in a tree, the buttons marked the years of the snake's life.

Justy shuddered at the memory of Dale's face, intent on severing the snake's head from the body. What was worse was the distant look Jake wore as he grappled with his secrets.

***

Jake headed toward town. The phone call from Carl Walters sat like a small fire within him, and he needed to quench it. He waited outside Hilltop until ten o'clock and then knocked and knocked until Helen finally came to the door. She didn't say a word but allowed Jake in. She set a bottle of whiskey on the bar and left him, returning to Juan. She checked on Jake every hour. He drank slowly, trying to find a way to put the call from Walters into his plan.

Someone, Jake didn't know who, had tipped Walters off about the plants. On the phone, Walters had merely suggested that everything on the ranch be in good shape because he and the company president planned a visit. But something in his tone told Jake what he was truly saying. Jake weighed the chances of Walters making a thorough search of the ranch and what would happen if he found the plants.

***

Jake drove the rutted road that night. The full moon sliced through the trees and he didn't turn on the lights. After stopping, his hands rested on the steering wheel, his thoughts jumbled. As he climbed out of the truck, he reached for the fiddle, which lay on the passenger seat. He studied the growing plants in the moonlight. He'd planned to play music to them as they grew, courting his future with song. But Walters and the rest of the mining people were maybe on their way to find them.

Jake played a slow waltz, a tune he created as he went, something to linger in the air and his memory. As he played, he watched the plants, growing in a circle around him. Near the end of the song, he saw movement at the far edge of the clearing. A deer gingerly stepped out of the tree shadows into the moonlight. The doe stopped next to a plant, and her soft eyes watched Jake with a careful stare. She took a step closer, her hide seeming to shine as she moved. Jake kept playing, thinking it was the music that drew the deer out of her skittish ways. While he kept the bow dancing on the strings, he studied the brown eyes and the delicate square of black that was her nose. He smiled and realized he'd never spent time with a deer like this. Before, he'd automatically gauged the distance a bullet would have to travel. The doe flicked the petals of her ears and her tail stood up straight. She looked one more time at Jake, then ran back into the trees, disappearing into the shadows, legs springing her away. Jake stopped playing and listened as she moved off in the darkness, and then the night was quiet but for the babble of the creek.

He dropped to his knees and stared at the spot where the doe had stood, wondering what message, if any, she had brought him. He laid the fiddle down and let his palms kiss the grass. The blades bent and the soil beneath was cool. His moon shadow spread before him. He lay down and rested his left cheek on the earth, pressed his belly into the ground. Sleep hovered close, but he didn't fall away to that other world. Instead, he lingered in the in-between place for half an hour, not entirely in the clearing but floating above his own body, watching it and wondering how to guide it. A breeze stirred the world around him. The night seemed suddenly full of noise, the grass bending in the draft, the branches groaning, the creek water slipping over stones.

He opened his eyes and felt the ground for the first time in minutes. He rose to his hands and knees and crawled to the nearest plant. The earth yielded easily, like it wanted to be rid of the plant. It lay soft and fragile in his hands, the soil clinging to the roots. He thought he could feel the possibilities beating through the tender stem. He measured its weight in his right hand and then tossed it into the deeper shadows of the trees. The next plant called him, and he moved, cradling it also before he flung it. When he'd completed the circle and all but one plant was gone, he sat and looked from the shadows to their source. The moon's fullness pulled at him, and he realized he found himself too often throwing things away. The plant he'd left waved in the slight breeze, and he decided to keep just that one.

A week later, Justy sat on the porch and waited for the bats to start flitting through the dusk. Jake was drinking at Hilltop while Kyle played his guitar to the smoky room. The VW van puttered up the road, and Mamie climbed out in a flowing shirt and those shoes that Jake called Jesus sandals. Micah and Justy helped Dale take the jars to Kyle's cabin, where they hid them under his bed, back behind his empty guitar case.

***

Evening crept over the mountains and into the valley. Dale called to Lacee, who came to the house slowly, dragging her feet, humming a pagan tune under her breath. She stopped under the apple tree, the fence between her and the yard. "Yeah?"

Dale stepped down from the porch. "Honey, would you trim my hair?" Dale pulled the rubber band from the braid, and her blond hair flowed from her head.

"Sure," Lacee said, trying not to smile. Justy knew she liked to be asked to do such things and wondered whether Dale was trying to win Lacee over.

"Great, I'll go wet it."

Lacee walked into the yard. Micah sat on the edge of the porch, his feet dangling. Dale returned with wet hair, a towel draped over her shoulders. She sat in one of the two chairs on the porch and held out a pair of scissors for Lacee. Justy wondered what it would be like to get her hair cut in the beauty shop that sat under the Kingdom Hall and next to Sullivan's. She'd seen older women walk into the shop and emerge an hour later with their thinning gray hair wound in tight curls that seemed to make them happy. Someday Dale's hair would lose its color and become something she'd have to tame and coax into cooperating. Or maybe not, not if the New System came before Dale's hair changed and her bones started bowing toward the ground, like Kyle's were starting to now. How much longer could he keep logging, Justy wanted to know, even if there were jobs.

"About five inches," Dale said, and all three children looked at her with surprise. Never before had Dale considered more than an inch, even when Jake had been the one to trim it. Lacee began edging the scissors under the blanket of Dale's hair. The sound of the scissors slicing seemed to fill the dusk, and Justy realized she'd been holding her breath. She closed her eyes and felt a kick from Jake.

Harris had approached him and Jake had been drinking hard, slamming the whiskey down. Justy felt his hands tighten into angry beasts, the anger blooming in him this time like a puddle and less like a flood.

***

Lacee took her time with Dale's hair, making sure each cut was exactly aligned with the previous one. Justy felt Jake and Kyle returning, and she breathed deep when she saw their headlights at the lip of the valley. Daylight still lingered in the air as Jake and Kyle walked unsteadily toward the house. Kyle grinned in a sloppy way, and Jake stared above their heads for a minute, a pint of Wild Turkey in his hand. Lacee pulled the scissors away and took a step back from Dale. Bats spun and flew over the pond's dark surface, dive-bombing for insects. Kyle patted Jake on the back. "What say, son? Should we fire up the guns and play a few?"

Kyle seemed blurred, just a little outside of himself. Jake turned slowly to look at him and nodded. Jake's careful movement revealed that he was the drunker of the two.

"Yeah," he said. "Let's play some music." He turned to look at Dale. He eyed her for a response while he drank. She watched both of them and pulled the towel from her shoulders, a cool gaze on her face, fear pooling in her stomach. Micah went to the truck and grabbed their instruments. While they waited, Dale moved to the edge of the porch, trying to break Jake's stare, but he did not look away until Micah handed him the fiddle.

"What'll it be?" Kyle asked Lacee. Her dark bangs hid her eyes until she tossed them back with a flick of her hand. The evening light was minimal, and she studied Kyle's face as if to gain a clue. Finally she sat down, scissors still in her hands, and said, "'Big Iron.'"

Kyle took the lead with the guitar, he and Jake singing another gunfighter song. Justy knew Lacee liked this one because she got to sing backup, purring words such as "big iron" and "after Texas Red" and "about to meet his death." Micah also sat on the porch, and they were all lined up, Dale off by herself at the farthest end. Jake and Kyle stood, and their voices brought a sense of calm, even though they sang about death. Justy leaned back to look at Dale, who strayed inward.

The song ended and Jake pulled the fiddle from his shoulder to take another drink. He passed the bottle to Kyle, and while he was still drinking, Jake started "A Hundred and Sixty Acres." He sang without music and danced to the words, moving over to sway in front of Dale. She opened her eyes but stayed perfectly still, her gaze tracking his movements as he crooned his wish for land. Jake cast a look toward Kyle and kept singing. The song ended, but Jake danced on. He reached a boot out and tapped Dale's bare foot. She smiled, as if she'd just noticed she had feet. Jake shuffled in the sparse grass, the only sound in the growing night. Kyle watched him out of the corner of his eyes, hands poised on the guitar. Jake set the fiddle on the porch next to Dale.

"How about 'Strawberry Roan'?" Lacee offered, a fragile smile on her lips.

No one said anything and Jake kept dancing the smoldering dance. Lacee tipped her head forward to hide behind her bangs. Justy felt suddenly aware of the smell of water, the dwindling heat leaving the soil, the Wild Turkey souring the air.

Jake swayed and tapped Dale's foot again. She smiled once more, the curve of her lips almost embarrassed that her feet might be nothing more than things getting in the way.

"What about a dance?" Jake asked. He extended his right hand and continued to move. Dale shook her head. Jake moved away from her, keeping his back to the family. When he turned around, his features were dark in the night, just a patch of paler color underneath his black hair. He shuffled over to the bottle, took it from Kyle and danced with it. Moving back to Dale, he took a drink and began singing "In the Valley." The words told her he was as sad as the willow that weeps in the valley since she'd gone. "Come back, come back, come back to the valley, come back to this poor cowboy's arms."

The short song ended and left him standing, cradling the whiskey and looking at Dale. She pulled her feet up and rested her head on her drawn-up knees. She closed her eyes.

"How about a drink? Maybe a little whiskey will help." Jake studied her eyelids.

Kyle strummed a chord, humming something under his breath. Jake slowly shook his head and then took another deep, long drink. The alcohol swished in the bottle as he lowered it from his mouth. "How about one song? Could you do that for me?"

Jake's voice had taken on a brittle edge, and he leaned forward. Dale kept her eyes closed, each breath harder for her to take. Micah moved to Lacee and she put an arm around him. Then no one moved for the longest time. Dale pushed her thoughts toward the day of her baptism and the deep comfort she'd felt when she dedicated herself to Jehovah. Jake walked away from her and spoke to the apple tree outside the yard and the pond beyond. "You see, she's waiting for your world." He took a drink. "What about *this* world? What about me?" he said. "What about all those other JWs growing dope in their backyards and knocking on doors?"

The silence grew and the bats continued to swoop over the water.

"And is there something about secrets?" Jake dropped the bottle and felt his hands growing at the ends of his arms. The bottle landed on the grass with a solid swish.

"What are you talking about, boy?" Kyle asked. He removed the guitar strap from his shoulder and held the instrument by the neck.

"Why don't you ask her?" Jake turned and, in the same instant, Dale scrambled to her feet. He ran and grabbed her legs and she lost her balance, falling off the porch. He crumbled under her, softening her fall. She started to crawl away. He seized her by the waist and swung her around and then they were face-to-face, on their knees. "Why didn't you tell me?" Jake yelled, and shook her shoulders to emphasize his words. Kyle dropped his guitar and Lacee stood, the scissors still in her hand.

Jake hissed at Dale, wanting to know why she'd gone behind his back. Dale told him it was just food for the winter. But Jake said it didn't matter what it was she snuck around doing. Micah began crying, and Justy scooted back across the porch, hitting the wall and huddling down. Dale kept her hands on Jake's chest, allowing herself this much resistance. Her uneven hair shook with his movements.

"Where are those jars?" Jake's fingers tangled into her hair and he pulled. She winced at the pain but shook her head.

"What's going on?" Kyle took a step closer.

"Ask your friend, here," Jake said, and pulled harder on Dale's hair. She took a deep breath but wouldn't look away from the wave of anger distorting Jake's face. "You better tell me, woman."

Again Dale shook her head. The look of hunger on her children's face from the winter before strengthened her, even though she could feel her hair coming out at its roots.

Jake slapped her. At the same time, Micah yelled, "Stop it!" Lacee moved close and studied the scissors. In a daze, she tried to use her free hand to pull Jake from Dale's shoulders. The three of them meshed together and then Jake howled. He let go of Dale and gripped his left hand where the scissors had pierced his skin. "How dare you?"

"Leave Mama alone." Lacee gasped for air.

"Don't tell me what to do." He stepped nearer to Lacee and back-handed her. Dale stood and moved at Jake. Lacee dropped the scissors and her hands curled into fists. Jake held Dale back with his arm. Kyle raised his hands in surrender and said, "Jake, this is getting crazy."

Jake turned and caught Dale's hair again and pulled her toward the door.

"Show me. Now."

Jake dragged Dale to the bedroom, and then thumps and whimpers came from within. Kyle pulled Lacee to him and held tight, his breath ragged and strained. When Dale called out, Lacee and Micah ran inside and yelled at Jake to leave her alone. He threw her Bible books across the room, and one grazed Micah on the head. Too numb to move, Justy listened as Jake threw Dale on the bed and straddled her, as his drunken nerves split and he grabbed her slender throat in his powerful hands and began to squeeze.

Micah yelled for Kyle and he finally moved. Dale narrowed her-self down to smaller and smaller breaths while Kyle ran to the room and pushed Jake from her. At the same time, Micah moved to the cabin and brought two of the jars of tomatoes to his chest. Carrying them like prayers, he brought them into the room. Dale lay silent on the bed, and Kyle had Jake shoved up against a wall.

"This is enough," Kyle said. Dale rose and staggered past the chil-dren, blind to their presence, as she made her way to Kyle's truck and locked herself inside. Lacee took the jars from Micah and held them out toward Jake. "Come and get them if you want them so bad," she said. Jake cut her a look and then Kyle pushed him harder.

"You calmed yet, boy?" Kyle demanded.

Jake nodded and Kyle studied his face. Finally, Kyle stepped away, his boot landing on a Bible. He almost tripped and looked down at the floor. From the porch, Justy felt Jake lunge and try to grab Kyle by the throat, but he was too quick, and Jake half fell against the dresser.

"You better scoot," Kyle said, and he herded Micah and Lacee back out to the porch. Again he took deep, ragged breaths. A swarm of stars dotted the sky, and Justy tried to count them. A Bible crashed through the bedroom window, sending glass flying onto the porch.

"Get," Kyle said to the children. "Go."

As Jake threw a boot through another window, Justy found her feet and asked them to carry her away. She and Micah made it to the truck and hunkered behind it before another window broke. Lacee stood by Kyle and refused to move. Jake came out on the porch and wavered on the edge, studying Kyle. "Where is she?"

Kyle shrugged, found the bottle of whiskey and took a thundering pull into his body. Lacee took a step back and yelled at Jake, "I hate you." Hate was the Devil's word, and maybe Lacee was right, maybe it was Satan who made Jake forget who he was and let his hands take over.

Jake jumped down from the porch and had to steady himself. He grabbed Lacee by the neck and said, "Shut your mouth." Lacee dropped the jars as she coughed against Jake's grasp. Kyle moved in between them. Dale tried to come back from the remote place she wanted to remain— but she couldn't open the doors, even knowing she should gather her children to her and drive away. The hot sting of Jake's thumbs pressed into her throat wouldn't leave, conjured up every other time his hands had come undone. Seven years before, he'd tried to choke back her words, lost in his rage, stopping short of killing her because Kyle had pulled him away. Then she'd wanted to protect the child growing inside her, wanted to keep all her children safe from every kind of harm. Now she couldn't even find a way to make herself move to their aid, couldn't stop the ache for everything in the New System that wasn't here now.

"There's nowhere to go," she whispered as Jake and Kyle tangled into each other again. Lacee picked up the jars and threw them at the men, but they shattered against the door, glass and tomatoes falling to the porch. Jake tried to grab her again and she ran away from him to the scissors lying in the grass. Jake moved toward her and Kyle stepped in between them again, pushing Lacee away. She screamed at them both to stop, waving the scissors wildly, her voice frayed by Jake's earlier hold. As Jake and Kyle fell into a brutal dance, Lacee jabbed the scissors. They tore into Jake's leg, and she ran to Justy and Micah, by the truck. "Come on," she yelled, and led them to the barn, not looking at Dale as they left her. They approached the shadows of the building, and Lacee laid the little ones down in the trough. They could still hear Jake yelling, his curses filling the night.

Justy felt Jake's hands pull the scissors from his thigh, drop them, then tighten once more, cutting Kyle's air. The raging madness in him swelled to fever and Lacee coughed again. Her assaulted voice pulled Justy from the way Jake's hands choked back every unkind word said to him, everything that boiled beneath his skin. His fingers tightened on Kyle's throat, taking Jake finally and completely into the place he feared most. All the words Jake never could find swelled in him, and Justy felt her own silence tear open. Everything wrong with this story bit at the inside of her skin and flew from her in a howl.

***

Justy sat up in the trough as Jake came back from the anger and realized that his hands still gripped Kyle's throat. He scrambled up and shook his head, slow and steady, sure that he was dreaming and that at any moment he'd find himself awake and not staring at his lifeless father. The deep night swirled around him, swam in his senses with the alcohol, convincing him that he was indeed asleep. He looked away from Kyle to the sky, saw the stars hovering above and then moved to the porch, where glass and tomatoes crunched under his boots. Something deep within him ached and he suddenly felt gut-shot. He ran to his truck and saw Dale standing next to it, watching him.

"I…"

She shook her head and said, "Don't even try." She walked past him and went to Kyle, grief welling in her. As she leaned down and placed a hand on Kyle's chest, Jake wiped blood from his nose, vomited and winced at the steady pain in his jaw. He wanted it to remain with him always and grow in intensity. He climbed into the truck and drove slowly, finally, from the house.

***

Dale came to the children, calling their names, her blond hair ghost-like in the dark. They sat up from the trough and watched her come to them, almost shy in her movements. She kissed each on the forehead and hugged them all close. Her warmth filled the air around them and they stood holding on to one another, waiting. The quarter-moon rose and then Dale finally led them back to the house.

"Wait here," she said, and the children sat on the edge of the porch. Kyle lay just beyond the reach of the lantern Dale lit inside. But they could see his cowboy boots splayed strangely. Justy kept watching to see him move, but nothing happened. Dale came back out to the porch with a broom and a blanket. When she had covered Kyle, she began sweeping, and Justy noticed Lacee studying the blood on her hands.

"Should we pray, Mama?" Micah asked. Dale's fingers shook as she tried to hold the dustpan steady, but she nodded. She laid the broom down, stepped from the porch closer to Kyle and cleared her throat. Her voice rose rough as she asked Jehovah to resurrect Kyle in the New System, asked for him to be waiting for the family when the time came. In the quiet after the prayer, Justy felt Jake tear the last marijuana plant from the ground and rip it apart. Lacee stood up from the porch and began to pace back and forth. She coughed and tried to spit. In the lantern light coming from the house, her eyes were only shadows. Her steps came to a halt and she tossed her hair. Dale stepped closer to her and the night paused.

"You was born on a wild night," Lacee said to Micah. Her words seemed to come from a faraway place.

"You see, Jake wanted a boy more than anything in the world, and the night you came, well, he was tickled inside and out." Lacee coughed again and placed her hand on her hips, daring Dale to move closer. "Having a girl, that was fine, but having a boy, now, that made him a man." She began to pace again. "You were born about six o'clock in the evening. Jake, he went to a pay phone and called Kyle. He told him to rosin up his buddies, that there was going to be a party, the blessed boy had arrived. By the time Jake gets to the house, ten, maybe fifteen people are already gathered there."

Justy looked away from Lacee's tear-stained face to the sky, seeing a slice of the moon. It looked like a horn to her.

"Jake got so drunk, he shot his pistol into the fireplace. After that, he got all the people out of the house, in the dark, and down to the barn. He saddled up his horse Sandy, barely doing it right with the whiskey. About this time. there were about twenty people standing at the edges of the corral, watching Jake trying to fit a boot into the stirrup. It didn't look so good for a while, but then he surprised them all and got on that horse in the middle of the night. He even enjoyed maybe a whole minute on that mare before she'd had enough of him and his drunk ways and bucked him off. Jake went sailing through the air and landed on his ass, and he's grinning the entire time."

"That's how happy he was, Micah. He finally had a boy." Her voice made Justy think of a coiled-up rattlesnake, ready to strike.

Dale took a step back from Lacee, her lips pressed tightly together.

Micah moved over to Kyle's body and hugged it. He started to cry again.

Under her breath, Lacee said, "The blessed boy had arrived."

They watched Micah until Lacee gently drew him from Kyle's body and Dale stepped down and tried to join them. Lacee allowed Dale's arm on her shoulder for an instant and then pulled away so that Dale was left to hug only Micah as wave after wave of regret washed through her.

Then Lacee said, "We have to call somebody."

Dale just nodded. Lacee blew out her breath and held her head in her hands.

"Time for bed," Dale said at last and leaned down to pick up Kyle's guitar.

Lacee took a step closer. "We can't just let him lay there like that," she said, her voice trembling.

Dale gathered the body of the guitar to her and held it like a shield. Lacee pulled hard on the neck until Dale finally let go, causing Lacee to lose her balance and take a step backward. Then Dale took a deep breath and looked Lacee in the eye.

. "It's time for bed," she said again. She picked up the fiddle and bow from the porch, then walked to the gun rack in the hallway. After hanging up the instrument, she came back outside and searched for Jake's glasses in the grass. When she found them, she told the children a third time to go to bed. Lacee stared at her and then nodded at Micah and Justy to move to the bedroom. They lay on top of the covers. Lacee turned away, so Dale kissed only Micah and Justy on the forehead, the salt smell of her dried tears filling Justy's senses and making her think of the Pacific. None of them could sleep. Justy lay, feeling Jake shove his hands into the earth, aching for them to be something other than they were. She listened to Dale standing in the dark bathroom. After taking a deep breath, Dale flipped on the light and studied her face in the mirror. Fat red marks still stung her left cheek, and her neck was bruising in a ring. But she could breathe, so she drew in all the air she could while she wondered who her people were.

***

On the floor in Kyle's cabin, Dale pressed her body to the wood beneath her. She stared at the ceiling, trying to read the darker whirled knots in the paler pine surface. Her prayer fell away from her mouth and she began to speak louder and louder, trying to block out the sounds of the night before. She wanted nothing so much as a quiet place to think over all she'd done wrong last night. The three masks on the wall watched her, and she shut her eyes against their noise. Quiet evaded her, so she kept praying and praying, hoping the sound of her voice would keep out the sound of Jake dancing in the grass in front of her, her own hands pushing the locks down on the truck doors.

***

In the morning, Justy walked past the garden to the middle of the grassy field. She stood facing west, the mountain range blocking her view of the ocean she wished to see, her tongue pressing Ochre's stone against the roof of her mouth, her feet glued to the earth beneath. Anything to keep her in place and help her hold the breaking pieces together.

The afternoon they buried Kyle arrived hot and windless. His fresh gravesite gaped in the far north corner of the new cemetery. Redwoods circled the headstones behind the Grange hall where a group of people gathered. Dale stood strong, her eyes taking in the coffin. Behind her, Joella and Lucas stood with their heads bowed. Joella's right hand gripped Micah's shoulder slightly and he looked older to Justy—Lacee's story about his birth creating a crease in his forehead. Lacee stood next to Dale, arms crossed and anger holding her head upright.

Loggers and other townspeople formed the rest of the circle around the coffin. Gil Walker sat in his wheelchair, next to Mark Sloan and Lefty Fry. Gaines smoked cigarette after cigarette while Juan led the service. He spoke in soft tones about the way Kyle scaled a tree faster than anyone in the county and how he could play the west out of his guitar. Helen watched him from beside Gaines, and Justy realized she'd never seen Helen outside of the bar.

Dale felt a decision rise within her. She shrugged her arms, trying to keep the thing at bay. Her hair fell down her back, two different lengths, testimony to the craziness of the other night.

Justy saw it all from afar, sitting on a redwood stump, trying not to think about all the bones Kyle had helped to bury. She pressed the stone into the stump, her right hand denting in the shape of the rock. While Juan talked, Justy tried to push out the thought that kept looping back at her, as if she were the water stuck inside the beer sign at Hilltop.

Juan asked Mark to step forward and sing something, since Kyle had liked music so much. Justy felt Dale stir and then move forward. She held out a hand toward Juan. A puzzled look flitted across his face for the quickest of seconds, and then he quietly told Mark to hold on. Dale moved farther forward and closed her eyes. Justy saw Joella shake her head and mouth Dale's name.

Dale swallowed, sent a prayer to Jehovah, asking him for understanding, and then she opened her mouth. Justy stood as Dale sang about going down to the river to pray, studying about that good old way. Dale's voice pierced the heat and the pain and sent chills over Justy's skin. The group bowed their heads as Dale's magnificent voice moved into the void of Kyle's death, reaching inside of Justy.

She had never heard Dale sing alone before, and the sweetness of it, the depth of it, the whole of Dale's voice, all of it boiled inside Justy. She wanted Dale to sing and sing, never stopping until the New System came.

And then there was Kyle, the man who was already gone from the entirety of who he had been. Already he'd become the man who had tried to stop the fighting between Jake and Dale and not the man who drank his evenings away with Jake, not the man who'd first laid hands upon Jake in a fight. Justy didn't understand how she could feel such a tender ache for Kyle's life and at the same time know he was part of the story that caused Jake and Dale to flow away from each other.

Dale finished the song, tears streaming down her pale face, her hands knotted into each other. Justy turned her gaze away from them to the cloudless sky, feeling Jake from a farther distance. Juan remained quiet for a few minutes. He finally cleared his throat and said a few words about the music that brought the Colby family together.

Lacee snorted, and Justy wished Kyle could appear one more time and tell them how to move forward in their lives. She didn't know which weaving of words would make her feel better about Kyle's death and the night leading up to it. She wanted Kyle to come and talk himself out of the story instead of being snatched away.

Then the group moved into the hall, where plates of food filled two tables. People spoke in hushed tones and no one seemed to want to leave. Justy sat outside on one of the wooden benches, clenching her teeth. She watched through the window as Helen approached Dale and the two women hugged. Helen's brown hands gripped Dale tight, and Justy thought about those hands and their fingers, how they'd reached out across the drunken nights to warn Dale about Jake's violent moods. When Helen finally released Dale, Justy suddenly hoped that Juan had held Helen when she cried over their missing son. Dale fidgeted with a tissue in her hands, not hearing the people who came to offer their condolences. Justy didn't want to feel Dale wish to be nearer to Jake, wish to know where he'd gone, so she walked down the steps, through the embracing shade of the redwoods and out into the sun and to the fresh mound of the grave. Justy felt the sun beat down on her. Squatting, she studied the soil that now covered Kyle's coffin. The earth was moist and brown and she lay down and covered her eyes with her hand.

She pressed her body into the ground and cried to merge into its dark coolness, as if it were the river. She tumbled the stone in her mouth and pretended she was it and her tongue was the Eel.

The sound of footsteps coming near did not stop her wish.

"Justy." A young boy's voice. A long minute passed. "Justy." She knew it was Ochre from the gentle pitch of his voice. She peeked at him. Sunshine and Nolan were with him. He knelt and placed a cool palm on her arm. His touch overwhelmed her, and tears filled her eyes, but she told herself she wasn't supposed to cry. She turned away and lay on her side, both hands curled into fists, knuckles pressed to her face.

"Justy." Sunshine's voice, careful and warm. Ochre placed his hand on her arm again and squeezed the slightest bit. Justy felt the soil digging into her other arm and the sun hitting her legs where they poked out from the under the dress. Ochre removed his hand and the silence stretched. A crow cawed from somewhere in the trees.

"Should we go?" Ochre whispered.

"No," Sunshine and Nolan said together. A hand reached out and touched Justy below the knees. By the size and warmth of it, Justy could tell it was Sunshine. Another hand landed on her ankle—Nolan's palm, warm and loose.

"This is when people need you the most," Sunshine said, and Justy wasn't sure whom she was talking to. Then Justy sat up and looked at them. Ochre's hair was out of its braid and flowing down his back. They watched Justy with that distinctive Raven look, not smiling, not frowning, just open. Ochre held out a small pouch. Justy felt the soft leather.

"It's deerskin," Sunshine said. "Ochre and I made it this morning. We put some good herbs in it." She mimed careful pouring into the small mouth of the bag. Justy opened the drawstring, reached inside and pulled out a pale dried disk.

"That's licorice root," Ochre said. Sunshine sat down cross-legged. Nolan and Ochre remained squatting.

Sunshine tilted her head, looked at the trees surrounding the cemetery. "Ochre asked me a couple of days ago what we could do to help you."

Ochre nodded at Justy, his blue eyes wide open.

"And I thought we could put together a little bag for you to carry wherever you go."

"A place to keep your worries, if you want," Ochre said.

"Or your wishes," Nolan said, his hand lost in his beard.

"And you can add whatever you want," Sunshine said.

"But the deal is"—Ochre leaned forward—"whatever you put inside, it's your secret."

Justy rubbed her fingers against the soft skin. She reached behind her and pulled some of the fresh earth from Kyle's grave and added it to the herbs.

***

Justy walked away from the house, away from Dale reading her *Watchtower*. Away from Micah sitting listlessly in the rope swing and Lacee trying to read a book on the far side of the pond. She followed the creek into the shade of the bay trees, letting their sharp smell be her world. Moss-covered boulders blocked her path and she climbed over them, feeling with her fingers for small holds in the rocks. The water level was nearing its summer low and the creek moved with lazy determination toward the larger Rattlesnake. All of the water finding its way to the Pacific. She wished she could keep going inland until she found the source of the river.

Even as she moved, she felt each of them once more. Jake pulled drinks into his body, somewhere not too far away. He studied his fingers, wanting to be able to coil them peacefully together. Dale stood up from the table and walked to Kyle's truck, heading to the river.

The places they lived inside Justy stormed and stretched with a sound like horses. She felt Dale step free from her clothes and enter the Eel, felt her swim against the current, pale arms stretching to pull her through the water. The river filled her and she felt calmed by the weightlessness.

Justy lay on the boulder and watched a spider work its way over the moss. She knew that soon she, too, would have to rinse herself clean. And like in her dreams, she'd find the season to let the river take her away. But on that day, the firm earth supported the full weight of her body. The stone in her mouth tasted like sadness. So she added it to the pouch.

This novel is in no way meant to be representative or indicative of the Jehovah's Witnesses religion. For accurate and complete information, please contact your local Kingdom Hall.

ACKNOWLEDGMENTS

Of course, I am extremely thankful to the many people who supported me. Without them, there would be no book.

My father, who is not Jake.

My mother, who is not Dale.

The immediate circle: Jerrie, Blaine, Cindy, Lance, Sydney, Samantha, Dan, Kathy, Keegan, Sarah Margaret, Tony.

The Upward Bound Program, the Colorado Council on the Arts, the Santa Fe Writers Project, especially Andrew Gifford, and the Mac-Dowell Colony. The many talented folks I met there: Chris Engstrom, Lawrence Chua, Carol Potter, Naoe Suzuki, Scott Frankel, Marina Berio, Jon Rappleye, Greg Woolard, Timothy Burton XX.

I thank: Joe, Lindsay and Phoebe Fox; Barbara Elliot; Daren, Tim and Charlotte Lewis; Heather, Eddie, Ben and Sam Kassman; Scott, Kirsten, Fred and Baby Maurer; Christine Funk; Martha Owens; Vicki Kerr; Cathy and Rich Ormsby; Mrs. Clara Phipps.

Colin, Colleen and Maura Anderson; Tim, Juliet and Myles Anderson; Julie and Harry Augur, Avery Augur; Nanci Beazley; Briana Byrd; Bernard Dix; Will, Lynn, Ben and Miles Dixon; Corbin Donahue; John Grissum; Charlie and Linda Hamlin; Jeff Henderson; Aaron Hunter; Jennifer Inge; Sheila Kelly; Merle and Burdette Knous; the Krugs, Tom LaChapelle, the La Garita Club staff, Jason, Amy and Kalen Lustig-Ya-mashiro; Schiavone McGee; Mrs. Clara Moore; Frank and Kate O'Brien and Max; Lauren and Jordan Reed; Lee Rogers; Scott, Jenny and Wailea Siler-Hom; Jim and Molly Smith; David Toole; Marie Tucny; the Veras; Jill Walsh; Christy Wafer; James White; Kurt Wolter and Anne Sullivan; the music of Los Lobos.

The Carpenter family: Stephen, Dorothy, Steve and Zoubeida Ounaies, Sean and Marty, Seth and Mi Hillefors. Dreux Carpenter: writer, comedian, companion and friend. Forever.

The other talented writers I know and am lucky enough to call friends: Kolin Ohi, Richard Rodriguez, Robert Buckley, Aisha Krieger,

Dayna Lane, Chris Markus, Steve McFeely, Mary Morrow, Melissa Nelson and Colin Parish, Leo Geter and Tim Mason, Beverly Ball, David Hicks.

My thanks to Sarah Manuel for the steadfast friendship that guided her careful editing hand. I love you, too.

I thank the following for help along the way: Inez Hernandez-Avila, Pam Houston, James D. Houston, Page Stegner, Tom Higgenbottom, Jane Vandenburgh, John Walsh. Jack Hicks and his direction of the Creative Writing Program at University of California, Davis. Louis Owens, who was there at the beginning and helped me find and believe in my voice. A better mentor doesn't exist. I am grateful to the good people at BlueHen Books: Caitlin Hamilton, Kim Frederick-Law, Greg Michalson. And I am especially thankful to Fred Ramey for his patience, professionalism, and most importantly, his perennial faith.

Charlotte Gullick is a novelist, poet, essayist, educator, editor, and public speaker. A native of the Leggett Valley in Mendocino County, California, she grew up during the area's transition from logging to marijuana production, and the resulting tensions inform much of her writing. Her awards include a Christopher Isherwood Fellowship for Fiction, a Santa Fe Writer's Project Grand Prize, a Colorado Council on the Arts Fellowship for Poetry, and a MacDowell Colony Residency. She is currently Department Chair of Creative Writing at Austin Community College in Austin, Texas.

GUIDE QUESTIONS

1. What is the significance of the novel's title? What role has the Eel River played in the lives of Justy's parents? What does it represent for Justy?

2. Discuss the themes of faith and sacrifice. What sacrifices or promises do the characters make to their faith? Jake's lack of faith seems to put him at odds with his family, but does he truly believe in nothing?

3. The author chose to give Justy qualities of both wisdom and innocence. Did you feel that this characterization was effective?

4. Were you surprised that Justy could "see" distant events? Why do you think the author chose to use that particular narrative device? What other mystical elements appear in the story?

5. How does the author evoke a sense of change throughout the novel? Consider the coming mine, the falling of the great redwood, and the changing seasons. How do the changes to the land degrade Jake's sense of self? What does this say about the larger community?

6. Compare the novel's opening and closing acts of violence. Was the final act inevitable? How would the story have been different if Kyle had lived?

7. Did you feel that the ending was hopeful? What is the significance of the deerskin bag and the stone that Justy places inside of it?

Also from Santa Fe Writers Project

American Fallout *by Brandon Wicks*

For Avery Cullins—library archivist, former teenage runaway, and gay man from a small Southern town—"family" means a live-in boyfriend and a surly turtle. But when his father, a renowned nuclear physicist, commits suicide, Avery's decade-long estrangement from his mother, now hobbled following a stroke, comes to a skidding halt.

> *"Compulsively readable...a really great book."*
> — *Matthew Norman, author,* Domestic Violets

Dissonance *by Lisa Lenard-Cook*

When Anna Kramer, a Los Alamos piano teacher, inherits the journals and scores of composer Hana Weissova, she is mystified by this bequest from a woman she does not know. Hana's music, however, soon begins to uncover forgotten emotions, while her journals, which begin in 1945 after she is released from a concentration camp, slowly reveal decades-old secrets that Anna and her family have kept buried.

> *"...this beautifully written novel defies its apparent fate: It weaves through the history of the bomb and the Holocaust without feeling depressing. To my mind, it is everything a novel should be."*
> —*Catherine Ryan Hyde,* Huffington Post

Fatal Light *by Richard Currey*

A devastating portrait of war in all its horror, brutality, and mindlessness, this extraordinary novel is written in beautifully cadenced prose. A combat medic in Vietnam faces the chaos of war, set against the tranquil scenes of family life back home in small-town America.

> *"One of the very best works of fiction to emerge from the Vietnam War.."*
> — *Tim O'Brien, author,* The Things They Carried

About Santa Fe Writers Project

SFWP is an independent press founded in 1998 that embraces a mission of artistic preservation, recognizing exciting new authors, and bringing out of print work back to the shelves.

Find us on Facebook, Twitter @sfwp, and at www.sfwp.com